VENGEANCE WILL BE HERS

Outside on the boardwalk, she drew her gun and quickened her pace toward the saloon. The memory of her son's lifeless face urged her onwards, oblivious of the stares she was generating. Her shoulder brushed the batwing doors aside as she entered the saloon. A red-hot need for vengeance was kindled in her mind. She raised the pistol and took aim at the man leaning against the bar next to John Wesley.

The first shot from her pistol crashed into the bottles behind the bar. Everyone in the room shouted and ducked for cover. Everyone but John Wesley.

"Mrs. Arnold!" he shouted. "You can't shoot him; he's my prisoner!" He walked toward her, blocking her view of the cowering, handcuffed Kid at the bar.

Dolly stared at him with burning hatred in her heart. "Get out of my way! I'm going to kill him!" She tried to move sideways to get a clear view of the Kid. The pistol was clutched tightly in both of her hands. "Get out of my way, John Wesley Michaels. I want that wretch dead."

"THE LAWLESS LAND is a gritty, fast-paced story about an outlaw gang's brutal depredations in Arizona Territory and the brave man who decides to stop them . . . A classic Western."

—W. Michael Gear and Kathleen O'Neal Gear,
authors of *People of the Mist*

St. Martin's Paperbacks titles
by Dusty Richards

The Lawless Land
Servant of the Law
Rancher's Law (coming in July)

SERVANT
OF THE
LAW

DUSTY RICHARDS

St. Martin's Paperbacks

This is a work of fiction. All of the characters, organizations, and events portrayed in this novel are either products of the author's imagination or are used fictitiously.

SERVANT OF THE LAW

Copyright © 2000 by Dusty Richards.

For information address St. Martin's Press, 175 Fifth Avenue, New York, NY 10010.

ISBN: 978-1-250-09197-0

Our books may be purchased in bulk for promotional, educational, or business use. Please contact your local bookseller or the Macmillan Corporate and Premium Sales Department at 1-800-221-7945, ext. 5442, or by e-mail at MacmillanSpecialMarkets@macmillan.com.

Printed in the United States of America

St. Martin's Paperbacks edition / December 2000

St. Martin's Paperbacks are published by St. Martin's Press, 175 Fifth Avenue, New York, NY 10010.

10 9 8 7 6 5 4 3

I dedicate this book to Charlie, who helped so much; to Linda, who typed the most; to Lynn, who corrected the most; to my wife, Pat, who listened the most; to Mary Alice, who bossed the most; and my wonderful critique group, who sure helped straighten out the kinks. Thanks also to the great staff and crew at Sharlot Hall Museum in Prescott, Arizona, for all their help in researching the past. Besides their great exhibits and research facilities, the museum hosts a wonderful cowboy gathering each August. Check them out on the Web. And to all my friends and fans, God bless you all.

Dusty Richards

PROLOGUE

Rinker's thick, muscular arm cranked the blower's handle. The acrid smell of burning coal from the red-hot center of the forge's fire wafted up his nose. With a pair of tongs, he plunged the horseshoe into the inferno. Radiant heat swept his sweaty face. When he was satisfied it was hot enough to be malleable, he removed the plate with the tongs and used a large hammer to shape the shoe on his anvil.

The pings of his blows rung like a bell under the building's shake roof. With a critical eye, he turned the shoe up for his inspection. Not quite flat enough yet to suit him. He stuck it back in the forge's heat and repeated the process.

When someone entered the sunlight-flooded double front doors from the street, he glanced up from his work. Marvel Ransom, a rancher from up on the Dry Fork, came inside leading a stout buckskin horse.

"He's thrown a shoe, Rinker. Can you get to him?"

"Be an hour or so before I can do it."

"That will work. I've got the time. Going to get some

lunch and then I have an order to turn in at the store."
The lanky rancher paused, looked around until he was
certain they were alone, then with a sly grin, he asked
"You still playing house with that widow Budd?"

"Yeah," Rinker said. "Her and that worthless kid of
hers."

"She looked all right to me. Don't know about the
boy."

Rinker shrugged. "She's all right." From time to time,
the bitch needed to be slapped around some, so she knew
her place. It was the kid, Bobby Budd, that he was thinking about. Kinda runty in size for his age.

"Yeah, but she's better than sleeping by yourself, I'd
imagine," Ransom said, and headed through the open
doorway into the glare from outside.

"Don't rush back," Rinker said after him, his thoughts
still focused on the boy. Where was that brat? He was
supposed to be there swamping out those stalls. He'd sure
bust that kid's ass good with a razor strap for laying out
on him.

As the horseshoe cooled in a pail of water, he bent
over to apply the plate to the horse's hoof. Thinking about
the kid had him worked up in the middle of the day. He
quickly drove the individual nails in their place, then put
the hoof on a stand. He nipped the pointed shanks off and
bent the ends of the nails over. The last shod hoof on the
ground, he straightened his tightening back and reached
for his uncomfortable crotch. Then with some regrets that
he still had hours of work left to do before any playtime,
he led the horse off to a stall. The gelding belonged to his
banker, Walton Bridges. Couldn't be too good to a banker,
never know when a man would need a loan.

Where was that hatchet-assed Bobby, anyway? He
brought Ransom's buckskin out to the center of the room.

An appraising glance down at the pony's feet told him the buckskin needed a small shoe. Maybe he had a used one that would fit. From the corner of his eye he caught some movement and turned to see who it was. He looked hard as Ina Budd strode through the back door, holding up the hem of her blue dress as she stepped over the board threshold. What the hell did she want at this time of day?

She knew he was busy working. Why did she come by to bother him, anyway? He hurriedly tied the horse's reins to the ring and turned to face her.

"What do you want?"

"I come to speak to you, Lighe Rinker," she said. Her eyes narrowed in anger.

"About what?" He cranked on the blower to contain himself from exploding at her intrusion. Something had her riled and he held back from his first urge to smack her a good one. She stood straightbacked a few feet from him, a tall thin woman in a blue checkered dress.

"Bobby told me what you did to him."

"What'd that little liar say I did?" he growled, ready to reach out and grasp her by the arm and slap the living fire out of her. He'd show that mouthy bitch and her skinny-butted kid what talking out of place got them when he got through with both of them.

"How could you?" she demanded.

He'd had enough. He caught her by the arm and whipped the back of his hand into her face; popped her so hard that her hair bun came undone. It spilled brown hair halfway down her back as his vise-like grip clamped her arm. He drew her up close to his face.

She threw up an arm to ward off any more blows. Then, cringing in his hold, she shook her head, on the verge of tears.

"You're an animal. An animal—" she cried.

"Shut up or I'll bust your damn teeth out, woman!" He held his coal-stained fist inches from her face. Trembling with rage, he shook her like a rag doll. "Shut your mouth. You hear me?"

When she nodded, he released her. She fell in a pile at his feet.

"Don't move!" someone commanded.

Rinker churned around at the boy's voice behind him. With a wide grin, he intended to complete his lesson of the day for both of them. They'd know better than to question his authority—

The cold sound of a hammer clicking a cylinder into place shattered the silence of the building. Despite the barn's oven-hot interior, a cold wave swept over Rinker and the beads of sweat beneath his sodden shirt turned to icicles. He blinked in disbelief at the muzzle of the .44 Army model cap-and-ball pistol that Bobby held up with both hands, aimed at his heart.

"You better point that somewheres—"

His words were cut off when he saw Bobby's jaw muscles tighten. It was too late for talking; the kid's fingers were already squeezing the trigger. The hammer fell and a chunk of hot lead struck Rinker in the chest like a powerful mule had kicked him.

A blue sulphurous cloud fogged the shop. Rinker felt himself being slammed into the buckskin horse. The gelding shied away and Rinker, dazed by the force of the bullet, sprawled on his back. When he looked up through the veil of smoke, he saw the coldness in the kid's blue eyes. Bobby stood poised ready to shoot again.

"No, Bobby," she screamed. "That's enough."

"Hell, Maw, this sumbitch needs killin'," Bobby said as the Colt bucked in his fist to spit lead and fire again.

Noise of the explosion, billowing gunsmoke, and the

confusion of the frightened, whinnying horses floated on the periphery of Rinker's thoughts. The second bullet struck him square in the chest and drove all the breath from him. He wanted to protest, but no words came from his mouth as he began to sink into a twisting whirlpool. In the distance, he could hear the boy and her arguing.

"One thing for gawdamn sure, he won't ever bugger anyone else," Bobby said.

Then through a misty haze, Rinker saw the kid bound onto Ransom's horse, duck his head to go out the front door and gallop away. The drum of the retreating hooves were the final sounds in Rinker's ears.

CHAPTER 1

Two days after his shooting of Lighe Rinker, Bobby Budd still looked hard over his shoulder for the posse's pursuit. Near noon that same day, he crossed out of Colorado into the New Mexico Territory. His pounding heart ached from the urgent panic and his empty stomach roiled like a nest of snakes from the cold fear of the hangman's noose. Somewhere near Fort Union, he traded the lame buckskin to a Jacarillo Apache for a scrubby pinto. In the months that followed, word drifted back to the Springfield, Colorado, authorities that the young killer was swamping out bars in Santa Fe. They sent warrants for his arrest, but the local officials either ignored them, or they never found him.

Several months later, information filtered back to Colorado officials that Bobby Budd was working for the army. They sent a deputy down to Fort Wingate, but the lawman returned empty-handed. More time passed and Bobby Budd vanished like a dust devil that floated over the horizon. The wanted posters became tattered and faded; the law lost interest in his capture. His crime became history and in turn joined a portion of the outlaw legend of the frontier. Murderer Bobby Budd, like so many other felons, had managed to evade justice's grasp.

Two years later, on a hot July afternoon, seventeen-year-old Bobby Budd rode up to the Bosque Grande's main house to see the most powerful person in the New Mexico Territory, John Chisum. He'd ridden down there to ask the big man for a job. Not for an ordinary ranch-hand position, but one as an *avenger*.

When Chisum's black houseman came out on the porch to greet him, Bobby tried to look past him. Where was Chisum? He had expected to impress the big rancher with his appearance when he rode up. Instead, he felt degraded having to talk to a black domestic servant.

"What you want, boy?" the man asked in a deep voice, a frown of disapproval written on his dark face.

"Chisum hiring today?"

"Hiring what?" the man snorted and looked at him in dismay.

"Avengers," Bobby said and squinted his left eye hard at the man.

"Why, you ain't old enough to be no avenger." The man shook his wooly head in disbelief.

"Let me talk to the man. You ain't doing the hiring, nohow." Bobby rose in the stirrups and tried to see past him.

He heard someone of authority clear his throat, then a man came out the front door of the two-story house. Very tall, he wore a sparkling white shirt, vest, and a tie. His full mustache was trimmed and so was the goatee; his eyes were dark as coal and had a hard look.

"So you came looking for work?" John Chisum asked, as he looked Budd up and down, appraising him.

"I sure did, Mr. Chisum."

"Rhemus," Chisum said to his man. "Go get five dinner plates for this man to shoot at with that hog leg in his belt. Every one that he hits is worth a hundred dollars to him and the ones he misses cost him two hundred."

"Yes, sah, Mr. John, I'll go get them, but I's says he can't hit no bull in the butt."

"Rhemus, that's no way to talk to a top gun. By the way, what is your name?"

"Bobby Budd. Up in Colorado, they call me the Coyote Kid."

"Coyote Kid, huh?"

"Yeah, in Colorado."

"Why, you must know Bill Bonney, the Kid. He has a big reputation in these parts."

"Never met him. Hope folks don't get us mixed up."

"They won't," Chisum said, as if he knew they wouldn't. Standing on the porch with his arms folded on his chest, the cattle king looked much bigger than Bobby had expected him to be.

"How old are you? Not that it would matter." Chisum straightened up and moved aside for Rhemus to come by with an armful of white china plates.

"Eighteen," Bobby lied. Still trying hard to impress the man, he stepped off his pinto in a swaggering manner and drew the ancient Army model Colt out of his waistband. This better be good. Here was his chance to get a real job and never again have to mop up puke or empty another stinking old spittoon. The thought of such work made a bitter sourness rise behind his tongue.

"I want it to be perfectly clear," Chisum began. "You know that each plate you miss costs you two hundred dollars and you'll have that held out of your wages working for me?" The big man paused and looked hard at Bobby for his reply.

"And I only get a hundred bucks for them I hit, huh?"

"Not fair, is it?"

"Not exactly."

"See, Bobby, I don't need another avenger, but from the looks of you, you really need a job."

Bobby nodded. The old sumbitch drove a damn hard bargain. Still, anything beat his last job swamping in a stinking saloon. His stomach churned and he felt weak below the knees over the prospect that he might fail to meet Chisum's standards. Somehow he had to hit those plates. They looked big enough.

"Rhemus," Chisum directed. "Throw up the first plate."

Bobby cocked the hammer, aimed, and followed the plate with his eye in the arch up and then downward, until it shattered on the hard-packed ground. He silently chided himself for not shooting. He didn't know why he hadn't shot. Was he spellbound?

"That's two hundred dollars you owe me," Chisum said coolly, while streams of sweat raced down Bobby's face. His armpits felt like rivers and he quickly switched hands with the Colt to dry his palm on the front of his pants.

It was an effort for Bobby to even swallow. The knot in his throat hurt each time he tried. He carefully studied both men and strained to imagine the next trick they had up their sleeves. His hopes for getting the job were fast evaporating in the hot sun.

"He wasn't ready, Rhemus," Chisum said to his servant as if Bobby weren't even there. "This time before you toss it, you give him a shout like, now!"

"Yes, sah."

"Ready, Bobby?"

"I am now." Bobby mopped his wet face on his sleeve and blinked his sweat-stinging eyes at the dazzling sunlight from under his floppy-brimmed hat. He drew a deep breath.

"Now!" Rhemus shouted.

The plate sailed high, wobbled, and Bobby shot. The cloud of blue smoke smarted his eyes, but he heard the undamaged dish hit intact on the ground and smash to pieces.

"That's four hundred you owe me. Way over a year's work as a stableboy. Want to quit?"

"No, sir."

"You're getting expensive, you know? You've already missed two of my good china plates. Should we quit?"

"Throw the damn plate." Bobby motioned the gun barrel at Rhemus to go ahead. He'd plugged that damn Rinker in the heart both times with this Colt. Maybe his aim was off. No telling about the old pistol. He bought it for two bucks from a Mexican back in Colorado.

"I'm ready."

"Toss it up slower this time," Chisum said to his man. "At this rate the poor boy will work the rest of his life for me for free."

"Now!" Rhemus shouted.

Bobby laid his gun butt on his left forearm, took aim, and fired. This time the stiff wind swept the smoke away from his face and he watched the plate shatter in midair.

Chisum stood applauding on the porch. The clap of his hands echoed from the adobe stables beyond. "Very good."

"That makes three hundred I owe you now," Bobby said, readying himself for the next one. "Throw it."

"Now!" Rhemus said, and instead of throwing it up, he tossed the dish flat ways away from him.

Bobby wanted to scream. They were cheating on him. He took a wing shot and fragmented the plate. Rhemus looked up at his boss, then he shrugged his shoulders as if to say, "I tried to trick him."

"Not your fault, Rhemus. That boy can shoot. One more," Chisum said. "Toss this one high."

The plate soared toward the tops of the rustling cottonwoods. Bobby knelt, rested it again on his forearm, and fired. His bullet disintegrated the white circle into a thousand pieces. He stood up, blew the smoke away from the muzzle, then jammed the Colt back in his waistband.

"Not bad," Chisum said, sounding moderately impressed. "You owe me three months' wages. Put that crowbait of yours in the corral with the other ranch horses. He is a gelding?"

"Yes, sir."

"Thank heavens, I won't want a colt out of him."

"What do I do first?" Bobby asked anxiously.

"You report to Dave McClure. He's the cow boss. If and when I ever need an avenger, I'll call for you."

"Yes, sir." He forced himself to conceal his excitement. He was hired to work for the biggest man in New Mexico. And Jesus, what lucky shooting.

"Oh yes, Bobby, the first three months you'll work for your keep and to repay me."

"I can count," he said, pissed that Chisum thought he was stupid or something. He led the pinto off to the corral. Pay or no pay, he was working for the big man and somehow opportunities would avail themselves. He jerked his rigging off the pony and turned him inside the pen. His tack piled on the top rail, he went off whistling to himself to find McClure.

Without money to gamble, buy drinks, or pay whores, Bobby still rode into town on Saturday night with the boys. Hanging around in the streets of Roswell, he soon met Rosa, a pretty Mexican girl close to his own age.

They danced for a few hours to the tunes of a small band in a park, then she snuck him into her bedroom. There she showed him the charms of her womanhood.

Sunday morning, when the hungover ranch hands came staggering out of Maria O'Brien's whorehouse, they frowned in disbelief at the beaming face of Bobby. He held the reins with their horses all saddled and ready for the sore-headed punchers to ride back to the ranch.

"Hell, he's sober and looks fresh bred," Cooly said as he coughed and spit in the dust.

"Yeah, the only smart one in the bunch." Phillips staggered off to the corner of the adobe house to retch up his guts with the wall of stucco for support.

"You riding or walking?" Bobby asked, bringing him his horse.

"Shit, riding, man. I couldn't walk to the edge of town." Phillips managed to get aboard by groaning, moaning and more coughing.

For Bobby's good deeds, such as saddling the hands' ponies and other chores done for them, he managed to borrow powder, balls, and caps for his pistol. Any idle time he had he spent target-practicing on brown bottles set up in a dry wash back of the corrals. Soon accurate shooting became as automatic to him as walking. It was point, shoot, and bust a bottle.

The more he practiced, the better he became. He went to smaller targets, like the base of the bottle tossed in the air with his left hand. The Colt in his right blasted it to smithereens.

"Not bad, kid," Phillips said from behind his back, breaking his concentration.

Bobby turned and nodded to the older man who had slipped up unnoticed by him. Phillips was old to be a puncher; men his age usually were foreman or the boss.

"Next time you go up against the old man, load your gun with birdshot and you won't ever miss."

"Good idea, Phillips. I'll remember it." Bobby shook his head in dismay. Why hadn't he thought of that before?

Late that night, he appropriated some shotgun shells McClure used on hawks that got too curious about the ranch's loose chickens. He knew where the foreman kept the spare brass cartridges in a desk drawer. It was ammunition that fit the late-model pump twelve-gauge on the wall in the adobe hovel he called his office. All Bobby wanted was the shot out of a few shells for his own reserve, in case he ever got another chance to shoot at plates in Chisum's front yard.

Saturday night, according to their usual ritual, the hands saddled up to head for Roswell. There was to be a fandango, so Bobby had washed his clothes and wore his suit coat. The sleeves were too long, but he didn't care, and Rosa wasn't that fussy how he dressed. Using a ranch horse for his transportation, he rode out the gate with the hooraying cowboys and his own designs for a night of frolicking with his Rosa.

At the edge of town, he parted from the crew with a foolish grin that spilled his secret plans to the others. His face felt heated for a moment as he realized they knew exactly what his scheme for the evening with her would be.

He rode off down to the water course. There, under some gnarled, rustling cottonwoods, he unsaddled and turned the horse loose to graze. He had plenty of time before she came to join him. With his back to the twisted tree trunk, hat brim pulled down, he planned to take a siesta. Wind stirred the treetops and birds chirped nosily. Somewhere, a jackass brayed mournfully.

A stray dog came by, sniffed at Bobby's boots, dodged

his kick and hurried off. He soon drifted into slumber. She would come for him at sundown with food and some wine. His Rosa. He visualized her smooth body, her firm breasts, and imagined making love to her.

He heard loud voices and his eyes fluttered slowly open. With great surprise, he panicked at the sight of several angry men standing above him with clubs. It was sundown, and in the canted red light he could see they were armed and angry. They had come there to do him harm. But why? What did they want? He went for his gun. Before he could draw, they threw a blanket over him and pinned him to the ground. Angry voices cried out in Spanish, harsh words that he shed like small hailstones. Then they began beating him with sticks and clubs.

Were they mad? Crazy?

Past midnight, battered and still dazed from his beating, Bobby managed to crawl to the river. Every muscle and bone in his body ached. A front tooth was broken off. He could feel the empty space with his tongue. His right eye was swollen shut and his left only allowed a narrow slit for partial vision. On the sandbar, he fainted.

He awoke shortly, spit out the grit in his mouth, and forced himself to sit up. Too groggy to clear his head, he wondered about the reason for the attack. He was a friend, an amigo, to many Mexicans. Plenty of them worked on the Chisum ranch. He always got along with them and knew enough Spanish to communicate with them.

He tried to open his aching eyes. He could only see the shimmering moonlit water of the Pecos from his left one. Had they harmed Rosa? No matter how bad he felt, he must see at once that she was safe.

After several tries, he managed to get up and stagger to his horse. Forced to use his left hand to throw the saddle on the horse's back, his right arm felt so bruised he could barely flex his gun fingers. The condition of that arm bothered him. Would he ever be able to use it again?

With all his teeth clenching effort, he managed to mount and ride into town, where he found the other Chisum horses in front of Flanagan's Saloon. He half fell out of the saddle, staggered across the porch, and lurched through the swinging doors.

"Kid, what in the hell happened to you?" Phillips shouted and jumped to his feet, upsetting a whore from his lap. He rushed over and helped settle Bobby into a chair. One of the girls brought a pan of water and a cloth to clean his cuts. Someone else shoved a glass of whiskey in his hand.

The rye burned like hell going down his throat. He drank some more and someone with a bottle refilled his glass while the *puta* very carefully cleansed the cuts on his face.

Word quickly went out to the others and the Chisum outfit soon filled the saloon around him. Like warriors anxious for revenge, they hung on their teammate's every word. Bobby told them the entire story, still confused about the reason for the beating. He tried to flex his right arm, but even the whiskey that eased his hurting had not helped to limber it.

Phillips took charge when he finished.

"Tootle, you and Cooly ride down there in messikin town and get a couple of them. Bring them back here and we'll get to the bottom of this mess."

The pair agreed and pulled down their hats. They waded out the batwing doors in their bullhide chaps and everyone else nodded in approval at the plan. They would soon know the truth. Bobby drank some more whiskey and tried to focus his good eye on the mirror beyond the bar. Whew, he sure looked beat up. Some good-looking young *puta* kept pestering him—didn't bother her how he looked.

In a short while, Tootle and Cooly returned with two sullen Mexican prisoners. They roughly shoved them inside the saloon.

"Here they are," Tootle announced. He parted the others standing around and went to the bar for a drink. The rest of the cowboys soon surrounded the prisoners.

Phillips rose from his chair, inspecting the two as he used his thumb to tip back his Stetson. "Why the hell did you beat up our pard here?" He pointed at Bobby.

The two Mexicans huddled together, obviously awed by Chisum's men. They shrugged as if they knew nothing.

"Get a lariat," Phillips said. "Maybe if we stretch their damn necks they'll remember something."

Yeah, Bobby agreed in his whiskey haze. Why in the hell did they beat him up anyway? He needed to know. One of the cowboys busted in the swinging doors, waving a coiled reata in his hand.

Then the shorter of the two men fell upon his knees, his hands clasped over his head as if in prayer and began babbling in Spanish a mile a minute.

"What's he saying?" someone shouted.

Cooly pushed his way in closer, then made a scowl. "He's saying something about Rosa being pregnant?"

"Rosa!" Bobby roared, bolted out of his chair and rushed to kick the man to death. How dare that bastard say anything about her. But the other cowboys restrained him.

"Bobby! Bobby!" Phillips shouted in his face to break through his blind rage. "It's no use. He says that she's gone to Las Cruces and has already been married to an old man."

Rosa married? How could he believe this liar? But it must be the truth or she would have checked on him by this time. Bobby's knees threatened to buckle. Blood left his face. Cold chills raced through his jaw muscles. The cowboys holding him helped him into a chair. For a long time he sat there in shock, absently drinking more whiskey and barely hearing the consoling voices of the other ranch hands and the whores around him.

A while later, dead drunk, he went outside, protesting that he wanted to be alone. He mounted his horse under the stars and rode down to the *barrio* where all the Roswell Mexicans lived side by side in adobe hovels.

Under the starlight, he cursed them at the top of his lungs for what they had done to him and, worse yet, for what they had done to her. Swaying in the saddle, he used his good hand and emptied his pistol at the dark buildings. Finally, he passed out and fell off his horse.

He awoke in a cell that smelled of old piss pots and realized then about his own captivity. Two days later, John Chisum rode into town and paid his fine. Like the father Bobby never knew, Chisum stood outside the bars looking aloof, while the deputy unlocked the iron door.

"Budd, you owe me four more months' work," Chisum said.

Bobby grabbed his hat and rushed out of the cell. "I can count."

"Good," the big man said, trailing after him to the front office. The other deputy returned Bobby's knife as well as his gun and holster. In his rush to get outside, Bobby strapped on the holster and strode through the door into the sunshine. Once on the boardwalk, he drew a deep, grateful breath of freedom. He never wanted to be in another jail as long as he lived.

Chisum stood beside him, looked up and down the empty street, and started off. "Let's go have breakfast at the Majesty Hotel."

"I already owe you four more months' pay."

"Quit feeling sorry for yourself."

Bobby jerked around and blinked at the man. "I ain't!"

"I need an avenger, not a crybaby."

Taken aback by the big man's word's, Bobby considered his good fortune. His headache fled and his ears were tuned to hear every word of the man's offer.

"First . . ." Chisum paused for a rig to go by and tipped his hat to the handsome women seated beside the driver. "Can I trust you to never implicate me?"

"I ain't stupid."

"If you ever get in trouble with the law while working for me," Chisum said through his teeth, "I'll hire the best lawyer that money can buy. Of course, he won't know who hired him."

"I understand—"

Chisum silenced him with a frown as they climbed the hotel's front stairs. "We'll have a good breakfast now," he said to settle the matter and guided him through the lobby.

Bobby drew the rich smells of the cooking up his nose. Yes, he would have a great meal in this fancy place with the big man and he was also about to become an avenger at last. Avengers made the big money.

The waiter was familiar with Chisum for he called the man by name, then showed them to a table and seated them. To demonstrate that he knew what to do, Bobby unfurled the napkin and spread it over his lap. Chisum nodded his approval, giving the waiter their orders for breakfast.

At length, Chisum leaned forward and spoke under his breath. "The first man I want eliminated is Arthur McKey. He's a rustler, small-time, but he's an example of the worthless ones eating and selling my beef to others."

When he finished, Chisum fished out his gold watch and acted busy with it. Finally he raised up his flinty gaze to look hard at Bobby for his reply.

"I'll find him and he will be no more," Bobby promised.

"That is what I expect. Of course, this is our last public meeting. Your money and instructions from now on will be in the Tank line shack. Check the northeast corner under the roof, reach up and feel for a snuff jar. They will be in it."

Bobby simply nodded to indicate he heard and busied himself cutting up his fried eggs. Saliva filled his mouth. After two days of jail slop, he could hardly contain himself to gobble up the real food on his plate. Instead, he attempted to relish each bite and listen carefully to what else Chisum had to say.

"Stay clear of the main ranch."

"I understand."

"You learn of any rustlers—" Chisum made a point with his fork. "I want them eliminated."

"I understand," Bobby said, carefully savoring his first taste of the fresh eggs.

"Get a new Colt, that old cap and ball might misfire. I'll give you money for one. Buy you a good horse, not some damn old pinto like you rode in on. And for Christ's sake, you don't need a flashy horse that folks will notice."

"Yes, sir."

"Find you a place to stay, out of sight and mind. If you don't mess with Sheriff Garrett, he won't mess with you."

Bobby nodded as he bit down on the biscuit. The brown crust melted in his mouth with a swirl of fresh sweet butter flavor on his tongue as he chewed. It was hard to conceal the excitement coursing through his veins.

"You're your own man from here on. You get drunk and land in jail, you figure out how to get out."

"Yes, sir."

Chisum grew taller in the chair. His eyes became dark pits, then he spoke. "You're smarter than most. But don't fall into a damn bottle again. I don't hire drunks nor do I keep them on my payroll. You got it?"

Bobby nodded that he understood.

After breakfast, flush with the roll of bills Chisum paid him, Bobby bought a stout bay horse and a good used saddle at the livery. Then he rode the new mount up the street to the Salinas Brothers' Mercantile, hitched him to the rack, and went inside.

He purchased a bedroll with a tarp, some coffee, bacon, dried beans, cheese, canned tomatoes and peaches, crackers, salt, and a canteen. Then he selected a new .45 center-fire Colt from the glass case, spun the pistol on his finger, hefted the balance and took an imaginary aim at a lamp.

"Give me four boxes of ammo," he said to the anxious clerk.

"Yes, sir," the boy about his age said.

"Oh, and a holster too." Bobby intended to wrap up his old cap and ball in its own holster and put it for safe-keeping in his saddlebags.

Bobby's glance fell on the split-tailed canvas coats hanging on the rack. They would shed water and wind and looked a lot more stylish than his old suit coat. He strode over and tried on the first one. The coat was way too large, but he kept trying them on with the clerk's help until he found one with sleeves short enough.

"Certainly looks dressy," the clerk said.

Bobby studied his image in the tall mirror. He reset

the weather-beaten hat on his head once or twice, then nodded. He finally looked and even felt the part of a real avenger.

A week later, after much scouting and planning, wearing a cotton sack mask with holes for his eyes and mouth, Bobby stealthily crossed the McKeys' porch in the late night darkness. Two days earlier, he had poisoned the rancher's dogs, so he knew there would be no barking to give his presence away. With care, he eased himself through the open bedroom window, the oily-smelling new Colt ready in his fist. A floorboard creaked under his boot sole and he paused to listen carefully for the couple's steady breathing. Satisfied, he continued. In the starlight, he could make out a man's form on his side of the bed. Beside McKey, his wife in a white nightgown slept in a fetal position.

Bobby cocked the hammer back and aimed it. A foot away from the man's face, he blasted the .45. Exactly like when he shot Rinker, the same coldness coursed his veins. Rid of another no-account, was all he could think. The ear-shattering explosion in the bedroom caused the woman beside McKey to jolt awake and she immediately began screaming at the top of her lungs. To be certain the rustler was dead, Bobby shot once more at point-blank range in the man's face, then he slipped out the window.

The gunsmoke was choking him. Outside the house and fleeing the porch, he stripped off the mask to escape some of the fumes still in his nose and throat as he hurried for the barn. In a long lope, he crossed the open yard, coughing on the gunpowder fumes. Anxiously, he stopped; caught his breath, and glanced back to check for pursuit. The house buzzed with the sounds of the hys-

terical family members. Satisfied McKey was dead, he
quickly mounted the bay and rode away.

One less rustler, Chisum.

The next day on his way back to his hideout, he paused
at a cantina and bought two bottles of good rye. Earlier,
he'd found an old shack in the hills. After driving out
the packrats and scorpions, he set up housekeeping in
the hovel. There was plenty of cured grass around it
for the bay and water, too, in some potholes down the dry
wash. Nearby, a small live spring filled a large ollah to
overflowing each day with his drinking-water needs.

The hideout was set back in the junipers, off the main
path. He considered the shack a good enough place to
cool his heels. General work around the place such as
gathering cooking wood kept him busy. It was the nights
that began to get to him.

All his life, Bobby had never missed a chance to sleep
soundly, either at siesta or at night. But more and more,
he saw Rinker in his dreams, not when he killed him, but
when the blacksmith brutally raped him. The man's hard
callused hand clamped over his mouth, smothering his
breath to silence his screams of protest at the excruciat-
ing pain. After the dreams, Bobby woke up in a clammy
sweat, his body quaking.

Then new dreams began to awaken him. A woman's
piercing screams filled his mind. He dreamt the dead rustler got up out of bed unscathed. Time and again, Bobby
would bolt up and hug his goose-bump-covered arms to
his body in the chill of the night. He peered hard in the
shack's darkness to be certain he was alone.

A few good swallows of whiskey sometimes chased
away the images as he struggled to slip back to sleep. The
next day, Bobby would dread the coming night and the
possibility that the nightmare would return. He visualized

McKey's last reflexes again as the lead smashed into his brain. His body's spasmatic jerks in death's throes. McKey was dead. Why did his dreams keep bringing him back—alive?

To try and escape the matter, he rode the next day to the Tank line shack and reached far back in the corner under the eave for the snuff jar. The glass clutched in his hand, he grinned at the sight of the thick roll of bills and carefully read his new orders:

> One down, many more rustlers to go. Verl Butler
> has a slaughterhouse at his ranch near Black Pine.
> Old man and both boys are rustlers.

Verl Butler and sons would be next.

Bobby's interest quickly turned to all the cash in the roll. He felt the crispness of the twenties in his fingers. Recalling what Chisum had said to do with those written orders, he held a lit match to the note and soon it was consumed. He dropped the flaming piece of paper short of burning his fingertips and with his boot sole ground the black ashes in the dust of the floor.

Riding back to his shack, Bobby speculated on how he would need a long-range weapon for this job. He stopped off in White Oak at a store and bought a new .44/.40 rifle and two boxes of cartridges. The smart-mouthed boy who waited on him asked if he was going to start a war with all that ammunition.

"Naw, just potshot nosy clerks that ask a lot of damn questions," he said, and took his purchase with him.

"No offense, mister," the clerk called after him. "I didn't mean—"

Bobby never even looked back. Filled with boiling rage, he pushed his way out the front door, ringing the bell as he left. At the hitch rail, undoing the reins, he glared back at the storefront, his heart pounding under his rib cage. Why, that stupid—

The next day, Bobby rode over to the small community of Black Pine. A crossroads with two cantinas, two stores, a livery, and some hovels where some Mexican families lived. Several small ranchers frequented the place and Bobby wore his worst clothes when he went there "looking" for work. Before he rode into town, he hid the rifle securely wrapped in a blanket under a thick downed juniper. Later he stowed away the new .45 and strapped on his old cap and ball to look like another busted cowboy in need of a job.

He dismounted in front of the cantina, with a four-day stubble on his face, and wiped the back of his hand on the whiskers. He wished he had a stiffer beard.

He pushed through the batwing doors into the dark cantina. His eyes were slow to adjust as he walked to the bar and ordered a beer. The man nodded and brought him one.

"You're new here?" the barkeep asked.

"Yeah, need me a job. Anyone hiring?"

"You build fence?"

Bobby made a sick face at the man, then lifted his beer and savored the first foamy taste. Bitter as hell, but it was cool and he was thirsty. The man must know that no self-respecting cowboy ever wanted to build fence. Get a damn Mexican to do that.

"Maybe Johnny Davis could use you for a month on his place."

"Where's his place?"

"Ride west a few miles and take the road with the D Bar D brand on the board nailed to a post. You can't miss it. That lane leads right to his headquarters."

"Good, I'll go see him. Someone mentioned the Butlers might need a rider."

"Who said that?" The bartender curled the corner of his thin mustache up in disdain.

"Some guy I met on the road."

"Naw, I don't think so. They got three of them and not very many cows. You talk to Jug Brown about that?"

Bobby shrugged as if he didn't know the man, and concentrated on his beer. "Never caught his name." He drank another beer then he thanked the man and headed for the D Bar D.

When Bobby rode up to the low-roofed ranch house, Johnny Davis, who looked half Indian, came out on the porch. A short potbellied man in his fifties, he spoke in Spanish first, then seeing Bobby wasn't fluent in the lingo, he switched to English.

"I could use you for four weeks to help me gather some long yearlings. I pay thirty and found." He waited for Bobby's reply as if that was all he paid and made no negotiations.

"Suits me." Bobby dropped heavily from the saddle. Why, he'd work for the old sumbitch for free to get the lay of the country and not draw a lot of attention. Chisum would be proud of him doing it like this. Killing three men wasn't like poisoning a few old yard dogs with strychnine, then riding up and shooting the cow thief in his bed. This operation would require much more planning.

Bobby quickly fit in as a cowboy for the old man. Davis's Mexican wife cooked them spicy-hot, rich food and Bobby wondered at his first supper if the beef they were eating wasn't some of Chisum's. The next day they shod four horses apiece to use on roundup, and Bobby's back wanted to give out. He could press with both hands all he wanted on his narrow hips when he tried to straighten, but the tightness remained. During the shoeing, Davis filled him in with gossip about the other ranchers in the area.

"Them Butlers are a little too handy with a long rope," the old man said, looking off at the mountains. Bobby knew Davis meant they stole cattle. The old man went on. "Best advice I can give you is stay clear of them. They pack sidearms and can use them. They've been in some bad scraps before back in Texas. That's why they're here, I guess." Davis bent over and went back to shoeing.

"I hear you." Bobby had learned plenty from his employer about the country and the Butlers. If they were tough rannies, it was a good thing he took the job. Near dark, they finished shoeing the last horses, went to the back porch and washed up.

"Oh, hungry hombres, your supper is ready," Davis's wife, Aleta, said from the lighted doorway and welcomed them into her sweet-smelling house.

"Hungry and sore hombres," Davis grumbled and she laughed.

Bobby envied the man for a moment, with his small ranch and good woman. The thought of her reminded him of Rosa and the recollection of his loss nauseated his empty stomach.

The middle of the first week, he, Davis, two other ranchers, Gill Checkers and Hoyt, were driving steers out of the canyons to bunch and sort on the flats when two riders joined them.

"Watch yourself," Davis said under his breath, riding past Bobby. "That's the Butlers."

Bobby nodded that he heard the man's warning and booted his horse off to keep the bunch of steers moving downhill. One freckle-faced two-year-old ox wanted to cut back, and he had his hands full. There would be plenty of time to meet the Butlers, but he felt better that before dark he would know his next victims.

The last steer finally in the herd, Bobby dismounted to loosen his cinch and let the lathered cow pony breathe.

"This here is Bobby Bleau," Davis said, using the name that Bobby gave him. "He's working for me through roundup."

The elder Butler nodded curtly, indicating that he'd heard the man, and acted like he didn't bother to talk to mere hands. Butler was a broad-shouldered man with a full black beard and wore a small felt hat with the brim turned down all the way around. Despite the heat of the day, he wore a suit, floured in dust. The senior Butler and Davis rode on to go through the bunch to see whether any animals in the herd wore Butler's brand.

"That old sumbitch Davis could have hired me to help him, 'stead of you," the pock-faced Butler boy of about eighteen said, grasping his saddle horn and rocking back and forth, watching the two men ease their way into the herd.

"The job's only for a month," Bobby said.

"Old sumbitch," the boy swore under his breath and stared daggers after Davis.

"My name's Bleau," Bobby offered.

"Zackeriahah."

Bobby decided the pimple-faced kid wasn't sociable because he'd taken the job that the boy wanted, but he figured Davis would never have hired that boy based on their conversation of the day before. What had he said? "Those Butlers were long on rope."

The fact that Zackeriahah wore two guns on his waist and his old man wore the same did not go unnoticed by Bobby. They were tough sons of bitches and he would treat them so. One more of the family to meet, then he'd start laying his plans for how to eliminate the three of them.

Davis and the old man found five head wearing Butler's brand in the herd. Butler promised to send Zackeriahah back for the rest of the week to help them. Davis agreed quietly to that, but Bobby could see he wasn't charmed by the fact.

When the Butlers rode off, Davis came over and dismounted. He hitched up his batwing chaps, cast a look down the trail where they had disappeared into the junipers, and then spit.

"I'd rather have a sheep-killing dog than that worthless Butler boy with us."

"Aw, easy, Davis. That boy may get kicked in the head and not show up in the morning," Hoyt said, laughing as he joined them.

"We ain't that damn lucky, boys." Davis went off shaking his head in disapproval.

Bobby grinned to himself and considered how that might be a good way for Zack to go. An accident would be better than them Butlers all being found toes up with bullets in them. Maybe he would work on that when the boy got there.

The next morning, Zackeriahah showed up at daybreak. Davis sent him with Bobby to scour some more canyons in the mountains.

They rode single file up the steep trail, Butler in the lead, bragging over his shoulder about how his old man killed four guys in Texas. Bobby looked back to be certain they were alone. Plenty of high bluffs; a man would never survive a fall from any one of them. A golden eagle floated about on the canyon's air currents looking for a meal and screaming at the intruders in his land. Bobby and Butler finally topped out in the pass and halted.

A fresh wind swept Bobby's wet face and refreshed him. He rose in the stirrups; it looked like a big draw above them to the left that they needed to ride up and check, despite Butler's complaining there was not any cow sign up there on the mountain.

"Davis said to check all these canyons." Bobby stepped off to tighten his cinch. He was busy with it when he noticed Butler pushing his horse closer to him.

"I say there ain't no cattle up there and we're going back," Butler said with a snarl.

Bobby turned from his task and looked up at Butler's flushed face. What was he so upset about? Must be a good reason why he didn't want them to go up there. Were there stolen cattle or incriminating evidence like hides with Chisum's or others' brands on them in that canyon or was he just too lazy to want to work?

"You don't hear very gawdamn good do you, Bleau?" Butler demanded, reining in his horse in Bobby's face.

Bobby felt himself being forced backward by Butler's crowding his horse into him. A quick check over his shoulder showed it was a long ways down and he stood only a few feet from the brink. He reached for his jackknife, easing it out of his pants pocket and letting Butler think the whole time he was winning this push-and-shove match.

The fractured layers of rock hung under Bobby's boot heel. He caught his balance, knowing the next step back would be life or death for him. The knife blade open at last, his sweaty fingers closed on the bone handle.

A golden eagle screamed close by and made a pass on the updraft. It was enough of a distraction for Butler to look away. Bobby moved like a cat, reached out as he sidestepped the animal and drove his jackknife to the hilt into the horse's tender flank. The gelding screamed with pain and, before Butler could check him, the horse leaped past Bobby and plunged out into the open sky where the eagle soared.

Brushed aside by the charge, Bobby fell to the ground and hurt his hand on the sharp rocks. But he knew from the screams that Zackeriahah Butler had gone to see his maker. Despite the aching in his palm, Bobby managed to crawl to the edge in time to see horse and rider hit the boulders below with a dull thud.

The two were sprawled lifelessly on the rocks. Bobby quickly considered how to get to them. It would take him a good half hour to work his way down there. He rose slowly and rubbed the grit from his palms. He wondered if his jackknife was still sticking in the animal's flank. If he could find it, he certainly needed to remove it, so no one would ever know. He remounted, gave a last quick look over the edge, but could not see Butler's body for he was not close enough to the brink to view them.

Whistling a dry tune, he booted the horse downhill. Had the others heard Butler's scream? Hard to tell. He glanced back up at the side canyon. What was up there hiding? Maybe nothing. The boy might have been plain lazy and didn't want to ride uphill anymore. Who knew? It had come close to costing him his own life. Feeling weak-kneed, he took a swig from the pint in his saddle-bags to settle his nerves, corked it and put it back. Too gawdamn close. He shook his head and ducked a low-hanging juniper bough.

I guess a bee stung Butler's old horse in the flank and he just leaped out into space. That would be his story and no one to question it.

"What in the hell happened?" Davis asked when he and the others met at the base of the mountain.

Bobby gave them his "bee story."

Davis nodded at the end and said, "Someone needs to ride over and tell Butler. Ain't much chance the boy's alive."

"I can go," Hoyt said and turned his horse.

"We'll go see what we can do," Davis said with a look of hopelessness. "Man falls that far—ain't much chance he's still breathing."

"He's in a tough place to get to," Checkers said.

"Yeah, we'll have to climb in there on foot for part of the way." Davis grabbed for his hat, pulled it down, and sent his horse through the dense junipers.

It took over a half hour for them to reach the area where the body lay. Out of wind and on foot for the last of the steep climb, Davis halted in the lead and mopped his brow on his sleeve.

"Whew, going to be hell to get his body out of here," Davis said absently and set out again.

Bobby came behind Checkers, who grumbled about climbing over every rock. The main thing Bobby wondered about was his jackknife. Was it still buried in the horse's flank? He wanted to be the first one there, in case. No way to do that with Davis leading the way. He drew in a deep breath and scrambled up the jumbled formation after the man. Something would have to work out when he got there.

At last, he could see the horse's legs and hooves stuck out overhead from the top of a building size boulder. They soon would know Butler's fate. The next thirty feet was straight up. Bobby could reach out and touch the talus rock to help himself scramble up it.

Davis bent over, picked up something and without looking pocketed it. Bobby's heart stopped. Had the old man found the pocketknife? Damn. He scurried past

Davis and went around the boulder, finding a way to reach the top.

Pulling himself up so he could sit on the edge of the flat surface, he could smell the horse. Obviously, the impact had forced out the contents of his bowels. The odor was strong and had already begun to gather flies. Bobby rose up on his knees to where he could see Butler's twisted body. The boy's head was smashed and bloody from the fall. Butler's blue eyes stared at the azure sky.

He was dead.

"Not much we can do for him," Davis said, huffing hard from the climb.

"No, I'll try to get his saddle off. I imagine his old man will want that?"

"Sure, guess we can wrap him in his own slicker and let him down the steepest part with a rope," Davis said as if thinking out loud.

"My lands, he took a helluva fall," Checkers said, at last standing on the top of the boulder. "Horse just leaped off up there?" He took off his hat, scratched his thin thatch on top, and gazed skyward in awe.

"Yeah," Bobby said, then he bent over and undid the latigos on the cinch. They couldn't prove anything different.

"Here's his knife," Davis said. "He won't need it. Found it down the hill. Just cut the girth on the other side, be easier to get the saddle off."

Bobby nodded to indicate he had heard the instructions and took the familiar Barlow from him. A cool wave of relief settled over him. His plan was complete. It was a horse wreck killed the poor boy. Smile, damn you, John Chisum.

* * * *

Bobby waited in the cedar brush until Reginald Butler left the whorehouse in Beecher's Canyon. The place was run by a German woman, Greta Stalz, who kept some Mexican working girls for the pleasure of the miners and cowboys in the area. Reginald was a few years older than his brother. Bobby met him at the funeral and despite the cold suspicious edge the Butler clan showed toward him over Zack's death, Bobby acted as if nothing was wrong.

His roundup work for Davis over, he drifted around like a typical unemployed cowboy. He spent a good portion of his pay from Davis at Greta's, drank "a little too much" at the cantina, complained about the cheap ranchers not hiring him. All the time, he was learning the Butlers' patterns, where they went alone and together.

It was mid-morning sun time when he spotted his quarry leaving Greta's. Reginald looked about done in when he stumbled out of the whorehouse and made three tries to get on his horse. He rode away from there like a sack of beans in the saddle and once almost fell off. Bobby observed him from a good distance, and became convinced he could ride up undetected and whack him over the head. Then a wonderful idea came to him. Reginald was about to have a terrible wreck. Dragged to death by his own horse.

Bobby rose in the stirrups, looked out across the country. Nothing, no one in sight, only scattered junipers. He spurred the bay on.

"Hold up!" he shouted and saw Reginald look back with his half-opened eyes. He soon joined him.

"Hmm," Butler sniffed and turned away. "It's you."

"Hey, I felt real bad about your brother dying that way."

"Yeah, I bet he'd be alive today if it weren't for you."

Yeah, he would be. So would you. Filled with rage, Bobby drew his Colt, gripped it by the barrel, drove his horse in close and busted Butler in the back of the head with the butt. Butler pitched face first onto the ground. Barely having time to catch the man's spooked horse by the reins, Bobby glanced over his shoulder to be certain Butler had not regained consciousness. He hurriedly led the man's horse back and dismounted.

He grasped Butler's right leg and with some effort forced his boot through the stirrup. Out of breath, he glanced down at Butler who was regaining some awareness.

"What the hell you doing?" Reginald asked, blinking his bleary eyes.

"Sending you to hell with Zack," Bobby said and lashed Butler's horse on the butt.

The animal made a bound, but when he discovered the dangling object at his heels, he kicked up and began to race away. Like a flapping rag doll, Butler was propelled along with his foot stuck in the stirrup. Bobby quickly mounted. He loped his horse down the dusty road after them to be certain the spooked animal did not stop too soon or that Butler's foot came disengaged.

No way anyone could survive the beating and stomping Butler was receiving. Bobby finally reined up. Butler's horse acted like he would run forever to escape the trailing object at his heels. Number two down, one left.

A small cluster of Black Pine's settlers attended Reginald's funeral. Greta and some of her girls dressed up respectable, arrived in a two-seat buckboard, and the *putas* crossed themselves several times during the services. A bald-headed Baptist preacher with a squeaky voice spoke the sermon above the hard south wind. Old man Butler gave Bobby a hard look when it was over, climbed on his horse and rode off.

The next day, Bobby waited in the brush until the old

man left the ranch on horseback, then he went in. Prowling in a shed, he found three hides with Chisum's Lightning brand on them. Proof enough for him that Butler had been killing Chisum's beef. He stood back in the shade of the shed and considered his options. This would be no accident; he needed to show folks the reason why. No one had learned a single thing from those boys' horse wrecks. The old man's death had to show that rustling Chisum stock didn't pay.

Stealthily, Bobby crossed the yard in the midday sun. Looking all about, he tried the front door of the house and found it unlocked. Carefully, he slipped inside. He found no evidence of a woman inside the house—it reeked of stale cigarette smoke, sweaty socks, and horse. The dry sink was piled with dirty dishes and the beds unmade. Filthy blankets were wadded up on the bare mattresses. Bobby found a great leather chair with oak arms and situated it so he could cover the front door and settled into it to wait the owner's return.

It was past sundown when Butler stalked into the dark house, lit a lamp, and then turned as if he realized he was not alone.

"Don't make another move," Bobby said, cocking the Colt in his fist with a loud snap.

"It's you!"

"It's me."

"You killed my boys."

"They killed themselves."

"You—" Butler raged.

"You stole the wrong man's cattle."

"Stole what?"

"Don't try to lie to me, I found the Lightning brands on those hides in your shed. Chisum, he really hates rustlers."

"Why, I'll—"

Bobby's first bullet doubled Butler over, the second one spun him around in the haze of bitter gunsmoke and ear-shattering explosions. Then standing over him, Bobby emptied the rest of the ammunition into his body.

Coughing and choking, Bobby fled outside on the porch and used the front of the house to lean on while he regained his breath. When he recovered he went for the hides in the shed, and brought them back. He dragged Butler's limp body outside into the starlight on the porch. Then he rolled his stiffening corpse in the hides, and bound him in his shroud with a lariat rope.

Bobby took Butler's horse from the corral, saddled him, and tied the body over it. Two hours later, he hung Butler's corpse by the neck in his funeral suit of mixed hides from a large oak limb near the crossroads.

With a last look at Butler's twisting form in the silver starlight, Bobby felt satisfied with a job well done and headed for his hideout. Word of this would get to Chisum in a few days and he planned to ride over to the Tanks, collect his money, and find out his next mission.

Three days later, hungover from his private drinking binge at the hideout, Bobby rode to the Tanks. He circled around on the hillside, making certain no one was there, then satisfied it was not occupied, he rode in, dismounted, and pushed open the door. He blinked in disbelief at his discovery. Seated on a crate was John Chisum, himself.

"I never—"

"Expected me to be here." Chisum closed his eyes as if pained. "You went too far, Bobby. Wrapping him in them hides with my brand on them!" Chisum shook his head in disapproval. "You've got the law all stirred up."

"Hell, I'll keep low for three or four weeks," Bobby protested.

"No. You're too dangerous for me to use."

"They'll settle down."

"No they won't."

"Hell, they can't prove—"

"Those were my hides that you wrapped the son of a bitch up in. It points at me!" Chisum looked at him in disbelief. "Why did you use them? I wanted him killed not a testimony that I was responsible."

"I figured—"

"You didn't figure shit. There is only one thing to do. You need to ride out of the territory and do it quick."

Bobby could not believe the man's words. Hell, he had murdered those two brothers, done it all so smoothly they could never point a finger at anyone. And he had used that damn old man's corpse to show the others that they shouldn't rustle his stock. Taken aback by Chisum's disapproval, he shook his head to try and clear it. His stomach balled into a knot. This couldn't be happening.

"Here's five hundred dollars. I want you to shake the dust of New Mexico tonight and not come back."

"Sure, sure," Bobby said, still in shock, jamming the roll of money in his pants. "You won't get a better avenger."

"Maybe I'll hire a smarter one. Now ride out of here before Sheriff Garrett finds you on my place."

"Fuck Garrett." Bobby turned on his heel and went outside. The same to you, Chisum. Folks always said that you turned your back on Billy the Kid the very same way after things got hot for him when he was working for you.

Bobby climbed into the saddle. For one last time, he considered with contempt and burning hatred the big man standing in the crude doorway. Without a word he turned away. He never wanted to see that rich bastard again. And after all he'd done for him. Seething with rage, he booted the bay horse eastward.

CHAPTER 2

"Another drunk," the officer said, shoving his latest arrest through the city marshal's office and toward the row of jail cells.

John Wesley Michaels looked up to observe his deputy, Mike Anser, half carrying the derelict past his roll-top desk. With a quick shake of his head, John turned his attention back to his paperwork. He cringed at the unmistakable sounds of the new prisoner's gagging and heaving. Anser's sharp words followed in protest. No need for John to turn around and look, the vile odors of puke had already assailed his nose.

He glanced up at the clock. It was only eight o'clock on Saturday night in Walsenburg, Colorado. There would be scores of other drunks to be herded through that front door before the Sabbath sun came up. Night after night, he and his deputies paraded the louts to the jail. At times, John grew so weary of the slobbering fools, he wished he had chosen another profession besides law enforcement.

Anser, a big man, came back attempting to wipe away the damage to his clothing with a wet towel.

"I didn't see it coming in time," he said and dropped heavily into the vacant chair. He shook his head wearily and sighed. "By damn, they've started early tonight."

"Saturday night. Payday always gives us a full house." John sat in the barrel-back wooden chair and tented his fingertips. "We will be full to overflowing by morning."

"Yes, we will. Aren't you going to the church social tonight?"

"If things don't get out of hand."

"Me and the boys can handle it, Marshal. It'll just be drunks."

"Yes," John agreed. "There will be plenty of them." He better be getting over there if he didn't want to be too late.

"You go ahead. We won't have a problem," Anser said again to reassure him.

John agreed, put the jail expense accounts away in the center drawer until later, and stood up. He strapped on the holster and short-barreled Colt, buttoned his coat, jerked it down by the hem, and put on his stiff-brimmed hat as he headed for the door.

"Send word if you need help," he turned and said to Anser. After the man's nod, he went outside.

From the city jail, he hurried the four blocks to Altersgate Methodist Church. The social was being held in the Sunday-school portion of the structure in the basement. He removed his hat when he entered the well-lit room and a smiling gray-haired lady greeted him. It was Sam Caughman's wife, Sarah.

"Oh, Marshal Michaels, so good of you to join us. The singing is about to begin. Get some ice-cold lemonade first, though."

"Thanks," he said, giving her his hat to put on the wall pegs with the others.

Several of the men waved to him from around the piano where they were finding their pitch. He held up his hand to beg a minute to get a drink. Bessie Jergen stood behind the giant lemonade bowl, ready to dip him a mugful.

"Good evening, John," she said and dropped her gaze to the floating chunks of ice and lemon rinds bobbing in the mixture.

A fair-haired widow in her thirties, Mrs. Jergen had spoken quite frankly to him on several occasions about the benefits of a spouse. Each time she apologized and said, of course, she intended nothing personal regarding herself.

Pale-complected, she stood ramrod tall with her head tilting forward of her body. A pleasant enough woman in looks and demeanor. He felt certain he could do much worse than arranging matrimony with her. However, he worried that his low pay as chief city marshal was inadequate to support a woman and two school-age children. A matter that he had never discussed with Bessie, since he felt talking about it would only give her false hopes. Still, he enjoyed her company and found the time spent with her a welcome change from the worthless sots he continually dealt with on his job.

"Warm evening," she said, handing him a mug of the yellow concoction.

"Yes, it is," he agreed. "If I don't get called away on duty, I would consider it an honor to escort you home afterward."

A pleased smile parted her lips. She nodded. "That would be nice, John."

"Good," he said, satisfied the matter was settled. With the mug of lemonade in his hand, he joined the other singers. They were already into the first verse of "Sweet Betsy from Pike."

John's deep bass blended in with the choral group. An assortment of businessmen, miners, ranchers, and railroad folks were melding their voices to the songs in the booklet. At the end of each number, the choir director, Mike Farr, told them the next page number so that no time was lost until they sung a new song.

Following the hour and a half of singing, they fell into friendly conversation and another round of lemonade and cookies before they began to disperse. Handshakes and good wishes were exchanged around the room, with promises to see each other at church the next morning.

John waited patiently while Bessie and some of the other women washed the glasses and put things away. He retrieved his hat. With his fingers gingerly holding the edge of the brim, he wondered what he would say to her. Filled with misgivings about how things were going uptown, he wished he had not asked her. Still, since no word of trouble had reached him, he felt obligated to accompany her home.

In the light from the kitchen door, he saw her hold up her chin and stride toward him. She wore a hat that reminded him of a hen's nest, and he wondered what would hatch from it.

"Marshal," she said, as if reporting for duty.

"John is fine," he reminded her and opened the door to the outside stairs. He followed her up and out into the starlight that shone between the large fir trees.

"I'm glad you weren't called away," she said quietly.

"So am I," he said. She would never know how grateful he was to be in her company and not dragging drunken derelicts to jail. He moved wide to avoid a spreading juniper bough. They continued their walk up the gravel street with light from the houses reaching into the shallow ruts.

"John, you have been very kind to me, but somehow I wonder if I have offended you, or else—"

"Offended me?"

"Did you ever have a wife or did you lose a girlfriend in your past? David and I were very happy. His departure was—well, very hard for me to accept, but after so long, I mean one should—"

"One should let it pass." He wanted to add, "And get on with one's life," but he didn't say it aloud.

"Yes."

"No, Mrs.—I mean Bessie, I have no one in my past. I'm afraid I'm a very practical man, and to take on the responsibility of home, wife, family, is more than I can afford at this time."

"Afford?" she managed as if the word had eluded her.

"Yes, it isn't you, Bessie or your fine, polite children. A chief marshal's pay is too low."

"But—but you could do other things."

"Not hardly. Since my discharge from the army, I've worked as a peace officer in some form or fashion. It's all I am qualified to do." No need for him to try and be something he wasn't and fail at it.

"Very well," she said in a small voice. They went the next half block in silence.

"I am pleased that is the reason," she finally said, looking down at her shoes. "And that you are that thoughtful."

"Yes, ma'am."

"Then you have considered me—I mean us—in your future?"

"Yes, I have, but you must understand my low salary makes it prohibitive."

"We could live in my house. It's paid for."

He nodded, acknowledging that he'd heard her.

"I could continue to sew, which is an honest living."

"Yes, but it still would not be enough—"

"I am a fair manager of accounts."

"I am certain that you are."

They were at her front door by that time. A crescent moon shone through the morning glory vines that ran up on strings tied to the porch roof. He removed his hat, feeling very uncomfortable; his stomach was upset, too.

"You may kiss me good-night," she said, looking down at her toes.

He leaned over and pecked her on the cheek. Then he jerked upright when she threw her arms around his neck, stood on her toes and pasted her mouth to his.

His eyes flew wide open. Then his arms went around her, and he could feel her willowy body against his. For a long moment, she pressed her lips to his in a strong kiss, then she stopped. Dropping down from her toes, she rapped on his chest with a knuckle.

"Don't be too long deciding, John." Then she turned and opened the door with a quiet "thanks" and disappeared inside.

He slapped on his hat. His conscience grated him for asking her to let him walk her home. He had been honest with her; she'd taken it wrong. He removed his hat and beat it against the side of his leg as he walked up the dark street, challenged by a yard dog or two that he shooed away. No way with his small salary could he ever ask her to marry him. There was just no way. When he licked his lips, he could taste her and the lemonade still on them. Sweetness and the sour part, like his life. He hurried toward his office; his deputies would need him by this hour.

John heard the shots before he reached the last block short of the jail. They came from farther down Main

Street, somewhere close to the Hurricane Saloon. He unbuttoned his coat and pushed it behind the butt of the Colt.
He seldom had to use his firearm, but at times the element
of guns and alcohol proved to be pure poison and some
innocent bystanders were usually hurt when it happened.

His boot heels clattered on the hollow-sounding
boardwalk as he hurried. Several of the curious came out
of the saloon doors and called after him to see what was
wrong.

"Don't know yet," he managed and rushed on.

"I'll kill the first sumbitch—"

John halted and spotted the big man, full beard, waving a smoking handgun and standing on the porch of the
Hurricane. Outlined by the glow coming from the
saloon's front doors, the gunman was dressed in cowboy
clothes, but was hatless and bald-headed, which reflected
the light. This shooter was no regular in town and John
did not recognize him.

"Get back," he said sharply over his shoulder to the
onlookers behind him on the porch of the Franklin Mercantile. He drew his Colt.

"Mister, either you throw down that gun or you can
prepare to die," John said, stepping to the edge of the
porch. He had the man in his bead.

"Who the hell are you?" The man blinked his eyes in
disbelief.

"Chief marshal, now drop the gun."

"That card shark in there stole my money. Cheated
me. He had cards up his sleeves," the man began to
whine.

"Guns aren't how you settle it." John advanced with
his body turned sideways to present as small a target as
possible. The Colt at eye level, cocked and ready.

"Yeah, well I did this time."

"Drop the gun!" he ordered.

"Aw, all right." The man let loose of the pistol and raised his hands. Anser rushed past John.

"I'll cuff him and take him in," the deputy said. "I had two fighters back at the jail or I'd have been here sooner."

"It's under control," John said to him. "What's your name?" he asked the big man, holstering his own gun.

"Horne, Isaac Horne."

"Well, Mr. Horne, you may get to learn all about Colorado justice. Now I better go see who is shot."

"He's a damn cheating crooked card player," Horne protested as the deputy shoved him toward the jail.

Inside the Hurricane, John parted the crowd and could see Doc Hampton was busy working with someone lying on the floor. The doc wore his small reading glasses, and when he looked up at John, he shook his head.

"Johnny Delco. He won't live till morning."

"Do what you can for him," John said as several men helped move the gambler onto a board stretcher.

"Take him up to my place," Doc said to the two men on the handles.

"If he makes a statement, take it down or send for me," John said to the physician as he looked over the crowd.

"I will—"

When the men started away with the wounded gambler, Delco's limp arm fell off the side of the stretcher and a playing card escaped from his snow-white shirtsleeve and fluttered to the sawdust floor. Doc saw it. John saw it. He bent over and picked it up. An ace of spades. It drew a wary loud murmur from the crowd.

"It still didn't give him the right to kill the man. Did Delco have a gun?" John asked, looking over the crowd.

"He went for one," someone said.

"How many saw him go for his gun?" John asked.

Several raised their hands.

"Was he standing—I mean Delco. Was he standing?"

"Yeah," Bart Yeats stepped forward and said. "They was shouting first. That Horne calling Johnny a cheat, and Johnny began bowing up."

"Who drew first?"

"That big guy was fast." Yeats shook his head. "That man you arrested is lightning. Johnny wasn't in his class."

"It ain't for me to say, but it looks like self-defense to me."

"I'd have argued about that, Marshal," Yeats said, "but not after I seen that card you've got there in your hand. I played with that Delco and thought he was straight."

"Cheating at cards isn't a reason to take a man's life." John frowned at the man.

"I'll bet you money and even give you big odds, ain't no jury in Colorado going to find him guilty."

"You may be right, but even the good book says, 'Vengeance is mine, saith the Lord.'"

"That guy Horne took his own vengeance out tonight."

"Maybe he did," John said. He looked over the crowd, then turned on his heel and pushed his way out the batwing doors. The prosecutor would want witnesses. Yeats could round him up a few. They wouldn't be worth much. He studied the card in the light from over his shoulder, then shaking his head with disapproval, he pocketed it. An ace of spades had cost one man his life.

Two days later, at the marshal's office, John was busy at his desk answering correspondence.

"You and that widow getting serious?" Anser asked from the doorway without turning to look at John.

"No, on my salary, I can't afford to pay attention on this job, let alone take a wife with two schoolchildren."

John shook his head and finished the letter to the Nebraska sheriff. He had been unable to find a killer that this sheriff thought might be in the area of Walsenberg. The wanted man's name was Ramon Ortega. A Mexican, short and swarthy, about five foot four with scars on the left side of his face.

"You could collect a weekly fee from each of the saloons. They're making money on these drunks we handle."

"That would be disreputable."

"Every other marshal in Colorado does it. You ever speak to the mayor about a raise?"

John looked up. Of course he had broached the subject, but he'd received no firm response. He studied Anser who was busy rolling a cigarette, his shoulder pressed to the facing so he could observe the street.

"I have spoken to Mayor Roy and he claims they can't pay any more," John said.

"Damn funny. In the rest of—"

"This isn't the rest, this is Walsenberg."

"John Wesley . . ." Anser dropped his voice and stepped inside the jail.

"What is it?" he asked, anxious to know what was causing his first deputy to act so strangely.

"Don't let them see you, but we have four men riding up Main Street. Brother, they're sure enough hard cases." Anser stepped back, anxiously studying whatever was wrong in the street

"Grab a shotgun," Anser said in a very serious tone. "Three of them just went inside the First National. They left one outside to guard the horses and he's cradling a rifle."

"Here," John shouted, rose to his feet, reached over on the rack, took a greener down and tossed it to his deputy.

Then he jerked out a desk drawer and began to fill his vest pocket with brass shells.

"You go down the alley—" But when he looked up, Anser was already gone. No, not that way, he thought, but he was too late. His deputy was headed right into their gun muzzles if they were robbing the bank.

John reached the doorway to see his deputy shouting orders at the horse guard to throw away his gun. A shot rang out. The lookout cut his deputy down with rifle fire. John rushed out in time to see Anser on the ground, and when he looked for the shooter, he was unable to locate him, hidden as he was behind the four horses. Though his conscience bothered him, he brought the shotgun to his shoulder and let loose a blast into their rumps.

His scattershot sent the robbers' mounts into panic. They bolted forward and crashed down the hitch rail. It gave John enough time to hook his hand under Anser's armpit and drag him to safety underneath a parked wagon. With no time to see about the man's condition, he fired the second round of his shotgun at the shooter who was fighting to control the panicked animals. Two of the animals stung by the pellets broke loose and ran away.

"Throw down your gun!" John ordered, uncertain whether the horse guard still had one or not.

One of the masked robbers emerged from the bank with a smoking gun. Bullets like angry hornets whizzed by John's head as he reloaded the twelve-gauge with buckshot. He fired back at the shooter. The blast doubled the outlaw in two and sent him flying back inside the open door of the bank.

The wild-eyed horse handler mounted, and took two wild pistol shots at him. John swung the barrel around to bear down on him, pulled the second trigger, and blew him headfirst off the pitching horse into the street dust.

At this point, John dropped the Greener and with his Colt drawn charged into harm's way.

The robbers inside the bank soon filled the air with cuss words. One came to the doorway and drew a bead, but his gun went off in the air when John's well-aimed bullet cut him down.

"Come out of there now!" he ordered and a hush settled in the street. Then came the sound of boot soles crunching over glass shards on the floor and a man in his forties, the red bandanna he used for a mask pulled down, came out of the door with his hands high.

"Where's the rest of them?" John demanded, holding the pistol at arm's length cocked and ready.

The bank robber shook his head like John couldn't count. "You got them."

"Turn around," John ordered, still not satisfied. Wary of the others, he moved in and frisked the man, took a knife out of his boot, then shoved him through the bank's front door.

"They've shot Mark Bridges," the teller, Amos Grimes, screamed and rushed up to him and his prisoner.

"Doc's coming, I am certain." John knelt and rolled over the one he'd cut down with the buckshot. The blast had torn him wide open. Obviously, from the man's blank eyes he was bound for the hereafter. After checking his prisoner to be certain he wasn't up to anything, John closed the robber's eyelids with his left hand.

"Get over there." John ordered the outlaw to stand by the front of the grilled cages. Then he kicked away the pistol from beside the last wounded one on the floor. He was still alive.

"That kid outside that you shot is still breathing," Rupert Jennings, his other deputy said as he burst in the door. "He isn't going anywhere, though, Marshal."

"Good, take this one to the jail." John indicated the unscathed one. "I'm going to see about Bridges," he said and paused. "What is your name?" he asked the outlaw.

"Ted Keith."

John nodded, waved his pistol at the two on the floor. "What did they call this gang of yours?"

"Didn't have no name. This was our first bank job."

"And your last," Rupert said and shoved him toward the door.

John found the wounded banker propped up by his desk. Someone had loosened his tie and the front of his shirt was soaked in crimson.

"Hurt bad?" John asked, squatting down and seeing they had used a towel to try and stop the blood flow.

"Not bad," Bridges managed.

"Doc will be here in a minute. Anything I can get you?" John asked.

The banker's eyes narrowed. "Tell Imogene I always loved her."

"You'll be fine—" John said, but the man's chin pitched downward and the bookkeeper, a thin man in his forties who squatted on the other side of Bridges, screamed like a woman, "Oh God, no, he's dead."

John looked up and saw a familiar woman coming through the front door. He bolted to his feet to catch Imogene Bridges before she could throw herself at her fallen husband.

"Mark! Mark! How is he?" she cried, trying to get past him.

"You can't do anything, Imogene," John said, struggling to overpower her. "He said he always loved you."

Then as if John had slapped her, she stopped trying to get by him. "He said he loved me?"

"Yes, the last thing."

"He never said that to me."

"Yes, he did, he said for me—"

"Damnit! Damnit!" she cried as tears rushed down her face and John was forced to hold her wrists to keep her from pounding him. "He told you, but in twenty years of marriage he never once told me."

Things went fast. Anser was carried to Doc's office, alive, but in critical condition. The two wounded robbers joined Ted Keith in jail and after Doc did all he could for Deputy Anser, he arrived at the jail looking bleary-eyed and began to work on the two injured robbers.

John had their names. Davy Brown was the kid holding the horses. He gave Las Cruces as his address. The other wounded robber said his name was Warren Bradley. Mumbled that he came from Texas. The dead man was Fred Brown, also of the Lone Star State.

When Doc finished tending to the men, it was ten after ten on the wall clock. He emerged from the cell block, and the volunteer guard, Matthew Riggins, locked the doors after him. The physician washed his bloody hands at the pitcher and bowl in the outer office.

"They going to live?" John asked.

"Sure, unless you cut their heads off, they'll live. Hard to kill those tough ones. Nothing I could have done for poor old Bridges today." Doc pulled off his reading glasses, stuffed them in his shirt pocket and shook his balding head wearily. "Guess we don't get a choice of who lives and who dies, do we?"

"No."

"They'll be all right to stand trial when the circuit judge gets here."

"Thanks, you've had long day," John said, concerned about his own deputy's recovery.

"I didn't have to drag my deputy out of the street under gunfire and face down those killers with them shooting at me like you did," Doc said, and poured himself a cup of coffee off the stove. He sank heavily into the chair opposite John's. "That took more cold nerve than most men have. This town is proud of you, John."

"That's fine," he said, then wet his lips. "That's my job, Doc. You have yours and I have mine."

"Word around town is pretty loud about you and Bessie."

"It'll have to get louder, Doc. No way I could ever afford to get married on my salary."

"The boys been talking about that. Most lawmen collect fees from businessmen to supplement their pay."

"Some own gambling halls and houses of ill repute too," John said leaning over and lowering his voice. "I don't belong to that kind of law enforcement, either."

Doc nodded. "John, we're going get you a raise. I can't say how much, but the whole city board and the mayor wants you to stay here."

"Good, I need to go check Main Street. I'll be up to see Anser after I make my rounds." John put on his hat to go out the door.

"John . . ." Doc rose wearily to his feet. "The last two marshals did this job for free and lived off the fines and kickbacks they pocketed. Folks don't want that kind of law again."

"I know," John said, and turning, spoke loudly to his new guard. "Keep an eye on things."

"Oh, I will, Marshal," Riggins promised.

John and Doc went outside. The sounds of hell-raising down the street rolled loud and clear. With a quick thanks and a goodbye, he hurried down the boardwalk. When John stepped from Branagan's porch to cross the space between it and the next steps, a rope whistled. The lariat snapped tight around him, pinning his arms to his sides. He realized with a gut-wrenching knot in his belly that he had walked into a trap.

"Sorry to do this," the leader of the three men in masks said as they bound him up.

"Let me go. You can't do this. Let the law handle it." John knew as they trussed him up that his words were like raindrops on a rubber slicker. They never soaked in.

"We had a trial and the jury's in," the man said as they sat him on the ground. "Mark Bridges was too good a man to die like that. Them bank robbers will pay the hangman's price tonight."

John fought at the ropes that bound his hands. Anger raged through his body as he sat on the ground in the dark alley. Vigilantes were in charge. It was his job to protect the criminal as well as the innocent, but there was nothing he could do in the alley, bound and tied.

He closed his dry eyes as tight as he could and strained. It was his job; he had to do something.

"Get me loose someone!" he shouted. But he knew not even the worst drunk would touch him until the "court's wishes" were fulfilled and the three bank robbers were hung from a tree.

John closed his eyes and prayed for them, both the vigilantes and the outlaws. "Dear heavenly Father, forgive them . . ."

The next day, Mayor Roy came by the jail with his hat in his hands and told John about the ten-dollar-a-month raise they would start paying him next month. John nodded and thanked the man politely, then he went over to check on Anser at Doc's. Sixty dollars a month was still not enough to make any wedding plans with. Not nearly enough. He shook his head, still seeing the vision of the three bank robbers hanging from the cottonwoods. The pay raise would not help them, or poor Mark Bridges. They would have his funeral that afternoon.

Hat in his hand, John entered the office. Doc looked up from his reading and John nodded at him. "How's the patient?"

"Getting stronger already, but he's sleeping. We better let him rest."

"Sure." John put on his hat and went down the stairs. Some good news anyway: maybe Anser would make it. He missed the deputy. His absence left lots of things for John to do by himself.

He went by his small apartment, took a sponge bath, and put on his best white shirt for the funeral. He brushed the dust off his suit coat and his hat. He considered how strange the mayor had acted earlier at his office. The man had seemed extremely anxious as he told him about the small increase in his salary.

Should he tell Bessie about the raise in pay? By his own calculation he needed a salary of at least a hundred dollars a month to support a wife and family. Sixty bucks was a long ways from that amount. He closed his eyes for a brief second at the hopelessness of solving the matter, then he started for the door. It would be sacrilegious to ask God for a raise. On the second-story landing, he stopped and studied the hills beyond the town.

To have someone pleasant for a wife, a person he could share his life with, was something he hoped someday to achieve. He simply wanted someone to come home to. He shook his head in disappointment and hurried for the cemetery and the final services for the banker.

After church on Sunday, John ate dinner with Bessie and the children. The boy and girl, Brent and Trudy, cleared the table and were excused to go visit some friends with a stern warning to be careful in their church clothing.

"And please recall that this is the Sabbath, so don't be rowdy," Bessie reminded them before they left.

"We will," they promised. "Good day, Marshal," they said politely and hurried out the front doorway.

"Nice children," he said to her absently and held the china cup of hot coffee close to his mouth.

"Yes, they have been raised right," she said stiffly.

A fiddle-tight string was drawn between them. He couldn't put his finger on the problem. Across from him, Bessie sat more straight-backed than usual. She reminded him of a china doll, so statuelike, so prim and proper.

"I received a small raise—" He stopped and considered the matter. "But hardly enough to make plans on."

"I should think they would be willing to pay you three times as much after what you have been through the past two weeks."

He sighed heavily. "Unfortunately they aren't."

"John, I had hoped—" She wet her lips and looked down at the white linen tablecloth. "I mean, I have wanted the two of us to reach some sort of . . . well, an understanding. Soon it will be fall—well, in a few months it will be and I—" Her green eyes bored a hole in him. "John, am I so ugly that you can't make up your mind?"

"No, you are a very attractive person, Bessie. But there is no way I could provide you and your children a fit living on sixty dollars a month."

"John, I will be very frank with you. You know Fred Bowles?"

"The rancher from west of here?" John recalled the man. Why, he must be close to sixty. Gray-haired and with ample girth, he came to town in a carriage driven by a Mexican driver. Bowles owned lots of cattle and sheep.

"He's offered to marry me."

"I didn't know that you knew him," John said, taken aback.

"I have made some shirts for him. Of course, my relationship with the man has been very proper." She raised her chin as if he had accused her of impropriety.

"I never doubted that. But I don't see—"

"No, John, you don't. I don't want to marry Bowles—" Tears began to well in her eyes then spilled down her face. "But I have no choice if you—"

"Bessie, you do what is best for you and the children." John rose to his feet. He knew as well as he had a week before, bound and tied in that alley, that fate would take its course.

"It will not be the happiest life, I am sure," she said and blew her nose loudly into a linen napkin.

"I am certain that he will treat you and the children well," John said to reassure her.

She dropped her chin and shook her head wearily. "Goodbye, John."

"Yes, thanks, and tell the children I said thank you." He rose heavily and could see she had no wish to accompany him out.

With a large knot in his throat, he put his hat on and headed for the sunny open front doorway. It was over between them. He could blame himself. He drew a deep breath of her fragrant flowers and stepped off the porch.

Headed the four blocks to his office, John looked up to see the ragged kid Amos in his baggy, hand-me-down overalls come hurrying up the dusty rutted street toward him. In his hand, the boy waved a yellow sheet of paper.

"Marshal. Marshal, I got a telegram for you," Amos lisped. "I been looking all over for you."

John frowned as he took the thin paper from the youth. Who was it from? He tipped the boy a dime and received a polite thanks and a smile.

Dear John,
Hiring men for a special agency in Arizona. Good pay and expenses. Are you available? Let me know at once.

> Major Gerald Bowen,
> Prescott, Arizona Territory.

Am I available? Yes, Major, I'm available. John hurried down the street.

CHAPTER 3

Ella Devereaux drew back from the curtained window of her second-story apartment in the Harrington House. She had been watching Major Gerald Bowen, the head of Governor Sterling's secret marshal force, striding up the hill for his own residence. Weary of the ongoing fuss between the legislators and governor over the formation of a statewide police force, Ella hoped that she had heard the last of the matter—and that potbellied Senator Green from Tucson who had pestered her so much to find out about them. When she finally managed to learn that Major Bowen had hired only one man called Sam T. Mayes and he had climbed on the stage for Tucson, she turned the whole matter over to Green, who lived down there. Let the pesky senator learn all about him.

Men became upset about the silliest things. Besides, she had much more important things to do than worry about what marshals the governor and major hired against the wishes of the territorial legislature. The everyday running of her sprawling mansion needed her close attention and supervision. Fifteen of the finest doves in the territory worked the upstairs bedrooms of her place, and downstairs, her clients also enjoyed two new billiard tables, recently imported from St. Louis, and the grand piano in the living room. At the palatial Harrington House, she stocked the finest liquors, spread the most exquisite tables of food, made available the finest cyprians of pleasure, and served the richest clientele in the territory.

"Missy, there is a man downstairs wants to talk to you."

Ella looked up and frowned at the black girl, Sassy. "Who is it?"

"He done gave me this card." Sassy handed it to her.

Ash Waddle. Westport, Kansas. What was he doing in Prescott? A tremor of fear ran up her spine. Of all the men in her life, she dreaded Ash Waddle more than any other. She swallowed the spittle in her mouth and wrestled up the front of her dress.

"Show Mr. Waddle up here . . . No, I will meet him downstairs."

"What should I do?"

"Stay out of sight," she said crossly at the girl for even asking, and swished out of her own apartment. She wanted to meet Waddle on neutral ground. What did he want? The question rolled over and over in her mind. In truth, she knew the very answer. For starters, he would want to take over the Harrington House. Lock, stock, and barrel.

Her fingernails cut into the palms of her hands, which were clenched tightly at her sides as she hurried down the hallway. She vehemently vowed she would see him dead before that happened. She had worked too hard to set up this place for her to ever again be put under the controlling thumb of Ash Waddle. When she paused at the head of the staircase, her legs felt as if they were filled with lead. She could see him pacing the hardwood floors in the entry. It was Waddle, all right; she would know him anywhere. And in any case but this one, she would have avoided him at any cost.

"Ash Waddle," she exclaimed. "Whatever brings you to the wilds of the Arizona Territory?"

He looked around as if amused. "Why, I came all the way to see you, my lovely darling."

"My, my," she said, forcing a smile on her face but feeling icicles inside. "All that way. When did you arrive?"

"A few minutes ago. I came on the stage from Ash Fork. They wouldn't carry my luggage—unfortunately it is coming by freighter from up there."

"How did you know I was here?"

Ash stood about five ten. He was a slender man dressed in a checkered yellow and black Prince Albert coat with a red silk sash tied at his throat and wore a fine bowler hat. His hard blue eyes undressed her as she descended the stairs. They bored into her with a hardness she recalled with deep bitterness. His smooth brown hair carried some gray now but it added to his distinguished look. For such a cruel pimp, she decided, his appearance looked much more benevolent than his real nature.

"A bird came and told me about you."

"And what was her name?"

"Don't recall now who told me, but the word is out back home about your lovely joint." He made a sweeping gesture with his outstretched bowler at the vestibule.

She paused on the stairs, wondering how he would start to manipulate her: gentle and friendly, or rough and cruel.

"Well, surely a man of your great means and talents is only passing through? I can find a lovely girl to rub your travel-weary back and entertain you—" She turned as if to fetch one.

"Get your ass down here!" His words, so sharp and chilling, brought out goose bumps on the backs of her arms.

She obeyed and soon stood face-to-face with him. Something cold shone in his eyes, reminding her of a diamondback rattler. The swift blow to her face sent her reeling into the curled end of the banister.

"Where's your apartment?" he demanded.

"Upstairs," she said, holding her hand to the fiery skin of her cheek and blinking her left eye to try and control the tearing.

"We're going up and move your crap out of there and I'll take it. Now how much money do we have? And you better not lie to me!"

Ella felt his fingernails dig like eagle talons into the flesh of her upper arm. The worst nightmare of her life had come true. Ash Waddle had come to take over her lucrative operations. What could she do? The law would never listen to her.

He roughly shoved her toward the stairs.

"Hear me good, girl. When I say move, you wag your ass or I'll remind you what else I can do to you," he growled in her ear.

His hold on her arm hurt deep into the muscle. How could she rid herself of this demon? Somehow she must find a way.

"But—but I thought you had a gold mine in Westport?" she said as she was hustled up the stairs. His breath smelled of whiskey and the cologne he wore was sharp-smelling, too.

"Ha, that all ended when the mayor's son got himself shot."

"You shot the mayor's son?" She blinked at him in disbelief.

"Shut up, goddamnit!" he growled under his breath. "You ever mention that again, I'll kill you. Get upstairs and be quick about it."

Propelled by her former pimp's firm grasp of her arm, she half stumbled on the steps, but his viselike grip kept her going. How would she ever get rid of him? He was not taking over her empire. Somehow, someway, she must eliminate him if she had to send him out of the house feet-first.

Ella promised herself she would do that. Ash Waddle was not ruining her life and ruling her in Arizona. Then the pain from his crushing grip made her head swim.

Two hours later, Ella sat despondently on the bed in the smaller room. Sassy and two of the doves worked to hang her clothing on the makeshift racks. Waddle had taken two thousand dollars from her house fund and headed off for Whiskey Row to gamble. Ella knew that amount was only the start; he would not be satisfied until he possessed all of her assets. How long could she hide the rest from him? Not long enough.

"Who is this Waddle?" Strawberry drawled, hanging up Ella's best red dress.

"I once worked for him."

"Looks to me like you're fixing to again."

Ella looked up hard at the redhead. "Looks can be deceiving."

Strawberry nodded, then stood on her toes to hang the dress on the wire they had stretched across the room for a hanger.

"This room don't get the breeze like yours, does it?" Strawberry asked, wiping her wet face on a cloth.

Ella shook her head, too upset to answer the girl.

"That's all of it in the hall," Sassy announced. "Want me to go look in that room for more, missy?"

Ella waved her away. "Let him have it."

"Where did he go?" Strawberry asked.

"Went to find a card game, I heard him say," Blue Winter said.

Yes, he did, and with her hard-earned money. He'd lose it all and be back for more, too. Ella knew him like a book. In the old days if he didn't have money he would use her body for collateral. Many a night she was forced to sleep under some grizzly old hunter who came to St. Louis and beat Waddle at cards. She shook involuntarily at the memory of those scenes and gritted her molars to stop the tremors in her body. They were nasty old bathless men who used her and were no better than boar hogs.

She had come all this way—by herself. Waddle was not going to take it away from her. Not spoil her chance to someday retire to San Francisco and live the life of a cultured lady. There, folks would never know her as anything else but that rich lady on the hill in the two-story brick house. She had seen that very neighborhood on a visit, before she found Prescott ready for the taking, and intended to retire in San Francisco in another ten years. But now her entire future hinged on whether she could control Waddle or get rid of him.

It would start with a telegraph to the Westport police. That would be her first step. If Waddle was a wanted man, she would be rid of him very shortly. The notion restored her confidence. Time for her to get to work. She shooed everyone out of the room but Sassy, so that she could dress in peace.

Ella rose and looked at herself in the mirror. His slap to her face still felt sore, but had left few traces that powder would not cover. Grateful for the fact she didn't have a black eye, she began spraying herself with expensive perfume.

"Which dress you gonna wear tonight, missy?"

"The blue one," Ella said casually, feeling at long last in control of the impossible situation. A telegram would do the trick. She would send Sassy with it to the telegraph office in a short while. In less than twenty-four hours, Waddle would be peering between the bars of the Yavapi County Courthouse. Filled with newfound confidence, she began to hum "Green Grow the Lilacs."

CHAPTER 4

Sun-cured bunch grass carpeted the rolling high country. Juniper-piñon-clad mounds rose like islands in the sea of yellow-brown. The two riders were headed south, avoiding the main road. The sun glinted on the brown whiskey bottle being passed between them.

Bobby Budd slouched in his saddle, weaving a little from side to side with his drunkenness. Beneath his weather-beaten hat, he bore a strong resemblance to the New Mexico wanted posters that depicted him as the Coyote Kid. He had seen one of them at Fort Wingate. That cheap tin star Garrett was only offering a hundred bucks for him. No-account stiff shirt needed a bullet . . .

Bobby glanced over and studied his sharp-featured companion, Leo Jackson, who rode beside him. Leo was loyal enough, Bobby decided through his liquor-dazzled gaze. Leo was a good sumbitch. They'd been together the past few months. Leo was like the brother he never had. He trusted him more than anyone, except his mother. She'd died, too, and he hadn't heard in time to get to her funeral. It happened when he was in the Indian Nation.

Made him sad to think about her being dead. For a long moment Bobby concentrated on the bottle in his palm, as he rode along loose in the saddle.

In disgust, he flung the bottle away, smashing it on a black rock. "Leo," he slurred accusingly, "that last whiskey that barkeep sold us ain't no damned good."

"Aw hell, Kid, we've drunk worse than that," Leo muttered. His stubbled face wore the growth of a three-day beard and brown tobacco juice stained his mouth.

"By gawd, we might've stole worse, but I ain't never paid two dollars for any worse." The Kid half laughed as he swayed in the saddle. "Hey, keep your eyes open for them Mexicans."

"You're plumb crazy, Kid. There ain't even a damn jackrabbit out here, let alone a greaser to plug."

Wavering on his horse, Bobby leaned over and grinned. "Don't you worry, Leo, we'll find some of them back shooters!"

"Damn, Kid. How come when you get real drunk you want to kill Mexicans?" Leo's brows furrowed and his mouth twisted as if he were displeased. "It don't make no sense. Most of the time you just shoot outlaws and troublemakers, I mean, that's what you're paid to do. But when you get drunk, all you want to do is kill greasers."

"Makes damn good sense to me, Leo!" The Kid slapped the pommel of his saddle with his palm. "Them damn Mexicans beat me up and they took the only girl I ever loved away from me. You remember me telling you about that nice man I worked for and how them chili eaters murdered him?"

"Sure, Kid," Leo agreed quickly. "You got any more whiskey?"

"Hell, yes." The Kid turned to get another bottle out of his saddlebags. He scowled irritably. Leo just didn't understand about them sorry devils. He was probably hoping they wouldn't find any. Leo didn't like him shooting them. But what the hell, after another bottle of this sorry rotgut, Leo wouldn't be worrying about who he was shooting at. The thought made Bobby chuckle.

Leo twisted to check their back trail, then looking satisfied, he turned back. "How far do you reckon it is to Arnold's Store?"

"Oh, about a bottle of whiskey away. What are you so nervous about? There ain't no law stupid enough to come after us. 'Sides, they can't prove we shot them two cow thieves back there. And we've got enough money in our pockets to stay drunk a month. When we run outta that, I know of a rancher down by Snowflake who would pay us a lot to get rid of some pestering rustlers."

Leo's eyes rounded. "Who?"

"You just never mind. Besides, ain't you done all right since you joined me?" Bobby demanded as he carelessly waved the bottle around.

Leo nodded. "Reckon so, Kid. I was just wondering."

"Well, goddamnit, don't wonder! There are lots of ranchers who don't like to admit that they hired us to get rid of rustlers and their little problems. Here"—he shoved the bottle toward his friend—"quit your worrying and have some more whiskey. Cy Edgar would be pissed if the word was spread all over the territory that the Coyote Kid worked for him."

Leo took the whiskey and apologized. "Sorry, I never meant nothing."

"It's okay, Leo." The Kid looked across the brown grassland. They had passed several of Arnold's cattle, which were branded with a AK. The cows and calves moved off when he and Leo rode near them.

Ben Arnold, the Kid recalled, was near sixty years

old. Arnold's Store was well stocked, and situated beside a big gushing spring that filled a dozen stock tanks before it tapered off into a dry gravel bed.

Old Arnold had a young wife named Dolly. The Kid had heard that she showed up at Arnold's with her baby boy a few years back. She was only a few years older than him. In the past, whenever she had waited on him, she had spoken curtly and been very businesslike. He recalled the nice turn to her hips as she walked away from him. He had speculated on her ripe body, but admitted to himself that it didn't look like the time would ever come when she would be willing to take him on, so he had just looked at her. Hell, the Kid swore silently, she had probably never heard of the Coyote Kid or Bobby Budd. That old Arnold must still have lots of fire in his chimney. It seemed a damn shame to him, though, that a good-looking woman like Dolly was stuck with an old fart like Ben Arnold.

"Here," Leo said thickly as he handed back the brown bottle, breaking into the Kid's erotic thoughts about what he'd like to do to Dolly.

He took the bottle and dropped his knotted reins on Buster's neck. Old Buster was well broke and would keep walking, which was just as well since he was becoming too drunk to guide the animal. It was getting difficult to concentrate on riding and drinking at the same time.

"Don't Arnold have a couple damn Mexicans working around his store?" he asked Leo as he abruptly grabbed at the rein to halt Buster.

Leo stopped his bay and turned the horse to ride back to him. "Yeah, I think he does. What's wrong? Why are you stopping?"

"I got to go." The Kid leaned over the side of the

saddle so far that only his quick last-minute grab for the mane saved him from falling off.

Swaying and weaving, he finally managed to dismount and fumbled with the buttons on his fly. Impatiently, he hoisted aside the scuffed holster that carried his guard-less .38 double-action pistol.

After relieving himself, he made three attempts to remount. "Stand still, you sumbitch," he swore at the sorrel gelding.

Leo moved in to hold the horse by the bridle. "You all right, Bobby?"

"Hell yes! I'm all right. Just right enough to shoot me a mess of b-back sh-shooting Mexicans." Finally back on his horse, he was panting heavily.

Leo chuckled. "You're drunker than a skunk, Kid."

"Huh?" The Kid looked at his friend, then began laughing as though Leo had said something hilarious. "We're crazy, ain't we, Leo boy?" Both men broke into loud guffaws. Tears welled up in the Kid's eyes, and he wiped them on his frayed shirtsleeve. Hell, Leo wasn't so bad after all, not after he'd had some rotten whiskey to loosen him up. Things were beginning to look better. He smiled widely, anticipating having more fun at Arnold's Store.

Dolly Arnold hung out the wash that she had just finished scrubbing. Ben was working inside the store. Dolly's six-year old son, Josh, played in the dirt alongside the building. Josh was a quiet child, content to build stick corrals and mountains of dirt. Dolly smiled tenderly as she pegged a pair of Josh's overalls to the rope line. Her son had been learning Spanish from Manuel and Rudy Garcia, the two orphan Mexican boys who worked for

Ben. They swept out the store, did the ranch chores, and rode for Ben at roundups. Although they were nearly out of their teens, they were very patient with Josh, who was quickly picking up their language.

She stared ahead and thought about how the two Mexican boys came to be at the store, long before she had arrived. Their folks had been killed by Comanches, and Ben had brought them from Texas to Arizona when he first settled there. Ben had a blunt way of explaining facts. He never doctored up his words, just stated the bare truth. But he was an easy man to please and seldom raised his voice in anger. He was good with Josh, and that counted for a lot in Dolly's book, even if she had never learned to love the Texan. Ben's first wife was buried at a site two days' ride east of El Paso. She had been a victim of bad water. Dolly surmised that was probably the reason why Ben treasured the ranch's big eternal spring. Why, in fact, he had built his store next to it.

Dolly shook her head to clear away the memories. She hung up the last article of clothing, then wiped her hands on her apron. It was near lunchtime and she hadn't started cooking yet.

Dust swirled around her ankles as she walked toward the back door of the store. At the top of the third step, she paused and pushed back a stubborn light brown curl. Shading her eyes with her hand, she peered in the distance at a trace of dust. Two riders were coming down the road. They were too far away for her to identify. She looked to the east toward the corrals and weather-beaten gray sheds that comprised Arnolds' store-ranch. Beyond them rose a green mound called Turtle Mountain. Ben rode there often to shoot a fat mule deer. He would always smile when he returned with the soft gray furred carcass draped over a packhorse.

"Hunting's still good in these parts," he would brag.

She squinted her hazel eyes again as she studied the approaching riders. They still didn't look familiar. She sighed and went inside the house. There was a cookstove to stoke and beans to warm. Along with her fresh bread with butter from the brindle cow's milk, that would suffice for her bunch, and she'd have enough to feed two more. Ben would expect her to serve lunch to the two newcomers. The big Texan obviously felt a kinship toward passing cowboys. Perhaps the empathy came from the time when he had punched cows in his youth.

A few minutes later, she set out plates, then began slicing her golden-crusted bread with her sharpest knife. Some intuition or maternal instinct caused her to suddenly put down the knife. She listened intently. The silence in the hot dry air was oppressive.

The Kid was the first to spot the two Mexican boys. They were lounging on the porch, dressed like cowboys. His jaw grew rigid with indignation. They had a hell of a nerve wearing clothes like that. Their manner of dress damn sure didn't disguise the fact that they were some of those ones that beat him up that night. He nodded decisively. They were some of those beaters.

"There they are!" He pointed and reined Buster in.

"Kid, wait!" Leo protested, blinking his eyes rapidly. "They're just Arnold's boys. Kid! Don't shoot! They ain't the ones!"

He ignored Leo's warning. He drew his deadly .38 and pointed it at the first Mexican, who stood wide-eyed on the store's porch. The other stood beside him, frozen in fear.

The gun barked and a puff of smoke surrounded the barrel. The heavy bullet slammed into the Mexican's chest and he collapsed on the ground. Buster reared on his hind feet at the explosion, nearly unseating the Kid. The horse's abrupt action caused his second shot to go wild.

No one noticed the soft cry of the child who had been playing near the porch. The second Mexican fled around the building. He's getting away! the Kid thought. He emptied his pistol after him, sending dust racing behind him like a brushfire.

There was a brief second of taut silence, broken suddenly by Leo's loud groan. "My God, Kid! You've shot that little kid over there."

Bobby twisted his mouth in disgust and tried to shove bullets into the pistol chambers while holding the upset Buster still at the same time. "Hell, Leo, you're drunk. I'm the Kid!"

"Damnit, let's ride, Bobby. You've killed him. He's right over there." Leo gestured wildly with his arm.

A big man working the lever action of a rifle rushed out onto the porch. Leo's wild shot shattered the window beside him.

The splintering glass jerked the Kid out of his drunken stupor. He quickly finished reloading his gun and shot wildly at the retreating man on the porch. For a split second, in his whiskey haze, he spotted the woman rushing from around the back of the store. He looked around frantically for the Mexican who had gotten away.

"Where'd that other damn one go?" he shouted at Leo, who was reloading at the same time.

"It don't matter a damn where he went. Kid, just ride the hell out of here!" Leo emptied his pistol at the store then he spurred his horse away. Buster almost jerked the Kid out of his seat when he galloped after Leo.

"Gawddammit," the Kid slurred, forced to hang on to

the saddle horn since he was unable to hold his pistol and pull up the gelding at the same time.

"You stupid ass, Leo!" He waved his gun at Leo. "I never shot no damn kid. Whoa! Dammit, whoa! I'm Bobby Budd, the Coyote Kid! Leo, wait!" He scowled at his friend's back on the racing horse and muttered savagely. Damn, he needed a drink. He needed to stop the crazy damn horse under him; he needed to holster his gun; and he needed to convince Leo that he was the Kid, and he hadn't shot one.

Dolly stood frozen on the back steps. Her cheeks felt drained. At the sound of the first gunshot, her heart had come to a thudding stop, and her legs refused to move beneath her. Then it seemed that all hell had erupted in the front yard. The shooting went on for hours to her, but she knew it had only been a matter of seconds. In her mind a vision flashed, one of Josh playing in the dirt beside the store. Trembling, she breathed in painful gasps as she searched wildly for her son. She swallowed hard at the sight of Manuel lying facedown on the ground, the dirt stained a rust-red around him. Then she saw Ben. He was bending over something beside the step on the far side of the porch.

"Oh God," she cried as she ran, tripping over her own feet. The distance seemed endless. She was choked for breath, her hair crawling over her scalp. Even the wispy dirt beneath her shoes impeded her progress. Finally she reached Ben. He was squatting, his broad back blocking her view. Biting her lip, she peered over his shoulder.

A moan erupted from her dry throat. "Oh God, my baby, my baby," she cried as she fell to the ground on her knees. Ben gently laid the child in her lap. Josh's head rolled back over her arm. A growing red stain darkened his white shirt. His straight brown hair was coated with a dusting of light dirt, and already his face held the blue pallor of death. Dolly cradled his still body and rocked him gently as she promised him vengeance.

Territorial Marshal John Wesley Michaels stared out of his boardinghouse window, waiting for a summons to Major Bowen's headquarters.

Uncertain of what assignment the major had in mind for him—since communication between the two had been so brief—John Wesley had packed an extra shirt in his saddlebag, along with his mother's worn, leather-bound Bible. Alongside the Bible, he had placed an extra short-barreled .44-caliber sheriff's model Colt, and with it, wrapped in sheepskin, he had put a spare box of ammunition. Earlier he had cleaned and oiled the weapon meticulously. The smell of the lubricant still reeked from the handgun.

Beneath the rooming-house window, the streets of Prescott, Arizona, bustled with the traffic of freight wagons and rigs. Beyond the booming village, John Wesley could see the surrounding hills clad with ponderosa pines. His gaze swept over the town, noting the Capitol building. A little farther down the street was Territorial Governor George Sterling's house. He knew that former army Major Gerald Bowen was a frequent visitor to the mansion.

Running his fingers absently through his coal-black hair, John Wesley smiled as he recalled his first meeting with the major, three days earlier. It had been a long while since the war days when he served under him, and at that reunion they discussed many things. On that first visit to Bowen's home, which also served as his headquarters, John Wesley had been informed about the organization he would be a part of. He recalled the major's conversation.

"John Wesley, we try to keep our position confidential," the major explained. "Republicans and Northern folks have a stigma in this territory with all these Texans and ex-Rebs. Governor Sterling does not want to upset the population with an unauthorized statewide law-enforcement office. You see, under the territory's constitution, the individual sheriffs handle criminals on a countywide basis. That system seems to work well for the most part, but it doesn't have the facilities or officers needed to handle the criminals that cross county lines. There have been border gangs, whiskey peddlers, and fugitives who have continually avoided the law." At that point the major offered him a cigar, which John declined.

After lighting the cigar to his own satisfaction, the major continued. "That's also why our force is so small. There are four marshals, counting yourself, who will report to me. The eldest is Sam T. Mayes, who you may recall was with us in Missouri and Arkansas during the war. He is off in the south after a border gang. He was formerly with a detective agency in Denver. Sam T.'s a resourceful, thorough man. Right now he has his hands full, but two of my former army scouts are assisting him."

John recalled Mayes from the war and tried to remember how he looked. Lots of water had gone under the bridge since those days. Mayes and his men had patrolled south of Cassville, Missouri, into Arkansas, while John and his outfit had tried to contain the bushwhackers in the Missouri hills.

Bowen continued. "Luther Haskell is another of my men. He's a former deputy U.S. Marshal from Fort Smith. Haskell's a Texas cowboy who can handle himself well. He's over in the eastern part of the territory investigating a brewing range war. And finally there's Shawn Kelly." The major rose and began to pace the room, and an amused smile lifted his carefully groomed mustache. "Shawn's a former railroad detective." He paused abruptly as a woman entered the room. "Oh, this is my wife, Mary. Mary, this is John Wesley Michaels. He's the town marshal from Walsenburg, Colorado, whom I told you about, and like Mayes, he served in the army with me."

Mary Bowen was a well-dressed lady of obvious breeding. She inclined her head in greeting and held out her smooth white hand to John Wesley. John took it gently in his own rough one and smiled at her. He surmised that behind the well-preserved oval face lay a shrewd mind. She had probably been a beautiful woman in her youth; the delicate bone structure of her face gave her a classic look of elegance.

"How do you do, Mr. Michaels?"

"Just fine. Pleasure to meet you, ma'am."

"I understand that you're a bachelor, Mr. Michaels." Her tone was gently probing.

"Yes, ma'am," John answered noncommittally.

She smiled warmly. "Well, you certainly have better manners than some of the other marshals." She glanced at her husband meaningfully.

The major laughed aloud. "We'll take some of your coffee, Mary. In the meantime, I think we'll leave Mr. Michaels to form his own opinion of the other marshals, including Shawn Kelly."

When Mary had moved out of earshot, the major shook his head and spoke wryly. "You'll get to meet Shawn later. Right now he's over at Crown King. There are lots of problems with claim jumpers and murders in the gold camps."

The major straightened abruptly and became brisk and

businesslike. "Now, the pay as I told you is one fifty a month, a lot more than most make. Of course, if you were a politician and held a sheriff's office, I think you could earn five times that amount. Surprised? Well, with fines, salary, expenses, and ten percent of the taxes they collect, I expect that the worst-paid sheriff in this territory earns around ten thousand a year."

John thought the amount exaggerated, but then he had no reason to doubt the major's word.

Bowen obviously sensed that he was surprised by the figure. "I can see that you are skeptical. That's why we are more or less a secret organization. The sheriffs are politicians, and any threat to weaken their authority will upset their old buddy legislators in the territorial government. So, I'd rather we call ourselves officers of the territorial court. And for that reason, I do ask that you not wave that marshal badge around unless absolutely necessary."

"I understand, sir," John agreed somberly. He didn't anticipate any difficulty ahead because of the need to keep a low profile, since he was a reserved man by nature.

"Good. You have a fine reputation as a soldier and equally good as a lawman, John Wesley. It's a sad fact, but the West seems beset with men who kill for hire or just plain orneriness. It's a disease, or at least a symptom of a system where a meager law enforcement agency is incapable of being *everywhere* to bring these men in."

Those words lingered in John's mind as he sat in his boardinghouse room, awaiting a summons to Bowen's headquarters. He had come to the conclusion that the major had studied the territorial criminal problem in depth. Bowen was a shrewd man, and he was looking forward to working for him again, but the current inactivity was becoming a strain. He sighed and looked around the room, realizing that it would probably be morning before he heard anything. John decided to fill in his time constructively.

He saddle-soaped and cleaned his handmade saddle, then disassembled and reassembled his short-barreled .38/.20 Winchester repeater. Lastly, as the day's sunlight began to fade, he read from Psalms in his Bible. His one goal in life was to be well equipped and ready at the call to serve either the law or his Maker.

Early the following morning, a young boy delivered a written message from the major to John. The major requested his presence at the Bowen residence at his earliest convenience after breakfast. John was grateful for the summons. At last he would learn what his first assignment as a territorial marshal would be.

Over a hearty boardinghouse breakfast, he listened to the monologue of a man called Gyp seated beside him, who spoke about the weather, a gold strike, the Apaches, and a few other things that held no interest for John. He replied to him in brief monotones.

"You an ex-soldier for the major?" Gyp asked, his small eyes scrutinizing John's face. John nodded and occupied himself with eating, hoping to discourage further comments. But the man of fifty years or so was not daunted. His voice held a whine that grated on John's nerves.

"Yes, sir, that major was an Apache heart eater," Gyp said with a chuckle. "You ever eat any?"

"No." John shifted irritably on the chair. Gyp seemed to have a never-ending supply of rambling conversation.

"This a reunion? You and the major?" Gyp asked, then slurped his coffee from a saucer. When John did not answer, he shrugged his thin shoulders and leaned forward as if to concentrate on more coffee.

John was relieved at last to get out of the boardinghouse and away from the talkative man. He strode down-hill toward the bridge over Walnut Creek and then past the end of the block that contained all of the saloons and houses of sin they called Whiskey Row. Grateful his days of arresting drunks were over and he was embarking on a new career, he drew in a deep breath of the strongly pine-scented air. A new stone courthouse had been con-structed in the square. He climbed the hill through the thin pine trees, noticed the large, luxurious two-story house with the high fence and wondered about the owner. A block farther on he turned onto the dirt street that ran past the major's bungalow.

As he approached the house, he noticed a long-legged chestnut gelding tied to the hitch rail in front of Bowen's house. He was an impressive animal and he stopped for a moment to admire him. Judging by the length of the stirrups, a tall man rode the horse. The rifle in the scab-bard was new. Alkali dust flecks caked the gelding's lower legs above the red-brown dirt from the Prescott roads, which meant he recently had been in the desert.

John stepped lightly up the Bowens' front steps, then lifted the heavy door knocker. He removed his hat and smoothed his black hair in place as he waited.

Mary Bowen opened the door. "Oh, good morning, John Wesley." She smiled pleasantly. "Gerald is upstairs in the den with Sam T. Mayes. They're expecting you."

"Yes, ma'am. Thank you."

"Come on in," she said, opening the door wider to al-low him entrance. She led the way across the hallway, then started up the stairs. She half turned and spoke over her shoulder. "Perhaps you'll be able to come to our so-cial at the end of the month?"

"I'll have to see what the major has in mind for me to do, but thank you, ma'am." He carefully hid an amused smile at her attempt to get him in a position so that she could play matchmaker. He had an idea that Mary Bowen enjoyed the cupid role.

"You did say you were of the Methodist faith?"

"Yes, ma'am."

"Good. We have a fine congregation here in Prescott, did you know?"

"Yes, ma'am, when I get time."

She shook her head and sighed softly, "It's just like the army. Always duty first. It's not going to be any different in this business than it was in the military."

She stopped outside an oak-paneled door, then pushed it open. "Here we are," Mary announced. "Gentlemen, John Wesley Michaels is here. I'll leave you to your business." She turned to face John Wesley. "Remember the social."

John nodded and stepped into the room. Major Bowen rose and stood in front of the yellowing map of Arizona that was tacked to the wall behind his desk.

A tall man wearing a brown suit rose from a chair in front of the desk. This was Sam T. Mayes, the marshal that the major had spoken of. "John Wesley Michaels, you know Sam T. Mayes," the major said, making the introductions with a smile.

John crossed the polished floor and stood on the colorful Navajo rug. Mayes's face looked more weathered and rugged then he recalled. Of course, everyone had aged since then. He held out a hand to the large man and met his direct, assessing gaze.

"Nice to see you again," Sam T. offered.

"Yes, my pleasure. It has been some time since the major's command in Cassville." John noted the large pistol grip that bulged out of the man's unbuttoned coat.

"John, Sam T. has just returned from Tucson," Bowen said. "He has the last of the Border Gang in jail."

John turned and gave the tall man an approving look.

"Sam T. is heading back to southern Arizona," the major said. "A man *believed* to have been Quantrel's captain is living the good life below the border."

"Good luck," John said.

"Thanks, I'll need it."

Major Bowen was up, pacing the carpet, his hands behind his back. "John, we have word that the Coyote Kid is in eastern Arizona. Did you ever hear of him?" Bowen turned and stared hard as if waiting for a reaction. John simply nodded and waited for the man to continue.

"Well, besides hiring out his gun," the major said with a scowl of disgust, "the Kid shoots Mexicans like they were whiskey bottles in a dump. He could've stayed over in the New Mexico Territory or ridden to Colorado, but unfortunately he came west. Last we heard of him, he was around Holbrook about the time that two known rustlers were found dead."

John nodded. He knew that the Coyote Kid had a notorious reputation that began years before with the cold blooded killing of a blacksmith in Springfield, Colorado. Later he was accused of hanging a cattle rustler for John Chisum in New Mexico. He also reportedly shot two men who were homesteading a water hole. Hired guns like the Kid were ruthless instruments used by powerful men to enforce their own vigilante law and to repel homesteaders.

Bowen sighed heavily. "He was taking potshots at some Mexican boys at a place called Arnold's Store, and . . ."—the major paused and drew a deep breath— "in the process, he killed a six-year-old white boy. No doubt the Kid was drunk, which of course, is no excuse for any killing."

John's jaw grew rigid with disgust. What kind of savage would kill a child?

"John"—Bowen spoke his name to recall his attention—"now we know that he rode south with an accomplice. So I would suggest that you start here." The major pointed to the map behind him. "Step over here closer and I'll show you the location." John followed the major's fingers as he traced a route on the yellowing, brittle map. "You'll need to take the train to Holbrook, then pick up a saddle and packhorse there," Bowen stated. "I think the Kid will stay in the back country for a while."

"Major, you do know that they'll probably hide him up there?" John asked.

"Beg your pardon?" The major looked at him in puzzlement.

John shrugged and said flatly, "These ranchers and other people that he's worked for will hide the Kid."

Bowen seemed to consider the possibility, then he nodded grimly. "I suppose that you're right."

Sam T. rose and walked over to the map. "He's right, Major." Knowingly, he repeated Major Bowen's earlier words to John Wesley. "It's a symptom of the disease. These hired guns are a festering boil in our society. Men like the Coyote Kid are a sign of these times."

The three men stood in silent agreement, their lips compressed in determination.

John Wesley was the first to speak. "Is there a good description of this Kid?"

"Behind you on my desk." Bowen gestured toward a pile of wanted posters.

John Wesley picked up two of the stiff, heavy papers and handed one to Sam T.

Mayes sighed and looked at John Wesley with a touch of wryness. "I'm beginning to wonder which of us has the most difficult task ahead."

John Wesley nodded. "It won't be a picnic for either of us." He watched to see if Sam T. thought he was making a joke, but the large man inclined his head in agreement.

John Wesley studied the paper in his hands and tried to visualize the man from the description.

"Bobby Joe Budd, alias the Coyote Kid. Age: mid twenties. Height: five feet ten inches. Weight: one hundred sixty pounds. Distinguishing marks: one front tooth missing, large brown eyes, brown hair. Is a careless dresser. Carries a guardless .38 double-action Colt. To be considered armed and dangerous." A lengthy list of law enforcement agencies on the sheet asked for his arrest.

John ground his teeth in brewing anger. No doubt it was that .38 that had so carelessly snuffed out the life of the young child.

CHAPTER 5

The Kid's head swam dizzily. He clung to a sapling for support. Past the stage of violent vomiting, he felt bitter bile rise up in his throat with a volcanic thrust, and forced his lower jaw to hinge and his tongue to snake out in a fruitless effort. His eyes were flooded with tears and his vision distorted. "I think I'm dying," the Kid gasped hoarsely. "I've been poisoned."

"You drank too much," Leo quietly scolded him. "You always drink too much."

Panting for breath, the Kid twisted around to focus his blurred vision at his companion. "Go to hell, you son of—" His words were cut off by the retching from his stomach as it tried to eject something alien. Hands on his knees, he spat phlegm, unable to free his mouth of the sour bitterness.

"You figure it'll be safe for us to ride into town?" Leo asked. "This bacon's moldy, and all we've got to drink is this bad whiskey we got from them three bootleggers back there."

"Quit your whining, Leo. I'm dying," he huffed, "and

all you can think about is damn food. Hell, if you'd told me there was a little kid out there by that store, I'd have—"

"Jeez, Kid," Leo interrupted defensively, "I never seen him either till it was too late. How was I to know some snot-nosed brat was sitting in the dirt there? I'm damn tired of you blaming me for this whole thing! You shot the little bastard, not me!"

A fit of coughing prevented the Kid's savage retort. Damn that Leo anyway. The Kid dropped to his behind on the ground, then scrubbed at his burning eyes. At last, he violently blew his nose between his fingers and flung the stream away. He wiped the balance of the snot on his pants.

"Well, it's a damn mess anyway! Word about it is bound to spread all over the territory. Maybe they didn't recognize us, huh?"

Leo shook his head in despair. "Yeah, I hope so. Way it is, we've got money and no place to spend it."

"I aim to go in and find out if they know it was us," the Kid said. But for the moment, he was more worried about his fading eyesight than whether some small-town law was looking for them. The blurry vision had sobered him. His fretting over the matter of his diminished sight had caused a fistful of worms to ball up in his already upset stomach. Despite his best efforts to strain his eyes and even squint hard, nothing looked clear, even the back of his own hand held inches away.

"You mean we're going to town?" Leo asked.

"Shit fire, yes! We need supplies." The Kid was determined to at least get out of their canyon hideout. He'd been denned up for four days with whining Leo and he was tired of it. After the incident at Arnold's Store, they'd bought that bad Injun whiskey. It must have been Injun whiskey all right, the Kid reflected sourly, 'cause no sane white man would have drunk it. Besides all that, he was getting on his nerves like a hill of red ants crawling on his perspiring skin.

"I'll go get the horses, I know you ain't feeling good," Leo said and hurried off.

Leo caught the horses and saddled them. While his cohort worked on getting ready to leave, the Kid kept trying to see, but everything looked fuzzy. He had never had any trouble with his vision before. What had caused this?

"You doing any better?" Leo asked, breaking into his thoughts. The man was ready to ride. The Kid reached out for the animal, finding a saddle strap to guide him.

"My eyes are screwed up, that's all it is," he said, feeling for the stirrup. "I must be sun blind or something."

"Here, I'll help you."

"No!" the Kid said. "I can make it myself. Say, why don't you just lead Buster with one rein till my eyes clear up a little. They'll get better in a little while." In the saddle at last, he handed the rein over to Leo. Then, with his fist grasping the horn and ready to ride, he could barely tell it was day light.

"Anything else?" Leo asked.

"No, I'll be fine in a little while."

"I sure hope so," Leo said in a small voice.

They started south. The Kid decided that if they had been smart they would have ridden on to Utah or Colorado, rather than staying this long in Arizona—especially after things got too hot for them to remain in New Mexico.

He could look back and regret how they had handled the matter of that pushy rancher, Howard. A fiery Texan by the name of Mark Taylor had locked horns with Howard over water rights. So Taylor hired him and Leo to solve his problem.

Simple enough; they had trailed Howard out of Santa Fe. Leo rode up and asked the unsuspecting man for a light. The Kid took advantage of Howard's vulnerable position, his broad back making a large target, and he shot the man twice. They left his lifeless body in the road.

Taylor paid them two hundred bucks in gold and thanked them. Afterward, the Kid reflected how he wished they had hidden the corpse. While no witnesses or evidence could tie them to the crime, the Kid noticed how Sheriff Garrett's old wanted posters on the Butler episode were reprinted and began showing up in many places. Things grew so hot, it soon became necessary for the two of them to ride over into the Arizona Territory until they calmed down.

Two weeks later in a Holbrook saloon, a ranch foreman sat down at the table with him and Leo. Obviously, this old man had something on his mind. His face was like saddle leather; his gray eyes were cold and calculating.

The old man asked if he was the Kid, and when Bobby said yes, he whispered that his name was Wagoner and told them how two rustlers had eluded him. He knew the pair was guilty, but couldn't get the proof to legally bring them to justice. Then he stated in a biting tone that these rustlers had to be stopped one way or another.

"It'll cost you a hundred apiece," the Kid informed him flatly.

"They ain't worth that much," the foreman complained, obviously holding out for a lower price.

Wagoner was a hard case, but if the rustlers had been so easy to capture, the man would've been able to do it himself without calling on the expertise of the Coyote

Kid. Bobby shrugged away the man's effort to get him down and stuck to his price.

"We've got our expenses."

When Wagoner realized he meant business, he complied irritably. "All right, all right. But I want the job done right and soon."

"It will be." Just who the hell did this old bastard think he was dealing with? He always did the job right; there had never been any complaints. Hell, just ask any dead man. Except for that damn fussy Chisum. The Kid curled his lip in cynical amusement when Wagoner tried to pass the blood money under the table.

"Who do you need to get rid of?" he asked, not bothering to keep his voice to a whisper. He laid out the bills on the table in a move of smug confidence and began to count it slow like, straightening the edges all even in the stack.

Wagoner cringed at the flagrant sight of the blood money and leaned forward. "Tom and Harry Slatter. They live west of town. They got a batching outfit in a shack." The ranch foreman gave the information quickly, in a hurry to get away from their company.

"Wait," the Kid said. This old buzzard was not getting off that lightly. "Me and my buddy Leo here ain't too familiar with the area. You better tell us exactly how to get there."

He felt important when Wagner squirmed uncomfortably on his chair. The longing looks he cast toward the batwing doors of the saloon filled the Kid with smug amusement. This old man wasn't any different than a lot of others who had hired him to do their dirty work. Once they handed him that money, they felt that they were clean of the whole thing. Hell, they were the real killers. All he did was pull the trigger.

Looking ill at ease, Wagoner wrapped his hands around the shot glass of whiskey on the tabletop, then spoke quickly. "You go west out of town, cross the wash, then you'll see some hills. The Slatters' place is in the second draw. It's almost hidden unless you're especially looking for it. When you ride up, you'll see a cow skull on a post. She has drooping, long horns." The man downed the whiskey, looked across the table at Leo, then at the Kid. "Think you can find it?"

The Kid glanced at Leo, who merely nodded. He never said much when negotiations were taking place, which was just as well, because Leo might have let tough guys like Wagoner beat down their price.

"Hold on a minute, mister," the Kid insisted as the man began to rise. "We want to buy you one more whiskey. Since we're working for you, it's only fitting that we buy you another drink."

"Oh, yeah, sure," Wagoner agreed. Obviously it wasn't because he wanted another one, but because he had no other choice. The Kid thoroughly enjoyed this man's discomfort. A guy like this usually gave orders. It was time Wagoner took a few; it might do him a lot of good. Besides, it was important that the man realized just who he was dealing with.

The following morning they went after the Slatter brothers. Like Wagoner said, they found the cow skull and rode right past it to the patched-up shack. Looking the place over, the Kid noted a couple of skinny horses in the pole corral. The homestead consisted of a ramshackle hut and a pole pen, reinforced with more posts to brace the weaker ones.

"Hey! Hello the house!" He shouted the customary greeting.

A grizzled face and a dull-barreled rifle appeared in

the doorway. Even at that distance, the Kid easily read suspicion in the man's piglike eyes.

"What do you want?" the man demanded harshly.

"Say, mister," the Kid began in a reasonable tone, "I ain't here for trouble." He looked around the area as if he were expecting someone else to be about the place. Where was the second brother? Must be inside, he decided. After settling back in his saddle, he continued. "Me and my pal Leo figured we could do some business with you."

The man kept the gun on them as he spoke. "Yeah, just what kind of business?"

"Put the gun up. I'm the Coyote Kid, and this here's Leo Jackson." With that announcement, he stepped off his horse. He felt certain that if the man had intended to shoot them, he would have already used the gun in his hand.

"What do the two of you want?"

"Leo?" The Kid turned to his friend and frowned in pain. "How many steers do we need to feed that survey crew?"

"It'll take at least one a day. They all eat like bears." Leo spouted their prearranged lie. " 'Course, we can always get them somewhere else."

"Wait, just a minute," the man said. "Come on in here where we can talk."

The Kid nodded to Leo in approval as they dismounted. Their plan was working. The two of them followed the man inside the hovel.

"I'm Tom. That there is Harry." The man pointed to a shape in the corner of the darkened shack. Then he laid his rifle across the bare wood table and peered at them as he asked, "Who sent you up here?"

The Kid drew closer to the table and spoke mildly. "We listened around the saloon. See, me and Leo here are guards and outfitters for that big survey crew. We need to make a couple extra bucks a head off the food that we buy for them. You savvy what I'm talking about?"

Tom looked back at his brother for his answer. Harry was seated on a bed of tattered quilts. At last, he scrubbed his face and said with keen suspicion, "How do we know you ain't the law?"

'Ain't you ever heard of the Coyote Kid?"

Harry looked at Bobby uncertainly. "Yeah, I heard of him, but that don't make you him."

With a grim set to his mouth, the Kid straightened and turned to Leo. "Leo, tell these yahoos who I am!"

Leo kept his voice to a low warning pitch. "Mister, he's sure enough the Kid, best not to rile him up."

As his partner spoke, the Kid assumed a bored attitude, casually looking around the dingy, smelly room and satisfying himself about the lay of things.

"Yeah, just because you say so, don't make it true," Tom said to Leo, keeping a wary eye on the Kid the whole time.

Filled with impatience, the Kid jerked his head up and gave the stupid man a scathing look. "What the hell do you think I do? Carry a damn wanted poster around with me?" He sighed in disgust and nodded at Leo. "Come on, Leo, obviously these guys don't want to do any business. Let's go somewhere else!"

"Right, Kid." They turned toward the door.

"Whoa, wait a minute, Kid," Tom said. "Harry, what do you think?"

"Well, we could use the money," Harry put in reluctantly. "I figure they're who they say they are."

Behind a hidden smile of satisfaction, the Kid turned back toward the men, sticking his thumbs in his belt and frowning. "Let's talk money."

"Yeah," Tom interrupted quickly. "How much you planning to pay us?"

"Twenty dollars a head." Then he said over his shoulder, "Leo, go get us some whiskey, so we can close this deal. It's in the left side of my saddlebags." He turned back and sat down on a nail keg, facing the two of them. "Me and Leo get five bucks; you get fifteen."

"Hell, no!" Tom protested. "We've got to do all the work and you and him get all the gravy. We're taking a hell of a risk as it is."

As if it made no difference to him, the Kid shrugged. He sure didn't want the two upset before he sprung his trap. "All right. You get sixteen; we get four."

"How come they're willing to pay so much for beef?" Harry asked. His questioning gaze cut back and forth from his brother to Bobby.

" 'Cause," he explained, "they don't know nothing about beef prices around here." He heard Leo returning and looked up in relief at him, seeing the brown bottle in his hand. A good shot of rotgut would settle his gun hand.

"Ah, good. Break out some cups," he announced to the brothers. "This here's real whiskey."

Harry found three cups and a bent can to put on the tabletop. He gave a chipped enamel one to Leo and the tin can to the Kid.

After the Kid poured the three drinks, rather than use the filthy can, he took a swig from the neck. "Here's to lots of beef," he toasted.

"Yeah!" the others chorused in agreement.

The Kid half stood and generously refilled the Slatters' cups. In Leo's, he splashed a small amount, then took a little swig from the bottle. The Slatters each pulled their chairs closer to the table, and were obviously relaxing their guard.

Then, as they had previously arranged, the Kid gave an inconspicuous nod to Leo. It was time to get this over with.

Leo rose. "I got to go piss," he announced in a tone so urgent that the brothers couldn't possibly suspect otherwise. Bobby poured them more whiskey after Leo went outside. Leo's actual mission was to check and make sure no one else was around the area.

"You've been working over in New Mexico?" Tom asked.

"We been lots of places." He grinned broadly, inviting the brothers to laugh with him.

"Yeah, I heard before that you was real slick," Harry commented. "I mean at getting jobs like this survey thing. What in hell they surveying for, Kid? Another damn railroad?"

The Kid paused with the bottle halfway to his lips. He blinked at the men and chuckled. "By God, I ain't sure," he said, as though the idea surprised him.

"Aw, hell," Tom complained, "you just ain't telling. Right, Harry?"

"Yeah, that's right. Come on, Kid, you can let us in on the—" Harry's wheedling grin was choked off abruptly and his face drained of color. Both brothers faced the Kid's .38 pistol across the table.

The Kid shook his head as though it pained him to ask. "You boys have been stealing beef, ain't you?" He didn't wait for their reply. "Well, you see these rancher friends of ours don't like that. Old Wagoner said he warned you, but I reckon you boys didn't listen too good."

He held the pistol steady and never took his eyes from them as he listened for Leo's returning footsteps.

The door eased open and a patch of bright light fell on the dirt floor. "It's all right, Kid. There's no one around," Leo said softly.

"What're you going to do with us?" Tom snarled, his fists bunched on the table. The rustler's eyelids were slits of smoldering anger at being taken in so easily.

The Kid raised a brow and pushed back his hat with the tip of the gun barrel. "Now, just what do you think I'm going to do? Goddamn, you sure are dumb, Slatter. We're going to kill you, what else?"

"Hey, Kid, you've got to give us a chance," Harry pleaded. "We'll clear out and be gone in a tick. And we'll never, never come back here. I mean vamoose! You won't ever have to worry about us again . . ."

He sighed heavily as if pained. "I know, Harry." Then he turned the gun on Tom, who looked the most dangerous and squeezed the trigger once. He swiveled the smoking muzzle at Harry, who let out a high-pitched scream before the loud shot cut his voice off. Harry grabbed his chest and slumped to the floor. The Kid rose slowly to his feet to study the wounded men in the haze of gunsmoke. He had shot Tom in the chest, but it was too high for a dead-on heart shot.

With slow deliberation, he aimed at Tom's chest as the man's eyes widened in fear and his mouth opened to protest. The loud report of the .38 and the thud of the bullet rang in the Kid's ears. Blood fountained out of the black hole centered on Tom Slatter's breastbone.

He glanced toward Harry, who by this time had rolled over on his belly and in desperation attempted to crawl away. The .38 jumped twice in the Kid's fist. The other Slatter crumpled and lay still. Satisfied, he sat down on a chair and laid the revolver on the table. Then he combined the brothers' cups of whiskey into one tin one.

"Leo, check and see how much money they've got on them."

"Sure, Kid." Leo busied himself searching the limp bodies while Bobby watched and carefully reloaded his .38. Then with care he placed the empty cartridges in his coat pocket, refilled five of the empty chambers, and snapped the hammer down. After holstering the gun, he poured himself another cup of whiskey.

"They got much money on them?" he asked Leo, knowing that most two-bit rustlers were usually busted. Leo put a jackknife on the table, making a dull clink on the worn surface. With a splotch of fresh blood on his hand, he tried to wipe it away with his kerchief and at last shook his head in disgust when he met the Kid's gaze.

"Shooting pushy ranchers is a lot better than this kind of thing," Leo complained.

"Yeah, reckon so," he agreed absently as he stared into the half-filled cup cradled in his hands. "But you've got to take the good with the bad." Someone had told him that once, he couldn't remember who. Of course, it didn't matter anyway. When it got dark, he and Leo would plant the bodies close to town as a warning to other rustlers. The foreman who had hired them would like that kind of detail. Then the whole business of the Slatter brothers would be over. Just another job.

"This one had forty bucks on him," Leo said in surprise, breaking in on the Kid's thoughts. "Guess we've got about fifty dollars altogether. Want me to look in their boots?"

"Sure." Bobby waved the tin cup. "Ain't no sense in leaving any money for the damn undertaker. Leo, you should know better than that by now," he scolded with irritation. He had to tell that dummy everything to do.

"Hell, I just figured that was all they had," Leo muttered defensively as he bent over to struggle with taking off Harry's boots.

"Are they good boots?" he asked, straining to see across the table. "These I got on have a hole in the sole."

"Naw, this one's sole's torn loose." Leo grunted as he worked the shoe off the corpse.

"That figures." He turned his attention back to the whiskey. He should have shot those brothers sooner, he reflected in disgust. They were a waste of good liquor. Oh well, in the morning he and Leo would ride south and pick up more whiskey on the way. They had a job to do for a rancher at Snowflake. There sure was no lack of work for them in Arizona.

The Kid tried to clear his sight as he came back to the reality of his blindness. Thinking about killing those Slatter brothers hadn't helped his damned eyes any. It had taken his mind off the fact that Leo had to lead his horse, but now it also reminded him of how dependent he had become. Despite the cool mountain air, his back was bathed in sweat. This helpless state filled him with a fear that made him weak. Although he was grateful to have Leo helping him, he resented the fact, too. His belly was still on fire and he felt dizzy-headed. A gray fog had settled over his eyes, and no matter how hard he blinked or rubbed at them, the wall of mist remained in place. Goddamn them rotgut-making bastards! He cursed them out loud. Those three whiskey runners who sold them that bad stuff would be drinking their own piss if he ever ran across them again.

Later as they rode, he could feel the sun on his left

side, and he knew it was late afternoon. But for him, it might as well have been midnight. He had gone completely blind, and the realization stabbed him with panicky fear. He had heard of men going blind on bad whiskey, but he damn sure didn't think it would ever happen to him. Before he went plumb sightless, he was going to find that trio of whiskey peddlers and make them pay for his condition.

"Leo, where did they go?" he shouted.

"Hell, Kid, I'm right here, ain't no need to shout," Leo said from beside him. "Who're you talking about?"

"Them damn poisoners."

"Who do you mean?"

"Goddamnit, Leo! Those three back at that log cabin sold us this damn bad whiskey," he screamed.

"I don't know what you want me to do about them."

"Well, by God, you're going to find them and kill them. They've served their last bottle of bad whiskey." He paused. His heart raced and his breath grew short from the tightness that encircled his throat. "Leo, I—I think I'm losing my sight completely."

"But I thought you said you were just sun blind?"

"I did—I thought I was—" he said, trying to keep the rising panic out of his voice, "But I'm going blind as a bat from that bad whiskey and I want them to pay. You understand, Leo?"

"Sure, Kid." Leo's voice was strained with concern.

"Thanks, Leo," he said, hating his vulnerability and his need to be so completely dependent on him. Just how bad was it going to get? To gain some control over the runaway anxiety clawing at his insides, he closed his eyelids tight. Maybe a doctor could help; maybe he'd never see another sunrise.

CHAPTER 6

Dolly Arnold stood at the corrals behind Arnold's Store. In small golden shafts, dawn peeked over Turtle Mountain. One of Ben's Shanghai roosters crowed near the saddle shed. Life continued, regardless of how dead she felt inside. It had been two weeks since she buried Josh. Her eyes still burned from all the tears she had shed, but now they were dried up like an old abandoned well.

The little red earthen grave that held Josh's small body was etched in her mind, refusing to be dulled with time or pain. At times she had tried to recall the words that Ben had spoken over the grave from his worn family Bible, but even that small comfort was denied her. She had been numbed at the funeral, such as it was. The only sense she possessed was the one that shot pain deep inside her heart. She knew there was grief in Ben's quiet voice, and she tried to derive comfort from the fact that he shared her loss, but that too was denied her.

Now slowly and inevitably, like the rising sun, her body was coming back to life. The gentle wind and the smell of the horses penetrated through her layer of frozen grief.

The rising piñon scent that perfumed the high country surrounded her in the wee hours of morning.

She turned her head slightly and looked toward the silent house that was attached to the back of the store. Ben would still be in bed. A bed she seldom shared with him, and not at all for the past two weeks. She was glad that he wasn't a demanding man. Perhaps it was due to his advancing age. Whatever the reason, she was grateful for his easygoing, sometimes tender manner. As she stood in the glow of sunrise, she fought a persistent feeling of guilt. She had made a difficult, but resolute decision, one she would not surrender. In twenty-four hours, she would leave the most peaceful place she had ever experienced in her entire life, until those drunken men shattered that dream forever. Growing up in austere poverty with constant domestic turmoil, her rootless family stayed on the move all the time ahead of the law and bill collectors. After her tumultuous upbringing, she survived the bitterest times in her life, working as a soiled dove for Sophie Maxwell. Five years earlier, she had fled all that with a newborn son and after a long trek, like a miracle, she found Ben and this place. In twenty-four hours, she would be leaving him and the only real home she'd ever known, to set out to find her son's killers.

The idea was not some ill-conceived notion. She could look back now and admit that at first, her instinct had been to ride immediately after those savages who gunned down her defenseless boy. It didn't matter that she had no weapons. Her rage was so strong she could have killed them with her bare hands. But now she could think and rationalize. She must control her anger. There would be a way to seek out those two men and avenge Josh. She might have to do things that she hated, things that she had given up long ago, but she would even resort to that, if it became necessary, to punish her son's murderers.

A fresh breath of pine-scented air blew across her face, disturbing the light brown tendrils around her strained eyes. Dawn's shadows fell past the objects around her, and the sun gilded the tops of junipers and bushes. Even the uncombed manes of the saddle horses in the corral were bathed in a dusky gold. The rooster bragged again for the benefit of his harem. Life continued.

"Dolly?" Ben had moved quietly behind her. "Did you sleep any?"

She glanced over her shoulder at him. "A little."

His weathered face showed new lines of strain, she noted in surprise. His milky blue eyes were red rimmed as though he too had done without much slumber. She watched his drawn mouth when he spoke. "If I've asked you once, I've asked you twenty times—can I do anything else?"

"No, Ben. I have to work it out by myself." She turned and straightened his galluses, which were lying twisted over his undershirt. "I know you tried to find them, Ben. But somehow it seems that the rest is up to me. I think it's my job now."

"Your job? Dolly, you wouldn't stand a chance against that Coyote Kid!"

"Ben, please listen to me and try to understand." She moistened her dry lips and narrowed her eyes as she stared into his face. "Ben, I'm leaving you tomorrow." There, she had said it. The decision was final, irrevocable. She tensed, waiting for her man's response.

He sighed heavily and looked beyond her. "I was afraid of that. Somehow, I've known that's how it would be. When I realized that it was the Coyote Kid and his partner, I looked hard for them. I looked real hard, girl, you've got to believe that. I knew if I didn't find them, I'd lose you."

She expelled a tiny breath of relief. There had been no need for her to be so anxious to tell him of her decision. He knew her better than she knew herself.

"I wrote the governor," he continued. "I thought maybe he might have an answer. I was pretty desperate, girl. Just imagine me writing a carpetbagger like Sterling for his help. My old daddy would turn over in his grave to hear that an Arnold had asked a damn Yankee for help. You know I want you to stay here. Me and Rudy need you, Dolly."

"It wasn't an easy decision, Ben. You've been generous to me, and you were always good to . . . to Josh."

"Guess we should have talked more," he said sadly. His eyes narrowed to slits, hiding whatever he was feeling when she glanced up at him again.

"No. We've had a good life together. I've got no complaints, Ben. I came here and we made a deal. You gave more than your share."

"Aw well, sometimes I'm not so sure I . . ." He trailed off and slapped the rail.

She shook her head and put her hand on his arm. "Come on to the store. I'll fix some breakfast for you two."

"Thanks, girl, that would be nice." He walked beside her and her hand fell away. She expected him to drape his arm around her shoulder as he had done in the past, but he didn't touch her. Perhaps, she thought sadly, he was already beginning to wean himself of her. They had talked more this morning than they usually did. She felt torn between relief and pain because he had accepted her decision.

Later they ate a silent meal. Ben chewed the fried mush

slowly, seeming to digest every forkful. After a while he pointed the fork at Rudy.

"She's leaving us, boy," he said flatly.

The youth's wide brown eyes swung to her in surprise. Then he looked back to Ben, as if he had not understood. "But where will she go?"

Ben avoided his pleading look by lowering his gaze to his food. "She wants to find the shooters."

"But I will go, Ben," the boy volunteered quickly. "They killed my brother."

"No, Rudy. Dolly must do what she has to do. We can't stand in her way. We only have each other now. You will understand someday."

"But she is our mother. Why must she leave?"

Ben shook his head slowly. "She's been like a mother to you, but now it is time for her to . . ." His voice wound down. She saw his eyes turn to the light coming in the small window. She recognized the signs. Ben was stiffening himself for the pain of the inevitable as he always did when he felt something deeply.

Long ago, she recalled, he had lost his favorite colt to a mountain lion. She had watched him withdraw into himself, closing up like a withering flower. It took him a long time to come out of his silent world. Now he was doing the same, withdrawing into a place where no one else was allowed entrance to see his pain.

Rudy bolted to his feet, and without a word or a glance at either of them, he left the room. He did not have Ben's strength. It was strange how close she had grown to the Mexican youth. She was surprised at how strong the urge was to go and comfort him; she had a hard time fighting that maternal instinct. She had taken Rudy for granted. He had helped her haul washwater, sweep up the store, and he did virtually every chore. His words of a moment ago now wrenched at her heart. "She is our mother!" Now, she was no one's mother.

Ben rose silently and went inside the store. She watched his retreating back, then she began gathering up the breakfast dishes.

A few minutes later she heard someone ride up in the yard. She tensed as she always did of late whenever someone entered the store. A ringing of spurs and a clumping of boots sounded in the small hallway that separated the store from the house.

"Dolly." Ben came through the doorway and spoke quietly, "This gentleman out here is a territorial marshal. He wants to talk to you."

Growing rigid at the words, she tried to gather her scattered thoughts. After drying her hands on her apron, she turned and looked up at the stranger who accompanied Ben. A nice-looking man, probably in his mid-thirties. He wore a black suit with a pristine white shirt and black string tie. A black Stetson crowned his ebony hair. He could have passed for a minister, but there was something in his shrewd blue eyes that soon dispelled the illusion.

Feeling her scrutiny, John Wesley took careful note of Mrs. Dolly Arnold. She was much younger than her husband, but her face showed lines of strain. There was a pinched look about her mouth as though she held herself in control only by determination. When he remembered that it had been this woman's child who was killed, he closed his eyes for a second in sympathy.

"Good day, ma'am." He touched the brim of his hat to her. "My name is John Wesley Michaels."

"Oh." She swallowed hard, wondering if this territorial marshal was an answer to her prayers. Although she didn't remember actually praying, she thought maybe God had read what was in her heart. Her mind raced frantically, causing her movements to become flustered. "How do you do, Marshal. Have a chair. Have you eaten?"

"Yes, ma'am." He removed his hat and pulled out a chair at the kitchen table. For a fleeting moment he wondered why his presence had caused her to become agitated, but he surmised she was simply still in a state of nervous shock due to the loss of her son. He lowered himself onto the chair, trying to read the changing expressions that crossed her thin face.

She felt certain that this man, this territorial marshal, had come to track down Josh's killers. To hide her growing excitement, she turned and busied herself with stoking the stove. "I'm sure you haven't eaten, Marshal. Why do men say they've eaten when they haven't? I'll fix you something; it will be just few minutes. In the meantime, you can have a cup of hot coffee." The smile on her face when she turned felt brittle. She hoped it didn't look as strained as she imagined it did.

He gratefully accepted the steaming cup that she placed on the table. He noted the slight trembling of her hands, and a flicker of anger stirred inside him. What kind of animals had killed this young woman's child? To hide his thoughts, he lifted the cup of coffee and blew gently across the rippling surface. "Don't bother fixing me any food, ma'am. I really don't need any."

"Oh, yes you do." The firm note in her voice caused him to look up at her warily, but she insisted. "You'll need every meal you can get, Marshal Michaels, if you're riding out after those killers."

He remained silent and watchful. The woman was obviously overwrought. She stood before him, her hands clenched around the handle of a black skillet, her head thrown back in what appeared to be defiance. A niggling feeling of uncertainty forced him to frown. He didn't care for the unspoken words between them, but some instinct told him to keep silent for the moment.

She placed the pan back on the stove, then turned and moved in front of him. She held his direct gaze as she sat down in the chair opposite him. Folding her hands on the tabletop, she gave him a level look. "Marshal Michaels," she asked in a clear, concise voice, "when are you leaving to track down those men?"

"In the morning." There was something about the set of this woman's jaw, and the purposeful manner in which she had asked the question that immediately put him on guard. "Why?" he asked flatly

She drew a deep breath, then plunged in. "Because, Marshal, I intend to go with you."

Although the suspicion had fleetingly crossed his mind, he had immediately dismissed it as ludicrous. He forced a small smile of amusement and cocked an eyebrow at her. "Mrs. Arnold, I hardly think that's a fitting thing for a married woman to do."

She gritted her teeth in irritation. Obviously the man was treating her as a willful child. She drew her shoulders back and jutted out her chin. "I'm afraid you don't understand, Marshal. When you ride out of here tomorrow to get those murderers, I'll be right behind you."

His mouth pursed into grim lines of disapproval, for he could see that the woman was serious. "Mrs. Arnold—"

With sharp resolve, she shook her head, and spoke quickly. "No, not missus. Ben took Josh and me in, but we've never married. He lived up to his part, I lived up to mine. Now, do you see?"

"No."

She fought down the urge to hit the stone-faced man. He was being deliberately stubborn. She gave up trying to explain her marital status. Placing her palms on the tabletop, she leaned forward and spoke intently. "You can like it or not, Marshal, but I am going with you. You can't stop me from riding fifty to a hundred feet behind you," she said triumphantly.

Blowing out a deep breath, he ran a hand over his forehead and prayed for patience. "Now look here, Mrs. Arnold. All right, you're not Mrs. Arnold," he said as she opened her mouth to protest. "You simply don't understand the situation. I am a lawman. It's my job to track down these men. I have a job to do and I do it in my own way, which does not include having a woman with me on the trail."

She closed her eyes and gestured expressively with her hands. "I don't care what you say. I have a job to do, too."

He looked up in relief as Ben Arnold came back into the room. "Mr. Arnold, would you please explain to your, er . . . wife that it simply isn't right for her to ride with me?"

Ben shook his head. "Dolly's a good woman, Marshal, but once she's made up her mind on something, hell won't stand in her way."

A sigh escaped her lips. You told him right, she thought. She looked at Ben and smiled. A good thing that she had spoken with him earlier. He understood her need to take part in tracking down her child's killers. Chancing a quick look at the marshal's chiseled face, she hid a smile of triumph. Whether the stiff-necked man liked it or not, he would soon find out that she was going to be a burr in his horse's tail. He would simply have to accept the fact.

John Wesley closed his eyes against her stubborn expression. He was not sure how he should go about asking God to help him, but it was apparent he would need an armful of extra spiritual strength to deal with Dolly Arnold.

CHAPTER 7

"Where the hell are we?" the Kid shouted at Leo. The sun had moved across his back, but he was so disoriented and uncertain of their direction of travel that he had no conception of time.

"Easy, Kid. We're going to Snowflake to find a doctor," Leo said soothingly. "It'll be somewhere south of us. You want to get down or something?"

Although his bladder felt swollen tight, the Kid gritted his teeth and answered curtly. "No, let's keep moving." He blinked his eyes, wondering if they had gotten worse. He could vaguely make out a gray shadow, and assumed it was Leo and his horse. But even as he strained to see more, that too was wiped away from his eyes, leaving a black world of emptiness. "Leo! Leo! Goddamnit, I can't see a thing. Not a damn thing! Those whiskey-selling snakes are going to pay for this. You've got to promise me, Leo, that you'll cut out their black hearts."

"Don't worry, Kid, I will." Leo's voice came from nearby. The concern and pity in it filled Bobby with helpless rage. He ground his teeth in futile frustration, hating his incapacitated state.

"Those stinking dogs. I want to eat their hearts, Leo. I want to eat them raw. You know what I mean?"

"Sure, sure, Kid. We'll find you a doctor in Snowflake, and he'll fix your eyes, right as rain again. Then we can go after them."

In his hands, the Kid clutched the saddle horn. A thirst for revenge churned his stomach, tying him up in knots. "No, wait, Leo. You've got to go get them whiskey peddlers. I ain't hearing of no doctor till we kill them dirty bastards."

"Aw, Kid, let's get you to the doctor first. You're the man with the gun. I ain't no match for them three. You seen them. Kid, those guys were mean. Not too mean for the Coyote Kid, but too mean for me. Please, Kid, let me take you to the doctor first, huh?"

"Aw shit, Leo, you don't even know if there's a doctor in Snowflake. And even if there is, what guarantee we got that he ain't a quack? Hell, I might end up deaf as well as blind." He reached up and touched his sightless eyes. His fingertips felt the moisture of his eyeballs, and for that he was grateful. He had seen men who had lost an eye. Their bad eyes had reminded him of a shriveled-up, punctured bladder.

"Are my eyes all gray, Leo?" he demanded, not really wanting to know the answer if they were.

Leo pulled the horses to a halt. The Kid could feel Leo's breath on his face as he obviously peered into the blank walls of his eyes. "No, they're still brown. They look fine, Kid. I think a doctor can save them. You'll see. I mean it. Why, a doctor will put some powder in them, and quick as a wink you'll see again."

The Kid swallowed a gulp of eagerness. "If you're lying to me—" His voice cut like a whip.

"I've never lied to you Kid. Hell's bells, I'm doing all I can. You hear me, all I can."

Forced to agree, he nodded. There was no need to get Leo all riled up and whining again. They were miles from anywhere, and he couldn't see to get away from an old woman let alone a whiny cohort. One thing he was determined about—one way or another those whiskey poisoners were going to pay. And pay heavily. Being blind was worse than being in jail. He hated jails. Jails were closed-up, smelly places. He had been in jail once, and that was enough to do him for a lifetime.

As Leo led his horse, Bobby recalled the eternity he had spent in that hellhole called a jail.

The whole incident began when he received a letter from a man by the name of Otto Pernell. Mr. Pernell had written for him to come to his ranch in eastern New Mexico. The name of the town was Arido, which the Kid knew meant "dry" or some such thing. He arrived by stage, then rode a horse that Otto kept at the wagon yard for his guests' convenience out to the ranch.

Otto was a pinch-faced man with a long nose nestled amid a bushy mustache. He reminded the Kid of a big barn rat. It had been cool in the living room of the spacious adobe house where they talked. The Kid sipped whiskey and smoked the cigar that Otto had given him.

"There is a man who steals my cows," Otto began in a German accent as they settled down to business. "But I cannot catch him. All year he eats my beef and then laughs when I bring a deputy to arrest him. You have no proof, he says, and he is right. This man is sly like a weasel."

The Kid blew out a stream of smoke. "Who is this guy?"

Otto was silent for a moment, then he shrugged his shoulders. "Gunther. His name is Noel Gunther."

"Well, you can quit worrying about Noel Gunther, Mr. Pernell. He won't steal any more of your beef," the Kid assured him confidently as he flicked ashes in the copper ashtray beside his chair.

"That easy, huh? No wonder they call you the Coyote Kid."

He drew in on the cigar and nodded at the rancher. The bothersome rustler would soon be sprouting grass. "Oh, I do charge two hundred and fifty dollars," he added casually.

"A little high, isn't it?" Otto asked doubtfully. "I thought . . ."

The Kid shrugged and looked back at Otto with his best poker face. "Of course, he could go on eating your beef. Be a few years before he eats that much."

Otto shook his head decisively. "No, by gawd, he is not eating one more head of my beeves."

"That's just the way I feel," the Kid said, smiling in agreement. "You can never cure these rustlers. Why, I recently handled one like him down south of here. This rustler wasn't out of prison six months before he was back to stealing cattle. See, they don't learn."

"I know, Kid. The sons of bitches are like chicken-killing dogs. By the way, did you see that yellow dog when you rode in here?"

"Yes, sir. He barked at me."

"Well, he's been killing my wife's chickens."

The Kid nodded. "Only one way to handle that."

"I know." Otto frowned heavily.

"No problem. You pay me to eliminate Gunther,

and I'll do the dog at no extra charge," the Kid offered casually.

The rancher paused for a moment, his face expressing shocked surprise. Then he expelled a sigh. "You're right. I'll get the money. You wait here."

After Pernell left the room, the Kid stood and strolled to the thick oak door. With the cigar still in his mouth, he opened the door and stepped outside on the shaded porch. The warm air washed over his face as he searched the dust-packed yard. He blew out a puff of smoke, then deliberately cleared his throat in a loud, openmouthed manner.

Two barking dogs came rounding the side of the house then stopped and growled at him in warning. The yellow dog came a step closer, with his wolflike teeth bared and a throaty growl rumbling through his lanky body. He advanced boldly, as if unaware of the .38 in the Kid's hand.

A single bullet smashed through the dog's head. It exploded a portion of the cur's right eye and half of his tiny brain. Then all was quiet in the yard, with the only sound that of the Kid ejecting the empty shell. The other dog had long before disappeared in a fit of yelping.

Mrs. Pernell came running out of the house shouting. "What's happening? What is going on?" Her eyes grew wide and her face turned ashen when she spotted the grisly sight of the dead dog at her doorstep.

"Sorry, ma'am. He was rabid," the Kid explained with a shake of his head. "He was in the early stages yet. I think the other dog is all right; we'll just have to keep an eye on him."

Mrs. Pernell's hands flew to her face in horror. She turned and rushed back inside the house. With a twisted smile on his face, he watched her go. Stupid old woman.

He shook his head and followed her. He needed another whiskey.

A little later when Otto counted out the money to him, the Kid noticed the man's hands tremble. The Kid stayed and visited for another hour, leisurely drinking Pernell's whiskey and smoking his cigars. He felt it was his duty to give the man plenty of time to back out of the deal. The extra time gave his employer an opportunity to dwell on the fact that he was actually sentencing Gunther to death and that made it even better. When he rode out later that afternoon, he was satisfied that Mr. Pernell understood that he, and not the Coyote Kid, would be the real killer of the rustler.

The Kid soon discovered that Arido was a small dusty adobe town with little entertainment. The cantinas were smoky stale caves. Spanish was the first language of the citizens. The hotel where he stayed seldom changed their linen, and the mattresses were gritty to sleep upon. The whores he saw were all slobs, fat and old and probably diseased.

To add to his disappointment, he soon learned that Gunther had gone to Sante Fe, hauling a load of freight, and wouldn't be back for a week. The delay cost him another trip out to Pernell's place. The extra time he must spend waiting cost the reluctant rancher another hundred dollars. The Kid sat in the same chair, puffing on a cigar, drinking Otto's good whiskey. "You got any more chicken killers?" he asked him conversationally.

"What?" Pernell jumped in alarm at the question.

"I just thought, since I'm here and working for you, if you had any more chicken-killing dogs you didn't want, I'd get rid of them for you."

"Oh no. Heavens no!" Pernell looked as though he had

Servant of the Law 115

just swallowed a rock. "The dogs are just fine—," he added hastily.

The Kid shrugged and drew in on a fresh cigar. "Okay, so long as my employer's happy, I'm satisfied."

Since Gunther was out of town, and the Kid had nothing pressing to do, he began to spend a lot of time in the Tolteca cantina. There was a pretty señorita who worked there, and he felt certain that she was not a full-time prostitute. Her name was Maria. She waited on the tables and kept her dignity with a sweetness that appealed to him. They became friends quickly. Whenever she had a spare moment and business was slow, she sat with him at his table.

"People say that you are a plenty bad *hombre*," she said quietly, her large dark eyes observing him intently.

He pursed his lips and shook his head. "Do I look like a bad man?"

"No, not bad," she said with a smile, displaying her beautiful ivory white teeth. Her brown eyes dazzled with pinpoints of starbursts under the lamp, like sunlight dancing on clear water. Her dark skin was smooth and inviting where the vee of her breasts disappeared beneath the fabric of her blouse.

"What do you do for a living?" she asked cautiously.

"Law work," he said, as though explaining to a child. "I serve the law, like you serve tables. It's my job. Sometimes there are bad men who steal and rob, and I must get them for the law. See, I'm not the bad guy. I don't steal or rob. I just catch the men who do."

"Oh, how wonderful," she exclaimed. "You are like the sheriff, no?"

"Yes, except that a sheriff must work in one place. I travel all over the territory to find these bad men."

"Oh, Bobby, I see now why these men do not like you; they are all crooks and thieves."

He beamed at the newfound star in his life. "Yes, that's it exactly."

"Oh, Bobby," she sighed with adoration. "You must come to my father's garden tonight when the moon rises. We will be alone. I swear that it will be safe. We can hold each other for many hours, yes?"

His brows shot up in surprise. He leaned forward and whispered urgently, "Of course, Maria. Where is this place, your father's garden?"

"Two blocks down, go to your left, then up the alley to the second gate. It will be unlatched for you." She glanced around, then continued with a rueful look. "I must go back to work, there are more customers. But you will come tonight, Bobby?"

"Yes, of course, I'll come," he assured her. She squeezed his hand and hurried off with a swish of her petticoats.

He glanced around the room, noting the glares and curious looks he was receiving. Yeah, he snickered silently, go ahead and stare at me, you stupid bastards. The Coyote Kid will pleasure himself with your prettiest señorita when the New Mexico moon rises tonight.

Later, he watched Maria leave her job for the day. The slovenly whore who replaced her offered one of her ample breasts to any man at the bar who seemed willing to fondle her. He tried to ignore her blatant display. Filled with contempt for her, he frowned when she came over to his table.

"So, you are the gringo who makes the pretty señorita laugh?" she said under her breath, her voice full of innuendo. She bent over and vigorously wiped his table with a rag, causing her partially exposed bosom to quack for his benefit.

"Maybe," he said curtly, not inviting further comment from the woman.

"Ah,"—she grinned knowingly—"you want the tender young chicken, huh, *gringo*?"

His eyes narrowed and a muscle flicked in his jaw. "Get out of my face, bitch!"

"Oh!" she yelped and drew back in fear. Her eyes like saucers, she stared at him in shock. Then shrugging her shoulders, she tossed her greasy head in a haughty gesture and flounced off to the other side of the room.

After he left the saloon, he loitered for several minutes in a shadow-darkened doorway, making certain that he was not being followed. He was foolish sometimes, he acknowledged with a scowl, but he wasn't so stupid as to forget that there were men who would like to brag that they had killed the Coyote Kid.

Near the end of the alley, a dog barked behind an adobe wall. He thought of Pernell's dog. If the wall had not been between him and the dog, he would have given this betrayer of his presence the same treatment as that yellow cur. Muttering under his breath, he moved onward. Soon he was at the second gate. Pistol in hand, he eased the gate forward with his shoulder.

"Oh, my Bobby, you came." Maria melted out of the shadows and came forward eagerly. The moonlight flashed on the barrel of the gun, and she squeaked in alarm. "Why do you have a pistol?"

"Sorry," he apologized as he looked beyond her, checking the silvery lighted yard. Hastily he holstered the gun, then took her slender form into his arms. He crushed his mouth to her perfumed lips, wanting to pull her soft body into one with his.

His hand cupped a small willing breast and desire pulsated through his veins. Soon he was smoothing her soft skin and their mouths were on fire.

She broke free abruptly and took his hand. "Come to my bed," she whispered. He blinked, not believing his good luck. The invitation was beyond his dreams.

He did not know how long or how many times he pleasured himself with his rose of the garden. But never had he been so successful, so *mucho hombre,* so virile in his life. Success rendered more success, and finally she pleaded for mercy. "Please, my lover. I will never walk again."

"Oh," he mumbled in shock, "have I hurt you?"

"No, but your love is so much."

"It will be dawn soon; I must go," he said regretfully as he raised himself above her.

"You will come back tonight?"

"Of course. Wild horses couldn't keep me away."

She almost squealed with excitement. "But now one more time, my great lover?"

"Are you sure?"

She put her hands behind his neck and pulled him closer. "I am sure if you are sure." They both giggled softly in excitement, then dissolved into the finale of the passionate night.

The next day he discovered that Gunther still had not returned from Sante Fe. Since he had had little sleep the night before, he decided to go back to bed. He dreamed of the creamy-skinned Maria who had awakened his sometimes less than virile manhood. He awoke once, bathed in sweat, and had to shake his head several times to clear his confused mind. Had he dreamed of all those pleasures of the previous night? But his bruised lips and sore muscles convinced him otherwise. He lay back down and smiled in anticipation of the coming sundown.

Later in the afternoon, he entered the Tolteca where she worked, noting that she had not yet arrived. He ordered a bottle of whiskey and retired to a rear table.

A disturbance at the door caused him to look up curiously. A group of loud men entered the cantina. They were obviously not Mexican, and appeared to be freighters. Apparently the leader or boss was the heavily bearded big man. He had a gruff but booming voice, like the growl of a grizzly. His companions were hard-eyed men. The Kid recognized the type, tough and ruthless.

Maria arrived soon after the men. She paused at the end of the bar and put on her apron. Glancing around the room and noting Bobby's eyes on her, she sent him a smile that would have melted a mountain of snow. A silent kiss flew from her lips to him, then she briskly moved around the tables to begin her work.

"Hey, *puta*," the large man shouted as he spotted Maria. "Come over here!"

The Kid jerked up from his lounging position at the man's disparaging tone. A muscle moved violently in Bobby's jaw and his hands were clenched at his sides.

"Whore, I said get over here!" the freighter repeated.

Maria glanced at the Kid, then at the big man uncertainly. Cautiously, she moved toward the freighter. "Pardon me, señor," she said with quiet dignity, "but I am not what you think."

"Goddamnit, get over here. I know a whore when I see one!"

The Kid lunged to his feet. "Maria, stand back!" he shouted. "These are the kind of men I am looking for."

His breath raged through his flared nostrils as his right hand rested on the butt of his gun.

"No, Bobby!" she screamed and tried to run toward him, but she was caught and held back by one of the big man's companions.

The freighter sprang from his chair, knocking it sideways across the floor as he glared at the Kid. "Just who the hell are you?" he demanded in a thundering rage.

"Doesn't matter," he gritted between his teeth. "Go for your gun, mister."

Before the man had cleared leather, the Kid's .38 spoke, the bullet smashing the freighter full in the face. His companion on the left took a bullet in the heart before he could come out of his chair. The other man, who held Maria, threw her aside and went for his gun, but the Kid's third shot caught him in the forearm.

Smoke rose in a thin wisp from his gun barrel as he advanced forward. Maria rose and stumbled into his arms. She clung to him sobbing hysterically. "Bobby, oh, my Bobby," she repeated over and over. He holstered the pistol and put his arms around her. The patrons of the cantina moved forward, glancing warily at him as they investigated the slain and wounded men.

Two ominous shotgun barrels were thrust between the swinging saloon doors. Behind the gun came the town marshal and a deputy sheriff. In his concern over Maria's safety, the Kid felt totally helpless to do anything as he stood holding her.

"Get back, everyone. You!" The marshal pointed the gun barrel at the Kid. "Get those hands up!"

"No!" Maria screamed. "No, not my Bobby."

He stuck his hands high in the air, but he looked down and smiled tenderly at the weeping Maria. "Don't worry about me, Maria." He turned and stared vacantly at the marshal. He kept his gaze directed straight ahead as they marched him out of the saloon and down the street to the jail.

Inside the marshal's office, he continued to protest his innocence, claiming self-defense.

"Listen, mister, the only way you're getting out of here is when Judge Hartwell says you're innocent and can go free," the marshal stated flatly. "We ain't having these kinds of shootings in Arido, you savvy?"

"When does the judge come?" the Kid asked.

The marshal shrugged. "Couple of months, I guess."

"A couple of months! Are you crazy?" he repeated in disbelief. "Why so long?"

"He's a circuit judge and goes all over hell trying cases. Now, that ain't my fault. You just settle down and behave. You've got plenty of time." With that said, the marshal pushed him toward the back of the jail, then shoved him inside the cell. The heavy slam of the steel door rang in his ears for a long time.

Time clicked slowly by. Each day, an old man, under the protection of the guard's shotgun, emptied his chamber pot. Once a week, Bobby was allowed to bathe in a wooden tub in the hallway while a guard pointed both barrels of a twelve-gauge at him. Then he shaved himself and returned the razor to the guard.

The marshal took no chances with him. Despite Bobby's constant vigilance, searching for an escape opportunity, none materialized. To pass the time, he read newspapers and magazines. One Denver newspaper's account amused him. It proclaimed that the Coyote Kid was in the Arido jail and he would soon hang for his notorious life of random murders. One such account cited him as being a member of a gang that had killed a former president. More lies.

Maria was allowed to see him twice a week, but they only permitted her to stand outside the bars and with a guard watching them from the door.

"There is a lawyer coming with this judge, Bobby," Maria said excitedly on one of her visits. "He is a very good lawyer. My cousin in Santa Fe wrote me this good news. You can hire this lawyer and he will help you go free!"

"Sure, angel," he agreed wryly. "They all want me hung."

"No, no, my lover. This is not true. Me and my friends at the cantina we will tell them how it was."

"Well, just don't count on that meaning a hell of a lot, Maria. Although I appreciate the offer." He stared at the dust particles dancing in the shaft of light coming in the barred window. The law in this place intended to hang him as a lesson for others; he could see the look of revenge in their eyes.

"Oh, Bobby, no. I am so worried."

He smiled and reached his hand through the bars to pat her gently. "Don't be. They've got a long ways to go before they stretch the Coyote Kid's neck."

Then came a day in the fall when the judge, a prosecutor, and the legal staff arrived in town. The day after his arrival the defense attorney John Evans came to see the Kid. He was an eagle-eyed man in his forties, wearing a store-bought coat. He sat in the hallway with his elbows propped up on his knees, listening without interruption to Bobby's side of the story.

When he had finished, Evans straightened and gave him a level look. "If you weren't the Coyote Kid, they never would have arrested you for this. Well, Kid, as I see it you have two choices. You can plead guilty to manslaughter and serve two to five years. Or you can plead not guilty and take a chance on hanging. Who knows?"

The Kid was not impressed with Evan's dry manner. He narrowed his gaze and he glared through the bars at the free man. "Not guilty," he said. "I didn't do it. I heard that if you were innocent that the laws worked for you."

"Well . . ." Evans shrugged. "Not always." With that disturbing statement, the man left Bobby to ponder his trial and fate.

The prosecutor arrived shortly after the defense attorney left and introduced himself as Roger Wilson. A pompous, blustering man, he stalked up and down the jail hallway, pointing his finger in the air as if he were shooting pigeons in a plaza.

"Coyote Kid, you are as good as strung up now. Your death will be a symbol that law and order has finally come to the territory of New Mexico. Praise the Lord. Law and order to these bastions of crime and disorder.

"Yes, your sentence will be carried out in Sante Fe, so all the heathens who worship firearms can see how their chief disciple ended his sorry life at the end of a rope." At that point, the people's attorney grabbed his own throat and gave a theatrical gasp. The Kid scowled in disgust at his playacting. The man preened and strutted like a bandy rooster until his antics nauseated the Kid's stomach.

"Coyote Kid, throw yourself on the mercy of the court. Free your soul and admit how you've pilfered and robbed, raped and murdered, innocent citizens the length and breadth of New Mexico."

The oration went on and on. Wilson seemed to be speaking to a greater audience than Bobby Budd and the two sullen Mexicans in the next cell who were serving a sentence for disturbing the peace. Back and forth, the demon chaser stalked his imaginary prey, seemingly unaware of his surroundings.

At this point, the Kid really lamented the loss of his gun. The .38 would have done an effective job of blowing away that word spewing opening on the man's face. He grinned to himself as he imagined placing the Colt's muzzle in Wilson's foul mouth. Well, he didn't have his gun, he acknowledged ruefully. 'Course, he could piss on the man, but there was a certainty that it wouldn't be enough to drown him. But the thought took root, and his gaze fell on the night bucket in the corner of his cell. Old Pablo hadn't been in to dump it yet.

A mischievous intent filled his mind. He glanced at the silent Mexicans in the next cell. After gaining their attention, he moved his night pail with the side of his foot toward the bars dividing their cells and gestured to them silently, clearly indicating his plan. The Mexicans nodded soberly and forced back grins. They moved cautiously, watching the orator's back as they dumped the contents of their chamber pot through the bars into his bucket. Although the air was rank with the stench, Wilson did not seem to notice.

The Kid waited until Wilson was on another track, his head thrown back and his voice droning on and on without pause. Then with the toe of his boot, he managed to push the bucket out in front of himself until it was halfway between his bunk and the bars. The hall was not wide, so if he were able to slosh Wilson head-on, the man would back up but the contents of the night bucket would still reach him.

"Wait!" he shouted, while still seated on the bunk. "I confess."

"What?" Wilson whirled and rushed to grasp the bars.

It was almost as if he wanted to pull them apart and grab up the repentant felon.

"I confess, oh yes!" the Kid shouted then bowed his head. He kept Wilson distracted so that he did not see the two Mexicans back away to the adobe wall at the rear of their cell.

The man flung his head back as if to seek gratification from heaven. Evidently he felt that his sermon alone had worked on the hardest criminal the court had ever known. Almost dancing with excitement, he pulled himself against the bars. "Tell me your sins! Now, my son," he hissed eagerly.

The Kid edged forward, his head still bowed. In a flash he had his hand on the bucket handle. Before the prosecutor knew what he was about, he shouted, "Here's my sins!," and threw the contents of the odorous bucket over him. "There, you son of a bitch. There's a sample of my sins!"

The blubbering, aghast prosecutor screamed. "Guards! Guards!" His face dripped with excrement and liquid, then his soles hit a slippery spot and he fell to the floor, floundering in the mess.

"Guards!"

When the shotgun bearer finally opened the outer door, he had to suppress a chuckle. "Wh-what's wrong?"

"What's wrong? Arrest that man!" Wilson shouted in a womanlike screech. He pointed and waved at the Kid, who was leaning against the rear of his cell, a wide grin on his face.

"Mr. Wilson," the guard said, pursing his lips to hide a smile. "There ain't nothing I can do. He's already under arrest." His nose twitched and he looked down on the floor with a scowl. "God, this place sure stinks."

The Kid and his jail cohorts laughed for hours each time they recalled the bath he had administered to Wilson. He felt it was almost worth the lingering stench in the jail just to remember the look on the mouthy prosecutor's face.

In the evening after the first day of his trial, he was not sure if all the things his lawyer Evans had said during the day's session would help or hinder his case. Evans scolded him. "Throwing that chamber pot on Wilson might have been a damned funny thing, but it just might get you hanged."

The careless manner in which he imparted that bit of news caused the Kid to clench his fist to keep from striking Evans in the mouth. He hoped that the judge had been more impressed by Evans's manner than he was.

At last, seated on his bunk, he heard a hiss from the window above him. He jumped up and glanced quickly at the door. The guard was not in evidence. When the Kid looked back at the window, he saw a rope snaking down the wall. Attached to it was a woman's small pearl-handled pistol. He pulled on the rope as a signal. Then he quickly untied the gun and jerked on the rope again.

"Ave Maria," he said with a smile. "You're a sweetheart."

The two Mexicans were still snoring, and a quick glance at the door showed him that the guard had not made his rounds. He checked the gun's chambers. Five shots. Five answers to his sentence. So excited the blood pounded in his head, he stuffed the gun into one of his boots, which were placed on the floor near the foot of his bunk. They would not find it, he felt confident. Sighing in relief, he lay back and closed his eyes. They would never hang the Coyote Kid, at least not this time.

At dawn, under the guard's supervision, Pablo brought him a breakfast tray of sorghum syrup over corn cake flapjacks and a cup of barley coffee. He ate the meal slowly and looked up in surprise when John Evans and the town marshal came hurrying in.

Evans smiled. "I've got good news for you, Kid."

"You're a free man, Bobby Budd," the lawman announced as he unlocked the cell door.

The Kid shook his head and studied the pair with wry cynicism. "Why in hell am I free all of a sudden?"

"The judge decided it was foolish to proceed with the trial since all the eyewitnesses have testified that it was a clear case of self-defense," Evans explained.

"It was." He handed Evans the breakfast tray. "Try the food; it's real tasty. Say, Marshal, how much do them two next door owe you?" He jabbed a finger toward the Mexicans.

"Thirty bucks. Why?"

"I'm bailing them out. Come on, turn them loose," he said. He waved off the two men's shouts of thanks as he went out into the office to get his personal belongings.

Before he strapped on his holster, he loaded the .38.

Prosecutor Wilson burst in the doorway. "My God, Marshal! You're not issuing him a pistol, are you?"

"It's his. He's free to go, so the judge says," the lawman said.

"Don't worry, fancy pants," Bobby said. "I won't waste good bullets on your ass. Just slop!" Wilson reddened at the laughter that the Kid's sarcasm drew.

"This is a travesty of justice," Wilson moaned, backing away.

"Hell, Wilson, I was so sure that I was going to be set free that I never even shot you when I had the chance." The Kid laughed and bent down to draw the small pistol from his boot. He smiled at the marshal's stricken face.

"Budd, how did you get that?" the lawman demanded.

"Get it?" he scoffed. "I've had it. See, the Coyote Kid plays by the rules. You all think I'm some hired gun or some sort of an avenger. I'm just a businessman."

"Sure," the marshal said, shock still registering on his face. "Where in hell . . ." Those were the last words that the Kid heard as he strode out of the jail.

Maria was not at the cantina. Word was that she had left for Santa Fe. He was anxious as he hurried to call at the house where she lived.

A frail old lady, wearing a shawl, answered the door and spoke to him sharply in Spanish.

"Está Maria aquí?" he asked the woman.

She shook her head. "Maria está in Sante Fe. Espera, gringo."

He knew she meant for him to stay put while she went inside the house. In a moment she shuffled back carrying a letter.

"Maria," she said as she handed him the letter. Her frail hands waved him back, then she closed the door with a thud.

He opened the letter with shaking fingers.

Dear Bobby,
I know I can never have you. You have much work to do for the law. There are many bad men all over. So, because I cannot have my *mucho hombre,* I want no man. I am going to a convent so I will always be faithful to you and my God. I will pray for you every day. Do not try to stop me.

Love,
Maria

Devastated by the news, he went to the hotel, checked into a room, fell across the bed and cried. All night long he cried. Sober as a judge and without restraint, he soaked a pillow with his tears.

At dawn, he went to find Gunther. After all those weeks in jail, he wasn't sure that Pernell still wanted Gunther dead, but it didn't matter. He had been paid to do a job and he had never reneged on a deal yet.

The morning sun shone on his back as he rode down the canyon. He dismounted and crept silently down the bushy slope. He paused when he heard a grating sound. After a moment he recognized it as a knife being sharpened on a whetstone. He parted the cedar bushes, and spied a half-skinned yearling hung on a single tree from a rope over a cottonwood branch. A man stood with a knife poised beside the carcass. In an instant, Bobby knew from Pernell's description that this butcher was his man.

He shot Gunther twice in the back, then propped his still body against the tree. To make a good scene, for whoever discovered the body, he placed the man's bloodstained hands in his lap, along with the knife and whetstone. The yearling carcass hung beside the dead man. The fresh hide on the ground spread like a blanket beside the corpse bore Pernell's SS brand.

Finished at last, he climbed in the saddle and rode off. "Pray for me, Maria. There are a lot more Gunthers out there," he said aloud.

Back to grim reality, he sat atop Buster and rode in total blindness. With Leo leading his horse, he repeated the same words, "Pray for me, Maria."

"What's that?" Leo asked.

"Nothing," he mumbled, not wishing to explain. "Nothing at all."

CHAPTER 8

A long-tailed rooster perched on the top corral rail crowed while John Wesley Michaels saddled the sorrel that he had dubbed Jacob. He found it difficult to concentrate on his preparations since he couldn't get over the shock of seeing Mrs. Arnold dressed like a man. She wore new jeans and a man's cotton shirt, and she was saddling her own horse like a man. Nothing he had said had dissuaded the strong-minded woman from accompanying him on this trip.

"You want me to put the pack saddle on?" she asked matter-of-factly. She had discovered that the only way to get a response from the silent man was to speak in a straightforward manner.

"Thanks, but I'll do it," he mumbled. The whole situation was getting out of hand, but he was at a loss as to how to deal with Dolly Arnold. He must look out for her, too. He would even have to go off the road to relieve himself. The fact embarrassed and irritated him. He was not accustomed to being around a woman all the time. The fact was, he did not frequent houses of ill repute, and loose women offended him. Not that he considered her wanton, but Mrs. Arnold was too outspoken for him to be comfortable with. He closed his eyelids for the solace of a moment of silent meditation.

Out of the corner of her eye, she watched Ben amble out of the house toward her. In the pale sunrise, he looked tired. There were times when he did not look his sixty years. Today, she noticed as he drew nearer, he looked that and more. Perhaps he had absorbed some of her youth in the past, but now that she was leaving, he had nothing to feel youthful about.

"You forgot your hat," he said guardedly. He evidently did not want her going back in the house. She understood. In any case, she had no excuse to go back inside. Everything that belonged to her, a few dresses, a hairbrush, some soap, a few changes of underthings, and a tintype of her and Josh that she had had made in Holbrook, were in the saddlebags. She sighed with guilt. Obviously, she was leaving with a lot more material things than she had brought with her years ago. But she was leaving behind a part of herself. Her son.

Rudy stood on the porch, a picture of dejection. "Rudy, you cook for Ben, and take good care of him. You hear me?" she said sharply.

"You will come back?" the boy asked pleadingly.

She shook her head. "No, I can't, not ever. Ben knows why. He'll tell you. It would be too hard on all of us." Only her steely determination forced her to hold her chin up. There was no going back. The things that were changed had to be left as they were.

His brown eyes filled with sadness, Rudy shook his head. "We will miss you."

"Me, too. Now go on inside, Rudy. It's hard enough without saying goodbye. And Ben." She turned to him, squinting her eyes to hold back the tears. "Thanks for everything, the pistol, too."

He nodded. "Be sure not to shoot yourself or that poor man over there," he said gruffly.

She laughed with a brittleness to her voice. "He ain't poor. A little stiff-necked maybe, but I figure he's tough enough or that Yankee governor would never have hired him."

Ben agreed with a grim smile. "And he's probably a Republican, too."

"I don't care as long as he knows his job." She plunked the hat on her head and turned toward her horse. It was imperative that she get away before she broke down completely. If she looked back, she knew she might never leave the two of them.

Once mounted, she set the gray mare in a short lope past Ben, past her home and the store, and out to the two fresh graves. She paused by the smooth mounds and spoke aloud. "Josh, I'll find them. I'll find them or join you trying, son."

She looked at Manuel's grave and said a silent goodbye to the boy, then she reined the gray around and rode south. Sooner or later that tight-lipped marshal would ride her way when he was ready to leave, but by then maybe her eyes would be dry.

John Wesley had loaded the packhorse that he called Thomas. Doubting Thomas was the big buckskin's full name. He'd earned his title in Holbrook when he refused to cross the Atchison, Topeka rails and ties. On several occasions he had shied at various other items, including a booming blue grouse, a scrap of paper on the wind, and a cottontail. John also suspected that both of his horses were gun-shy.

The dealer in Holbrook had appeared honest, but John had had little time to haggle over prices. He needed two horses that were sound and ready to go. He had grown fonder of the sorrel Jacob, and he even decided that Thomas was not completely incorrigible. With time, the buckskin would settle down, and then he would eventually get the horses accustomed to gunshots. Until then he would secure them with stout ropes or hobbles when he had to shoot.

Glancing around, he could not see Mrs. Arnold. Where was she? Oh well, perhaps she had changed her mind and decided not to go with him, he hoped. She had loped off on the dish-faced gray mare and had, no doubt, reconsidered the error of her ways. Maybe she was going to remain with Ben and that young Mexican who seemed to adore her.

But a little later, he was not really surprised when he caught up with her. Nor was he surprised that she sat astride the mare as she rode in the worn tracks that half resembled a road.

"How far will we go today?" she asked quietly without looking at him.

"Until the horses get tired or we find someone who has seen the two men."

"Good. I won't ask you a bunch of questions. I know most men need quiet to think."

"A very nice concession," he said stiffly. "I appreciate that."

They rode a while, then she spoke again. "I do know most of the ranchers on this road. So, if you want to ask them something, I'll be glad to introduce you to them, Marshal."

"Please don't call me that. Major Bowen, my employer,

says that 'officer of the court' is a better title. As you may know, Governor Sterling wants to keep in everyone's good graces."

She shrugged. "Seems kind of stupid to me. First there ain't no law, and then when it does come, you can't call it the law."

"That's not quite correct, Mrs. Arnold," he reproved her quietly. "I'm an officer of the court. Please remember that."

Beneath her wide-brimmed felt hat, she wrinkled her nose at his stilted manner, but she answered meekly, "Yes, sir." Privately, she thought it was still silly. But that was a typical man's way of thinking, she supposed. She had known a lot of men in her time, but she found it difficult to understand the way some of their minds worked. They definitely did not think like a woman, and the one riding beside her was a closed book. Resigned to that fact, she shrugged, recalling her earlier thought that she didn't care if he said two words, as long as he got the job done.

They rode in silence. It wasn't exactly a companionable silence, but that did not seem to matter.

In the distance, a fork in the road drew her attention. She pointed to it as she spoke. "That way there leads to Milton Devers's place."

"What's he like?" he asked, following the direction of her finger.

"Just a small rancher. He's a bachelor like you. You two would probably have lots to talk about." She looked away and scowled. "What do old bachelors talk about?"

He chuckled at the reference to his age. "Mrs. Arnold, I really don't have any idea what they talk about. But let's ride up there and see Milton Devers. Anyone can be a lead. I . . . er, we can't leave any stone unturned."

"Yes, Mr. Michaels," she said, beginning to feel a measure of respect for his logical thinking. Perhaps if she kept quiet, she might even learn something from him. There was always a possibility that she had underestimated him because of his stiff-necked manner. "You know I want to find those two killers."

"So do I. So do the major and the governor. We all want to see the Coyote Kid and his partner in jail and tried for their crimes."

"Yeah, me too." She bit her lip, wondering why that had come out so flippantly. I do want the killer of my child, she vowed silently. I want him looking down the barrel of the .32 double-action Colt that Ben gave me. It was a small gun by most standards but accurate enough for her needs. She wanted to be close enough to see the killer's eyes when she shot him.

"Is that Devers's place down by the sycamore?" John Wesley asked, breaking into her vengeful thoughts.

She nodded. Milt Devers would be shocked when he saw her with this man. Oh well, she wasn't riding with John Wesley to improve her social image.

He spotted a beanpole of a man laboring at setting a corner fence post. As they drew nearer, he watched Devers remove his sweat-stained gray hat and wipe his leathery face on the sleeve of his shirt.

"Morning, Mr. Devers," John said politely.

"Oh, howdy. Guess Mrs. Arnold there told you my name? You all right, ma'am?" the older man asked with genuine concern.

"Fine, Milton. This is Mr. Michaels. He is an officer of the court and is asking about Josh's killers," she explained.

"Oh." Milton nodded, his expression reserved. "Well, get down. I've got plenty of cold spring water. Help yourself to it."

"Thanks," John Wesley responded absently. He frowned as Mrs. Arnold reached for the reins of his horse and the lead of the packhorse. He handed them over with a little shrug, feeling a bit uncomfortable as he did so.

"You go ahead, Mr. Michaels." She motioned him toward the spring. "I'll water the horses in the creek and wait for you. Milt won't talk much with me around."

"Yes. And thanks," John agreed. She was probably right. If Devers knew anything, he would probably talk more freely out of her presence. John watched her ride off leading both of his horses.

The rancher spoke behind him. "Shame about her losing the boy. Plain mean men done that." John Wesley turned and kept silent, although he watched the man's expression carefully. "Yes, sir," Devers continued, "I rode with Ben to look for them. Guess he told you that we lost them down in the Mustang Range. We seen three tough-looking whiskey peddlers, but they weren't talking. Ben even offered them money for the information, but they refused and acted pretty mean. Did he tell you about them?"

Although Ben Arnold had said nothing to him about the peddlers, John Wesley nodded and remained silent, waiting for Devers to continue.

"Well, I guess the two killers just kept riding. Them kind don't have no roots, Mr. Michaels. I seen a grizzly like that once. Even the Apaches were afraid of him. He'd kill a cow but wouldn't bother to eat her. Then he'd go on, and a quarter of a mile or so farther along, he'd kill another one. No sense to it. You savvy? Well, if you've never seen one that bloodthirsty, you wouldn't have believed it."

"Mr. Devers, I've seen such things. Could I ask for your help?"

"Sure. Anything I could do to help you."

"About these whiskey peddlers," John Wesley asked thoughtfully, "who are they?"

Milt scratched at his red neck. "Well, all I know is one is named Gar, and it appears he's the boss."

"Gar what?"

"Danged if I know, but he's plenty mean. When I see them coming, I ride over the ridge. I ain't afraid of much, but them three ain't worth hog spit."

"Where are these men?" John asked as he walked with the man toward the rock tank.

"Oh, up there in a place we call the Mustang Mountains." Devers tossed his head in that direction. "You ride southwest, cross a big open place, then you'll see an old deserted ranch house made out of logs. The folks who lived there have been gone for ten years or more."

"Do you reckon this Gar would hide the killers up there?"

"Mister, they'd do just about anything for money, and that includes killing, too." Both men took turns dipping the gourd into the small spring box and drinking the cool water.

The chilly water slid down John Wesley's throat like liquid silk. "Could you take me close to their place, Mr. Devers?"

Devers was intent on watching Dolly in the distance. "Can I ask you a damn personal question, Mr. Michaels?"

"I suppose so."

Devers jerked a thumb in her direction. "It's about her. How come Mrs. Arnold is all get up like a man and riding with you, instead of being at home at the store?"

John took a deep breath. "She's determined to ride with me. Nothing that I or Mr. Arnold said could dissuade her.

He said that once she made up her mind, she stuck to it. I believe him."

"That's too bad for Ben. Now, if she were leaving me, it would break my heart." Devers's eyes remained on Dolly who was still attending the horses. "In a way she is kind of leaving me, too." He nodded as if considering the matter deeply, then swung his gaze back to John Wesley. "I'll ride with you. It'll take me a few minutes to get my bedroll and saddle my horse."

John gave the man a grateful look, then sipped slowly from the gourd.

"Thanks for your help. This is good water, Mr. Devers."

"That's why I stayed here. Always wanted a woman out here, but I got so busy fixing things around here that I never had time to go find me one." Devers shook his head as if dismissing some memory. "Reckon she'll go back to Ben when this is all over?"

"I really can't say."

"Well, I'll get ready and meet you in a few minutes."

John nodded absently. He walked slowly toward the sycamores along the creek. Devers was almost as upset as the two back at the store. It seemed that Dolly Arnold had no shortage of admirers.

Dolly leaned her back against rough cottonwood bark. The horses stood hipshot, swishing their tails at pesky flies. They acted grateful for the short respite.

"Did you learn anything?" she asked when he drew nearer.

"Yes. Did Ben mention seeing whiskey peddlers?" he asked.

She shook her head, wondering what whiskey peddlers had to do with the killers.

"Perhaps Ben thought them unimportant," he mused

aloud. "Mr. Devers is going to take me to the place in the Mustang Mountains where those peddlers are hiding out."

She stepped away from the tree and narrowed her eyes as she stared up at his face. "Don't figure on going there without me."

"Mrs. Arnold, I think it might be best if you stay—"

She cut him off sharply. "I told you, Mr. Michaels, either I ride with you or I follow behind." When he said nothing—simply looked at her with a hard glint in his eyes—she folded her arms. "Now, why are we going after these peddlers?"

"First of all, they may be hiding the killers, or maybe the killers may have been there. Secondly," he added in a hard voice, "rounding up whiskey peddlers is part of my job. I can't ignore the men who sell untaxed whiskey, Mrs. Arnold. I have my duty."

Glaring at him, she swore silently, then stalked off. Her soles slid on the gravel and she barely managed to recover her balance as she strode beside the trickle of a stream. At this rate, she thought, scowling, she would be ninety years old before they found the pair of killers. In disgust, she kicked at the gravel with the toe of her boot, venting her displeasure and impatience on the loose rocks.

After some of her anger had evaporated, she walked back to where he was squatted on his boot heels. She refused to address him, and he merely nodded, acknowledging her presence.

Devers rode from the house to join them. He smiled, unaware of the strained atmosphere. "Howdy, ma'am. Reckon I'm ready to go." His smile became wider. She sighed inwardly. Milt looked plumb silly with that grin on his face, but she knew it was simply because he did not know quite how to behave around women. She gave him a polite smile, then moved to the horses.

After they mounted, she took the buckskin's rope and led him. John Wesley accepted the idea that she would take care of the packhorse. He and Devers rode ahead. He suspected that she had deliberately maneuvered herself into that position to give them a little privacy or simply to ease the strained atmosphere.

"You do a lot of law work?" Devers asked, to be conversational.

"I'm new in Arizona," John answered casually as the horses plodded onward. "Before this, I worked as a town marshal in Colorado."

Devers nodded as he appeared to digest the news. "Well, I never got to Colorado. Always aimed to go there, but stopped here and stayed. Must be lonely, though, being a lawman? No roots."

"Sometimes," John agreed. Then he wished he had denied it. Because it suddenly occurred to him that he wasn't lonely anymore. He didn't like to think it was because Dolly Arnold was riding with him. He had never spent much time in the company of women like her; they usually made him uncomfortable and tongue-tied.

He recalled Bessie Jergen. How on his last day in Walsenburg, he had seen her in Fred Bowles's buckboard; no doubt they were headed for Bowles's ranch. She never even acknowledged that she saw him, if she did. As he stood by himself on the boardwalk, he hoped her children could attend school out there. He even recalled how he couldn't swallow the knot in his throat and when the rig was gone from his sight, how grateful he was to be alone on the street.

He had blown his nose hard twice and wiped his eyes, before jamming the kerchief in his pocket. Then he strode away to close the rest of his business in Colorado. He'd never had a chance to tell her about the new job in Arizona. Just as well. Like smoke in the wind, Bessie was gone in the buckboard with another man.

"We can camp at Muddy Springs," Devers said, breaking into his thoughts.

John blinked his eyes to dispel the image of the blue-eyed widow. "How close will we be to the peddlers' place?"

Devers didn't answer immediately. Looking at him in puzzlement, John noted that he was squirming uncomfortably in his saddle. The expression on his face was almost comical, and John realized what his problem was before Devers spoke in a disgruntled fashion. "I'm going out there somewhere. What do you do with her along?"

John hastily swallowed a smile and spoke dryly. "The same thing you're doing." He watched Devers move toward a bushy piñon to his left. He didn't trust himself to look back at Mrs. Arnold, for fear he would chuckle out loud.

When Devers rode back to join them, he spoke as though John had just asked the question. "We'll be half a day's ride from the peddlers when we get to Muddy Springs."

John glanced around the Arizona landscape then he turned and spoke decisively to Mrs. Arnold. "We'll camp at Muddy Springs."

She sighed gratefully at his words She was not used to being in a saddle for such a long time. The stiff new jeans were chafing the inside of her thighs, and it would be a relief to put on a dress.

Later, she boiled beans and bacon in a small pan over the fire.

Both men seemed to find things to do to avoid sitting

by her at the campfire. Even dressed now like a woman, she had not put them at ease. She gave up trying, and poured herself a cup of strong coffee. Glaring at the two bachelors' backs, she decided if they wanted some coffee, they could get their own. It would be sundown soon, and she had other problems on her mind. One was her growing fear of sleeping on the ground. The mere thought of a snake caused her to shiver in spite of the warm fire in front of her. It was going to take a lot of grit and determination not to squirm and complain when the time came to bed down on the open ground.

Her brows drew together when she looked at John Wesley's rugged face as he talked to Milt. With Devers along, she knew she wouldn't get much opportunity to find out anything about John Wesley, and for some reason that fact irritated her. Curiosity nagged at her. What was he really like? Did he have a family?

A twig crackled in the fire and she shrugged. It looked like she'd have plenty of time to find out about the silent lawman, because at the rate they were tracking the killers, the snow would be flying before they caught up with the murdering pair.

In Prescott, Ella Devereaux stood in her former apartment behind the lace curtains and studied the sunlit street below. The skin on her neck crawled. Her ex-pimp Ash Waddle was gone for the afternoon to play poker. To no doubt lose some more of her hard-earned money. Why, he must be the hit of Prescott, throwing that cash around on Whiskey Row as if he owned the U.S. Treasury. Her only hope to escape his vindictive hold on her and Harrington House was the telegram she had sent to those police officials in Westport, Kansas.

If he had killed the mayor's son there would be a

murder warrant out for him. If not that, then he must have committed some high crime for him to ever leave the business behind. Why, he owned the best sporting place in the country. Didn't make sense that he'd up and leave it for a chance of horning in on her place in the sticks.

It was off season in Prescott. When the legislature came to town, her business flourished. All the important folks flocked to the Capitol and the Harrington House during that time. Why, there were more things about those sessions decided in her parlor than on the floor of either the house or senate. The pockets of those trying to influence the politicians were bottomless, paying the tab for huge banquets, champagne, liquor, and frolicking with her girls.

There were gray-headed old men who found their youth had not died. Filled with new steam afterward, they came downstairs, hugged her shoulder, and shoved a crisp bill in between her cleavage for a tip, with heartfelt gratitude. "Thanks, it was the best I ever had."

She drew a sharp breath watching a freight wagon lumber uphill under mule power. Why hadn't the Westport law answered her telegram inquiring about Waddle? There had been plenty of time for one to come by this hour. Perhaps the wire was down? She would send Sassy up there and see about it.

"Sassy," she shouted from the top of the stairs.

"Yes, missy?" The girl came running into the vestibule and looked up at her.

"Go up to the telegraph office and see if there are any messages for me."

"Now?"

"Yes, now."

Sassy rolled her eyes at the ceiling and nodded that

she would. Then she rushed out the front door before she drew her boss's wrath.

"That girl at times—" Ella said aloud in despair and started down the stairs. Some way or other she was ridding herself of this parasite Waddle. She could only hope the law handled him for her. Getting rid of his body might be hard to do—no, the law thing would work, she felt certain.

Sassy returned in a short while. Ella was busy in the kitchen overseeing her culinary staff when the girl reported, "Missy, they said there ain't been no telegrams for you."

Ella nodded that she had heard her. Damn, oh damn, she couldn't stand him blowing her money much longer. For a long moment, she stared at the cut-up potatoes on the counter. Something else might have to be worked out to rid herself of this festering parasite, Ash Waddle.

Tuesday nights were usually slow, this one dragged on. Two inebriated drummers sang sea chanteys about the girl from Fray in the parlor until she told two of her girls to take them upstairs and do whatever was necessary to shut them up. It was late and she doubted there would be any more business coming by, so she sent the rest of them off to bed and went upstairs to her room.

She was half undressed and standing in her corset when, unannounced, red-faced Waddle burst in the door.

"You bitch!" he shouted, waving a yellow piece of paper and closing in on her. "You lying, damn rotten whore!"

For an instant, she thought of the .22 in the trunk among her things, but there was no time for her to get to it. He shoved the telegram in her face.

"Goddamn you. If my friends hadn't been working the desk shift at the police department when you wired them about me—"

Her heart sank. That was why she hadn't heard. His friends at the police station had intercepted the one she sent. Her heart stopped. She saw his quick move and the savage look on his face. Despite her effort to avoid and repel his reach for her, Waddle ended with a handful of her hair and jerked her toward him. The pain of his grasp caused her to catch a scream in her throat.

"I'll teach you to try and double-cross me!"

Then he swung his fist into her midsection and drove the air out of her diaphragm. The worse was yet to come and she knew that unless she did something quickly to stop him, he would give her the worst beating of her life. Helpless, she tried to think of something to say to make him quit—but nothing came to mind.

Never would she beg for mercy. Gawdamn him! Never—

Once, she saw what looked like her opportunity and she kicked hard, but he deflected her foot and she missed her goal—his crotch. His wrenching hold on her hair jerked her around again and he delivered another hard blow to her midsection. Desperate for air, she gasped for breath. Her knees gave way. She felt him pounding on her back, then she found herself sprawled facedown on the carpet.

For an instant, his ferocious attack let up. A wave of relief coursed through her body, but it was short-lived.

The first slap of his belt across her bare shoulders felt like a fire brand on the exposed skin. She tried to scoot away, but the lashes only grew more fierce. Then he repeatedly kicked her with his boot. Deeply in pain, she drew herself into a ball under the relentless onslaught of his belt and boot toes. At last, unconsciousness took her away from the pain and she passed out.

CHAPTER 9

His whole world was totally black. Fear caused his heart to race uncontrolled. The Kid desperately clutched the saddle horn's cap under his palm to keep from falling from the sway of Buster's gait.

"Where in the hell are we now?"

"Oh." Leo paused and brought the horses to a stop. He was still leading the Kid's horse. Bobby could hear the leather creaking and knew Leo was looking around. "Dammit, Kid, I don't know. There are some more pines now. I think we'll be at Snowflake tomorrow."

The Kid noted the uncertainty in Leo's voice and cursed to himself over his own helplessness. He was fairly certain Leo would not leave him. Leo was a follower, and since having taken up with Bobby, he had stuck tightly. No, Leo wouldn't leave him. When his blindness was healed and everything was over, he vowed silently, he would do something for Leo. Something really special.

"Kid, I think we'd better stop for the day," Leo said, sounding concerned. "We'll ride up one of those washes and make camp. It'll take me a while to get the fire started and to take care of the horses. I'll get you settled first. Is that okay, Kid?"

"Sure, Leo. Sounds fine. I'm counting on you."

He dismounted heavily and Leo helped settle him on a bedroll with his back against a sun-warmed rock. The Kid recalled that he had heard those same words "counting on you" from someone else years before.

After Bobby quit Chisum, he went over in the Indian Territory for a while. Satisfied the law had forgotten him, he rode back to New Mexico. Los Gatos was the first place he had stopped when he reached the territory. It was a wood-frame town without any trees except for a few spindly ones that dotted the nearby river. The stream was a typical sandbar affair with a strip of water so narrow that it could be leaped across anywhere.

In the empty saloon, he drank a ten-cent beer and ate boiled eggs with sourdough bread off the free lunch board. He had very little money left, and knew he would soon have to find some work or starve.

"Anyone around here hiring?" he asked the bartender.

The man wiped his hands on his apron. "And just what can you do?" he asked mockingly.

"Mister, I can ride, shoot, and punch cows pretty good."

"How good can you shoot?" The man looked at him with deep skepticism written on his face.

"Pretty fair."

"Which says nothing," the bartender scoffed. "Tell you what; business is kinda slow. You come on out back, and we'll see how good you are."

Feeling a little put out at the man, Bobby trudged after him. In the backyard of the saloon, the man motioned for him to wait.

The saloonkeeper took several brown whiskey bottles from a big pile outside the back door, and set them in a row on the edge of the grassy hill. Then he walked slowly back.

"How many of them can you hit?"

"Which ones you want hit?" he asked the man seriously.

"Just take out as many as you can."

The Kid nodded, then drew the .38 he had traded for in the Nation. He fired the gun in a slow, methodical manner until five bottles were splintered pieces of glass. Then he busied himself reloading his .38. He knew the bartender was impressed with his skill, because each time he had hit a bottle, the man had softly exclaimed, "Oh."

"You're good," the bartender admitted with a surprised smile. "What's your name?

"Bobby Joe Budd."

"Where you from, Budd?"

"Oh, the Indian Nation."

"I think I know a man who could use you to shoot wolves and varmints."

"Really?"

"Yes, I'm sure he'll hire you. His name's Peter Townsend. He owns a ranch south of here. You ride out there. Tell you what, I'll give you a note to take along, sort of an introduction. You're some shooter."

Bobby had shot lots of ammunition through this revolver and liked it better than the larger .45 Chisum had issued him. He loved the double-action Colt and practiced for hours with it. He never doubted his ability. If he wanted to hit something, he simply took aim and fired.

Four hours later, he found the ranch for which the bartender had given him directions. The moment that he laid eyes on Peter Townsend, he knew that the man was a gentleman. Townsend was dressed in a suit even though he was working around the corral. He came forward with a polite smile of inquiry.

"Good afternoon. Can I help you?"

Bobby nodded. "The bartender in Los Gatos said you might be able to use me." He passed the folded note to the rancher.

The man read it, his eyebrows rising in obvious surprise. "What's your name?"

"Bobby Joe Budd."

"Willis says you're a marksman." Townsend tapped the paper in his hand.

He felt flush faced with embarrassment. "Oh, I reckon I'm . . . a fair shot."

The man smiled at his modesty. "Fine, you're hired. Go put your things in the bunkhouse, then get a bath. You can start work tomorrow."

Get a bath? Bobby echoed silently. Hell, the man had hired him to punch cows or shoot. What did that have to do with taking a bath? Oh well, it might not hurt him. It was still warm outside, so maybe he wouldn't catch pneumonia.

So he went to work on the Turkey Track Ranch. The other hands were congenial, although there was an occasional bunkhouse squabble. It was a good job and a fine place to work. Townsend expected everyone to take a bath twice a week, which was unheard of in New Mexico, Texas, and the Indian Territory. But the rancher paid better than most, so it was worth the small inconvenience. Later on, frequent bathing would become a habit with him.

Townsend ran two-year-old steers that he brought in from Texas. Bobby calculated he ran a few thousand or more head. The cattle did good on the rich grass and sold for a healthy price in the fall. Then the following spring, Townsend went back to Texas for more steers. Of course, the man could have laid everyone off in the winter, but he didn't operate that way.

Folks were drifting into New Mexico. A lot of riffraff came and squatted around Turkey Track watering places, which proved to be an irritation to Townsend.

"There's not a blessed reason for that bunch to squat over at the Blue Hole," Townsend told him. "They can't farm that ground."

"Probably be closer to your cattle if they get hungry," Bobby said with youthful cynicism.

The rancher nodded grimly. "Exactly. They eat our beef and then sit on their bottoms."

"Maybe I could ride over there and suggest that they go to California or somewhere," Bobby offered.

Townsend looked at him intently, then smiled. "A fine idea. We don't want no trouble, mind you. Just tell them how poor this land is to farm. Take one of the other men with you."

Bobby considered the idea before he spoke. "Mr. Townsend, I think I can handle it myself."

"Just be careful."

"Oh, I will."

Bundled in a jacket against the north wind, he saddled up and rode out to the place where the good spring water was. He wore a scarf around his neck and a knit sailor cap pulled over his head for warmth. The sun was weak and gave precious little heat.

When he arrived at the top of the mesa near the spring, he saw the wagon bows. They looked like bleached steer carcass ribs. Smoke swirled up and was swept away from beneath the rise that hid the squatters' outfit.

He rode up to a dug-out canvas tent and could smell

the cow-chip fire. Wind whistled past him and popped the tent roof.

"Hello!" he shouted from his position on the horse's back. His answer was a hexagon barrel of a rifle poked out of the side of the canvas door. "What do you want?"

"Hey," Bobby protested with a halfhearted laugh. "It's cold out here; can we talk inside?"

"You just keep riding, mister. We don't have nothing here for you." The man had a slight accent.

"Can't do that. You better come out here and talk to me." His words carried a distinct warning.

"Don't try nothing. I'll get dressed and come out."

Bobby looked around the small encampment, then pulled his cap over his ears and hugged his arms for warmth.

A tall man, wearing a quilted coat, appeared with a rifle in his hand.

"What do you want?" he demanded, his eyes narrowed in suspicion.

"Mister." He twisted around as if to examine the land. "This sure ain't farmland. You'd be ten times better off somewhere else."

"Yeah, we know that."

"Well, why are you staying here, then?"

"Costs money to move on. We can't go until spring."

"Would you go on west if I gave you a little money?" Bobby asked, confident that the man was not looking for violence.

"Sure, if we had the money, we'd go. How much you talking about?"

"Ten dollars," Bobby offered; almost certain that Townsend wouldn't mind paying that much to get rid of the squatters. He had already said he didn't want any trouble.

"When will I get the money?"

"When you get the wagon loaded and ready to go."

The man frowned in thought, then nodded his head decisively. "We can be ready by the day after tomorrow. This is a bad place. Thank you for the offer and your generosity, mister."

"That's all right. You're welcome."

Townsend was amazed and pleased by the outcome of his visit to the squatters' place. That was the beginning of his new job of moving the honyockers off the Turkey Track. The position suited him. It sure beat splitting firewood or mending corrals, and in the summer it would be better than herding and checking steers.

One outfit that he approached left for free. Bobby rode over and told them it was a damn sight warmer over west of the Rio Grande. In less than a week, they were gone.

In early spring, he rode east to a place called Two Rocks. By midday, the sun had warmed considerably. There was a man and woman who had been camping out at Two Rocks since early fall and it was time to get them to move on. Bobby had observed the woman at a distance as she collected cow chips and stockpiled them in small mounds near their camp. At the time he had been gathering steers to move north with two other hands, and he didn't have an opportunity to visit them.

He finally found the time to ride out to the place and check on the pair. By mid-morning it was hot enough for him to shed the heavy blanket-lined coat that he had put on earlier. The patches of snow in shady places had evaporated, with the exception of a small mound or two under a ledge or sagebrush.

He rode up to the tent. It was a neat walled affair with a protruding rusty stovepipe. "Hello, the house."

The woman who appeared wore nothing but a short

night shift. His eyes widened in shock as he looked at her. At a glance she was nice enough looking, but when he drew closer he noticed the deep pockmarks on her face.

"Hello there," she said with an overly friendly smile. He grew apprehensive. The smile was not the kind a lady gave a stranger. Maybe, he mused with growing suspicion, she was covering up so her husband could sneak up behind him. A quick glance around dispelled his suspicions.

"I have some coffee. Come in and have some," she said with a provocative twist of her thin body.

"Ma'am, is your husband here?" he asked loudly.

"Oh, I'm sorry, but he's not here right now. Did you need to speak to him?" Her voice sounded full of innocence. Too danged innocent, he thought grimly.

She continued, sounding almost apologetic. "He left early this morning for Los Gatos to see Mr. Beamer at the bank about a loan."

He hid a start of surprise. The woman was obviously lying. He had heard lots of stories. In fact, he had made up a few of his own at one time or another, but hers about the banker business took the prize. He decided to play along. "I see," he said flatly.

"Could I help you?" she asked with a tilt of her arched brows.

He speculated on her obvious offer. If her man was really gone to Los Gatos, he'd not be back until after dark. But if he was the jealous type and caught them together, he might well shoot first and ask questions later. It seemed unlikely that her man would return before he was done with her. Bobby drew a sharp breath up his nose and decided it was worth a chance.

Inside the tent she gestured for him to sit on a canvas cot and then went to get him a cup of coffee. He noted that she was barefoot and the short hem of her nightshirt exposed a generous amount of her legs and slim ankles.

"My name is Claire," she said as she handed him the coffee. She was standing so close he could see the dark brown nipples of her breasts through the thin shift. He swallowed hard when she sat down on the other cot directly opposite him.

"What's your name?" she asked in a husky voice.

"Oh, er . . . Bobby Joe." His face reddened in embarrassment as he tried to draw his eyes away from the smooth mounds beneath the thin material of her night gown.

"Is there something wrong?"

"No. Actually . . ." Bobby looked down at the steaming coffee. "I came here to ask you to leave. You see, this is Turkey Track land," he explained quietly.

"Oh, I'm sure Chester, my husband, did not know that this was your land," she said sweetly.

He shook his head. "Not my land, ma'am."

"Claire."

"Yes, ma'am, Claire. It's Mr. Townsend's land . . . er . . . sort of."

"Sort of?" she repeated softly as she rose and moved to sit beside him on the narrow cot. When her hand touched his thigh, he spilled a little of his coffee.

Clearing his throat, he avoided looking at her face. "Well, it is his and it ain't. Except—"

She cut him off by placing her fingertips against his lips. "I hate to worry about legal things, don't you?"

As she leaned against him, he was reminded of how a woman smelled. It had been so long, he had forgotten about the musky scent of a near-naked woman's body. The pressure of her soft skin against his and her earthy fragrance acted like a fire upon his brain.

Of course, with his limited knowledge of women at that time, it was really a squirming flash-in-the-pan affair. But he managed to prove his manhood twice. Then the same odor that had drawn him to her rushed to his nose and nearly gagged him with revulsion. Exhausted and weary of the scar-faced woman with the stringy hair, he pushed himself up and threw back the covers.

"Will you come back, Bobby?" she asked as she lay blatantly naked and unconcerned about the fact.

"Sure," he said quickly, thinking it was a lie.

"Will you, ah, leave me a little money?"

"How much?" He sighed and avoided looking at her as he dressed.

"Two dollars for two times?" she asked with the first note of uncertainty in her voice. Then she sat up and gathered the blanket to wrap up under it.

He dug the money out of his pocket and threw it on the bed.

"If we don't get a loan, I will need this to go on," she explained softly. "Otherwise, I wouldn't ask you for it."

"That's all right. You be sure and tell your husband about this land belonging to Mr. Townsend."

"Oh, I will." She stood and wrapped the blanket around her body. "Bobby, will you kiss me?"

He turned and looked at her in puzzlement. "I guess. Why?"

She didn't look up. " 'Cause men don't kiss sporting women goodbye."

He furrowed his brows. Who didn't? It was news to him. He usually kissed them before he left, especially if he was drunk. He lifted her chin and dropped a quick kiss on her dry lips. She was no sporting woman, he was certain, or she would have stuck her tongue in his mouth.

Later, mounted on his horse, he circled around and

studied their camp for a long time. From his vantage point, Bobby was able to see a man climb out of the wagon, look around, then enter the tent. Bobby turned his horse westward. He wondered how many trips he would have to make until they had enough money to go west. There was no need to worry Mr. Townsend or the boys about these nesters. He could afford their stake.

Mr. Townsend was proud of his patrol. With spring upon them, Bobby stayed out riding the range, moving stray wagons of pilgrims off the Turkey Track. Claire and her hidden husband left in April with nearly thirty dollars of his money. Bobby had cut the cost to a dollar after that first trip, regardless of the number of times he used her.

The wagons did not make good time. Sometimes they traveled as little as five miles a day. Then the squatters would rest and graze their stock. But he made it clear to them that they weren't to stay in one spot for more than two days. Or else. His "or else" was seldom more than a threat.

One evening he rode into the main ranch, bone tired, and dismounted at the corral.

"Well, how's my security force?" Townsend asked jovially.

"Good, sir. I hope I've been handling the problem to suit you?"

"Oh, yes." Townsend walked beside him. Bobby's arms were loaded with his saddle, and every step he took sent a jolt of pain through his body, but he noticed his employer seemed very preoccupied with some troubling thought.

"Something wrong, Mr. Townsend?" he finally asked.

"Well, actually there is, Bobby. There's a Texas outfit planning to drive a couple thousand head of cattle up here."

"Here?"

Townsend nodded. Bobby noted the grimness in his voice when he continued. "We may go meet them and try to change their minds."

"You think that'll work, sir?" he asked doubtfully.

"Bobby Joe, I'm just not sure. These men are not dirt farmers. They wear guns like you do, and I'm sure they know how to use them."

From his experiences in the Nation, with Texans, he had some misgivings about them backing down. He had seen lots of drovers pushing their cattle across the Indian territory. Wild sky shooters, he privately called them. They all rode half-broken horses and stampeded anything that got in their way. They certainly were not dirt farmers in an inhospitable land. This was grassland and the Texans knew it. It was the kind of range that they would be looking for, and they wouldn't give a damn who laid claim to it.

Townsend made up his mind to go out and try to change their notions about crowding his range. He and Bobby rode southwest for three days until they spotted the rising dust of distant cattle.

"Whatever we do, Bobby Joe," Townsend warned, "I don't want any gunplay." Bobby thought his boss was being overly optimistic, but he had noticed from the first time he had met Peter Townsend that he was unarmed. He had looked almost naked to Bobby. At times he felt embarrassed to be riding beside a man without a sidearm, but that seemed to be Peter Townsend's way of life. He might send others out to shoot wolves or coyotes, but he was never armed himself.

The leader of the Texans, Rod Dailey, was a tough old man with a snow-white handlebar mustache. His eyes were flint hard and his back hunched from years in the saddle. "Mr. Townsend," he stated flatly, "we're headed for New Mexico."

Bobby noted his tone of voice and grew uneasy. This was no threat, no wild raving, just mere facts. They were coming with their herd regardless.

"Mr. Dailey," Townsend warned, "there isn't enough grass to last the summer. Not for all these cattle."

"Well, then, when it's gone, we'll move on to Colorado."

"Mr. Dailey, be reasonable. I have steers to fatten, and I can't have them pushed around all over the place."

"Townsend, you, sir, are a damn fool," Dailey declared with contempt. "You come here, unarmed, with a sniveling, snot-nosed kid who's armed with a broken pistol, and you tell me I can't graze up there. Well, you go home and get the rest of your army ready because I'm coming!" The meeting grew worse, the words flying fast and furious.

Only Townsend's flat refusal to unleash Bobby saved the Texan Dailey and his Mexican vaqueros from death. The vaqueros stood around with their hands on their gun butts, and spit out tobacco carelessly. Slant-eyed dogs who accompanied the Texan, ready to snap at anything upon Dailey's command.

Townsend looked defeated when he and Bobby rode out. Even when they pitched camp later, neither man had anything to say. Bobby fixed some half-cooked salty beans for their meal. Then after the horses were hitched for the night, he and his boss rolled out their bedrolls and fell into a restless sleep.

Bobby wanted to tell Peter Townsend a lot of things. Those bullies would never reach Turkey Track if he had his way. There would not be any more talk, just action. They would see what a sniveling kid could do. But that was not his boss's way.

From deep sleep, Bobby woke to rifle fire. It sounded like fifty of them blazing in the night, shooting up the camp. He scrambled on all fours and managed to get away into the darkness. Bullets screamed around him as he continued to crawl from the camp.

"Don't shoot!" he heard Townsend cry, but their guns were reloaded and kept up the orange barrage. Blasts and sour gunsmoke filled the night sky. At last the Texans rode off. The night fell silent except for the retreating horse hooves. Not one word had been spoken. But as Bobby lay in the stiff grass, trembling, his leg burning from a slight wound he had received, in the distance he made out a faint few words in Spanish from Dailey's vaqueros. They bragged about what they had done to Townsend and him. Good, they thought he was shot up, too. They would pay, if it cost him his life. At dawn, he buried Peter Townsend on a rise; tears of grief clouded his vision. He mounded rocks on the bullet-ridden corpse. He had no shovel and knew of no other way to hide his employer's body from the vultures and coyotes. Without a prayer book, he looked up at the sky helplessly.

"God, he's yours now. Those bushwhacking bastards are mine."

The Texans had fought Comanches, but they had never fought anything like the ghostlike avenger who stampeded their cattle with his wild coyote howls. One by one, he picked off riders and killed them as they tried to stop the runaways. Each night became a fearful time for Dailey's men.

Once, Bobby sent a dummy on Townsend's horse racing into their camp. The "rider" quickly had over a hundred bullet holes in him. Only later did Dailey discover that the dummy was dressed in the clothes of one of his own men. They found the naked man's corpse the next day, his skull bashed in.

Two days later, Dailey rode in the lead of the herd, directing the few remaining vaqueros, when a lone rifle shot cracked across the sea of grass. Spooked cattle raised their heads, poised to race off. Blood ran down the leathery face of the Texas rancher, Rod Dailey. He slumped and fell off his horse amid the sagebrush. Dead.

The vaqueros dismounted around his body. They pointed in all directions as they argued where the bullet had came from.

Bobby watched them through an eyepiece. As if spooked by the sight of their dead employer, the vaqueros hastily remounted and rode off.

Riding up, he looked down at the bloody corpse. He did not bother to ride after the others, nor did he bury Dailey's body. He left him for the buzzards and coyotes. Satisfied the man was gone to hell, he raised his head and howled. He yapped like a real coyote, hoping the vaqueros would hear him. From then on, he decided, that's who he would be, what they had called him, the Coyote Kid.

Leo was talking to him and his concerned voice brought him back to the reality of the moment. "I have some supper here for you. You all right, Kid?"

"No, I'm blind as a bat. You reckon that I'll see at night like bats do, Leo?" he tried to joke.

"God, Kid. I don't know. My head's been pounding all day too, but I can still see. Guess I didn't drink as much of that poison as you did."

"Hey, thanks for the food, Leo," Bobby said, taking a tin plate from his friend. His fingers felt clumsy as he tried to feed himself.

"I'll help you," Leo offered.

"No." Then the Kid cocked his head at a faraway

sound. A coyote raised his yipping cry. Coyotes rarely howled in the daytime. With stark realization, he knew it was dark and he was not like a bat, he could not see in the darkness, either. He was truly blind.

CHAPTER 10

Dolly knew that Milt Devers would never ride across the valley and all the way up into the Mustang Mountains. He was like a tethered dog. If another dog came inside his circle, he would fight it to the death. But if you turned him loose, he would go back and lie down in his own yard. He probably wasn't afraid of the whiskey peddlers. It was simply the fact that he fought better on home ground. Some men were like that.

John Wesley was the opposite. She had noted that about him their first night out. He adapted easily to new places and situations. The one possible exception was having a woman riding with him. And he had such methodical ways that irritated her. Every night he checked everything in a certain manner. He went over the animals, then inspected the cinches and pack saddle, and finally his weapons.

Devers had curled up in his bedroll after a polite word or two about her cooking. Soon he was snoring. After she washed the metal plates, she sat on a small log and tossed twigs into the dying fire.

"Are we going to take turns guarding?" She addressed John Wesley's back, which was bent over the pack saddle.

"Oh, I don't sleep very deep."

"If we do need to take turns, Mr. Michaels, don't concern yourself with me. I'll take my turn."

His shoulders heaved as though he were sighing in exasperation. But his voice was casual when he spoke. "No need for you to bother about guarding, Mrs. Arnold. I'm used to fending for myself. And as I said, I'm a light sleeper."

She was already piqued because he had not said one word about her cooking, and his attitude caused her anger to grow out of proportion. Maybe he was a better cook than she was, she mused acidly.

Unaware of her growing anger, John Wesley spoke over his shoulder, "Oh, Mrs. Arnold, if you want to ride back with Devers it might be your last chance. What I mean is the last chance for someone to escort you home—"

She glared at his broad back and spoke through clenched teeth. "No, thank you. I am staying here." Her dress swished as she stalked past him. Obviously the hardheaded man still did not believe that she was going with him. For Lord's sake, she argued silently, did he think she was playing a game? He had not seen her child lying on the ground with the life draining out of him from those killers' bullets. Even now, the memory brought a stabbing pain to her heart that she could only transfer into hate and a desire for revenge. It was the only thing that kept her going. And if that . . . that stiff-necked marshal—*excuse me, peace officer of the court,* she corrected herself grimly—if he thought she was playing some sort of game, then he had better think again.

A sudden suspicion struck her. Surely he wasn't planning to sneak out on her? Maybe that's just what he had in mind. He would slip out quietly before daybreak, leaving her with old Devers. No way, Mr. Michaels! She turned with fire flashing in her eyes. Her molars ground against each other as she watched him carefully cleaning his gun. She sent him a silent warning, which he did not see.

In the early hours before dawn, John Wesley saddled Jacob in the darkness, his movements quiet and confident. He turned and almost bumped into a figure that appeared out of the tree branches.

"I told you, Mr. Michaels," Dolly said quietly, "that I was going with you."

His breath came out in a resigned sigh. He dropped his hands, which he had automatically put out to steady her. "Yes, Mrs. Arnold." There was nothing for him to do, other than tie her up, and he was reluctant to exert physical restraint over her. He handed her the reins to his horse. "I'll saddle your gray. We'll leave the packhorse and our other stuff here so we can travel faster."

"Thank you," she said coldly. If she had to cook, then he could worry about saddling the horses. Besides, as fussy as he was about saddling, there was little chance that he would let anything hurt her mare's back.

In silence they led their horses out of the trees, past the snoring Devers. They mounted by starlight; John took the lead. He intended to cross the vast open flats and be in the timber before dawn.

"Watch yourself," he warned her, "there could be gopher holes. Those mounds could cripple a horse."

"Thanks," she retorted with heavy sarcasm. "If I see any I'll let you know."

Irritated by her sassy manner, he spoke sternly. "This is serious business. I intend to be across this open stretch by the time the sun rises."

"Yes, sir."

Her meek answer caused his brows to draw together. He suspected she was mocking him, and he didn't like the idea, but he did not know how to deal with it. He cleared his throat and reminded her, "You didn't have to come on this ride, Mrs. Arnold."

"I told you—"

"And I keep telling you," he interrupted sharply, "that I will get the killers and bring them to justice."

"I'll be there to back you."

He rolled his eyes toward the dark starlit heavens, praying for patience with the sharp-tongued woman. Since she was bound and determined to have the last word, he decided to ride toward their destination in silence.

Dawn began to stretch its lazy fingers at the edge of the sky when he stopped and dismounted in a grove of pines at the foot of the mountain. He looked up at Dolly and held out his hand to help her dismount.

"I am perfectly capable of getting on and off a horse by myself, Mr. Michaels," she said coldly, still stewing from his silent disapproval.

He stepped back as she dismounted. "You want jerky and water for breakfast?" he asked.

"Yes, thank you." She led the gray mare to a large rock. Then, when she was seated on it, she frowned at the steep craggy slopes above them and at the spindly pine trees.

"Here." He gave her a few strips of brown beef jerky. "Might not be as good as your cooking, but it will do for a while."

She raised her brows in surprise at his mention of her cooking. But she soon dismissed his praise and gnawed on the leathery jerky, shifting restlessly on the boulder. The jeans still chafed the insides of her thighs, but they were becoming a little less uncomfortable than they had been.

After a little while, he rose and gestured her toward her

horse. It was time to ride. "See way up there?" He pointed to the higher ground. "Devers said that's the way to the valley that those bootleggers are hiding in."

"Good." She motioned for him to lead on.

They had to ride single file up a narrow game path. The horses cautiously picked their way across the rock shelves that tilted dangerously to the side. She tried to avoid looking down. The height was soon dazzling, and although the top of the mountain seemed no closer, the bottom appeared to be farther away. Pine trees scraped against her denim-clad legs, leaving sticky sap streaks for flies to buzz around. The mare was forced to hug so closely to the trees that the boughs nearly unseated her.

A new scent teased her nostrils. It was not pine resin, or horse, or her own body. It was the pungent odor of wood smoke.

"John, they aren't far. I can smell smoke." In her excitement, she was not aware that she had called him by his Christian name.

After his initial surprise, he turned in the saddle. He sniffed the air and frowned. "I can't smell it, but thanks."

"Oh, anytime," she muttered under her breath. Was she supposed to be grateful that she had been some small use to him? Maybe he wanted her to get down and sniff around the ground from now on, a sort of assistant deputy assistant bloodhound?

As she stared holes in his back, he turned and nodded. "I can smell it now."

"Well, bully for you, Mr. Territorial Marshal."

He gave her a questioning scowl and went on.

Finally at the crest, the pair rode into a narrow grassy valley situated between two pine-clad slopes. He kept them close to the timber in case they were spotted and needed to take cover quickly. He reached down and drew out the Winchester .35/.20 repeater. Men had laughed at the small caliber he used, but he felt the gun was ideal for his work.

They rounded a bend. Directly in front of them rested the log house. Before either of them could comment, someone on the porch took a shot at them. He saw the telltale muzzle flash and spark.

"Get in the woods!" he shouted. "Take cover!"

The two of them bent low in their saddles, drove their horses into the timber. He hurriedly dismounted and gave her the reins for his horse.

"Stay here and keep down," he ordered, then immediately darted through the trees. He moved like an Indian, fading in and out of the pines, crouching low and making little noise. The rifle was in his right hand, and the tip of its barrel was the last thing she saw of him before he was swallowed up by the tree trunks.

She quickly tied the horses to a small pine. Satisfied they were securely hitched, she drew the loaded pistol from her holster. From her saddlebags, she took a box of extra shells, then she started down the dry slope carpeted with pine needles.

The pop of a gun sounded in the distance. She saw John behind a huge fallen tree trunk. Three smoking guns were firing at him from the cabin. Half running and stumbling, she raced down the incline to his hiding place. Her arms flung out to help her retain her balance, the pistol whipped the air as she stumbled the last few feet.

"What in heavens—" he croaked as she plunked down beside him.

"Well, here I am, ready to back you up," she stated breathlessly.

He gave her a withering look. "So I see." He glanced down at the pistol in her hand, and tried to mask his displeasure concerning it.

"What do you plan to do with that?" he demanded. Not giving her time to answer, he directed his attention back to the cabin from where bullets were still flying. They buzzed overhead and sprayed bark dust off the log onto them.

She expelled a deep breath. "Tell me something, John Wesley," she asked curiously, "do you just plain hate women?"

He glanced over his shoulder at her. "What has that got to do with this?"

She shrugged. "Nothing, probably. But answer me anyway, do you hate women?"

A bullet zipped over them, sending down a shower of pine needles.

"No, I don't hate women," he said as he pushed her to the ground, his arm familiarly around her shoulders.

She half rose on her hands and spit out some pine needles. "Are you sure?" she persisted.

He ducked low and growled at her. "Yes, I'm sure."

"I don't think you're sure at all," she said thoughtfully. "I think the only way you like women is when they're in the house wearing dresses."

He ducked low again, then spoke with exaggerated patience. "Mrs. Arnold, I do not intend to discuss my—"

"Your private life with me," she completed his words. "That's fine by me. By the way, why are we hiding behind this log?"

He flung his arm across her back as she tried to rise. "Because we don't need to get ourselves shot." His words seemed to be emphasized by the bullets that chewed into the bark of the log in front of them.

"Oh," she said, her mouth forming the word in surprise. "Yes, I see." She flattened herself against the ground. After a few minutes of discomfort, she rose up and peeked over it. A ricocheted shot whined past her and she quickly ducked again.

"John Wesley," she asked dryly, looking the few inches between them into his eyes. "How long are you planning to do this?"

"Do what?"

"Lie here on this bed of sticky pinecones?"

He gave her a considered look and his mouth twitched for a moment in what might have been laughter. "Not long. You shoot at the cabin every once in a while so they think we're both here. Just reach over and shoot, but be sure and keep your head down."

"I won't be able to hit anything shooting like that."

He shook his head. "Mrs. Arnold, just reach up and shoot in their direction."

"All right," she conceded ungraciously. When he began to crawl away, she called to him, "Hey. Be careful, John Wesley."

He crouched low, and began to move along the hillside to reach the rear of the cabin.

She knelt on her knees and watched him go. The .32 gripped in both hands, she fought to control her breathing and her racing heart. He needed the distraction of her shooting at them. Quickly she rose up, took aim at the cabin, and then fired.

A man screamed from the cabin, "Gar! I'm hit! Hit bad."

She dropped flat, her eyes wide in horror. Oh Lord, had she killed one of them? The idea made her sick, but she tried to shrug it off. She had no time to worry about it, because she had to shoot again to give John Wesley cover. Her movements were automatic as she rose up, took aim, fired, and ducked down. She repeated the process several times until her ears rang with the percussion of the gunshots and the wounded man's screams.

Her breath came out harsh and ragged. The sulphurous smoke of the shots burned and watered her eyes.

John's authoritative voice came from the direction of the cabin. "Throw down your guns and raise your hands, or my posse out there will cut you to ribbons."

"We give up!"

"They already got me," one man grumbled.

She crawled over the log, then ran down the valley toward the cabin, the pistol still tightly gripped in both her hands. "John Wesley, you old law dog," she whispered breathlessly to herself as she hurried toward the cabin. "We did it. We did it."

"Mrs. Arnold!" John called out as he emerged from the house with the three disarmed men. "We'll need the handcuffs from the saddlebags."

She stopped short, her legs nearly buckling beneath her. Dumbly she nodded and waved the pistol as a sign that she had heard him. She turned and holstered the sidearm as she hurried back to the horses for his restraints.

"You mean to tell me a woman shot me in the ass?" she heard the grumbling man ask in disgust. Yes sir, she silently answered him, the same woman who intends to capture the Coyote Kid.

When she returned with the handcuffs, John Wesley had the men lined up. The big one, Gar, cussed vividly until John was forced to shut him up by hitting him with a pistol butt on the shoulder. She winced as she heard the dull thud. It silenced his foul language.

When John finished cuffing them, he assured her that the wounded man was all right. Though he didn't tell her, obviously the bullet fragment had creased his rump. She watched the man sit down gently and to one side. He looked barely twenty years old. The other two men called him "Dip Shit," but she was certain he had a real name. She privately dubbed the whiskered man, who flapped his gums, Toothless. So they had Gar, Toothless, and the wounded Dip Shit sitting around in irons. She wrinkled her nose. They did not look so dangerous seated on the ground and handcuffed.

John insisted that she hold a gun on them while he interrogated them. She did not fully listen to his questions, but glanced around occasionally to make sure there was not another member of their gang lurking nearby.

Finally John came over and hunkered down beside her. "Mrs. Arnold, a couple of weeks or so ago, they sold the Coyote Kid and his partner some whiskey. Then those two rode south."

She inhaled sharply.

"What's wrong?" he demanded.

She shook her head. Now that she knew they were definitely on the trail of her son's killer, she wasn't sure if she was glad or frightened. Feeling John Wesley's gaze on her, she shook her head again. "Thank you for telling me."

"Sure." He watched the changing expressions cross her face. Now she had a hard glint in her eye and a determined tilt to her chin. The fact that she knew the Kid on sight might prove beneficial when they found him. On the other hand, she just might decide to take justice into her own hands.

"We'll have to take these three into Snowflake. Maybe we can pick up some news of the killers there," he said.

"Yes, I realize that. Thank you again. And, John . . ." She looked up at him steadily. "I'm sorry about my earlier outburst."

He waved away her apology. "No, that's all right."

"No." She put a hand on his arm, determined to have her say. "I talked out of turn. I was wrong."

He felt uncomfortable and shook his head. "We can talk about it later."

She scowled at his retreating back. Men! There were times when she wished them all in hell. Now, as if having to make a detour to Snowflake wasn't bad enough, she had three grubby whiskey peddlers to cook for. It would take them at least three days to go back and get their packhorse, then ride all the way to Snowflake, and in the meantime the Kid's trail would be getting cold. Milt Devers was the only one who made any sense at all. He'd probably gone home.

John Wesley used a pine-knot club to bust the peddlers' stash of whiskey. He was careful to retain two bottles as evidence. When he had finished, he smelled like a whiskey still himself.

He glanced at Mrs. Arnold, noting the strained expression around her mouth as she held his rifle on the prisoners. The whiskey peddlers grumbled about the waste of their whiskey as John helped them to mount their horses. She rode out in front of the procession and John brought up the rear.

As he watched his prisoners sway on their horses, he thought about his first arrest as a territorial marshal. Three whiskey makers had been captured with the assistance of Mrs. Dolly Arnold. How was he going to explain her presence to the major? How would he word the letter to Bowen? he wondered. *Dear Major, I have this immoral woman riding with me, but I am not being immoral with her.* No, he sighed, better forget trying to explain her to his employer.

CHAPTER 11

"Kid, we're at the doc's place," Leo said quietly as he helped Bobby dismount from his horse. The Kid cocked his head, detecting dogs barking and children laughing. He stumbled as Leo guided him onto the boardwalk. Straining his eyes, he thought for a moment things weren't entirely black, but his confidence was wavering: he could make out no forms, nothing distinct.

"What's the matter with him?" a man's scratchy voice asked loudly. "He been in a dynamite blast?"

Leo drew the Kid to a halt. "No. Are you the doctor?"

"Yes. You can read, can't you? Come this way."

"You're doing fine," Leo said confidently, guiding him by the right arm. "We're going into his office."

"Here now, be careful with him. Does it hurt much, young man?" The man's voice came from right beside the Kid's ear. He calculated the physician was standing beside the open door.

"Over there please, on the table," the doctor directed. "Set him down easy." There was a shuffling of feet then the Kid smelled the doctor's tobacco breath on his face.

"Now open your eyes real wide, young man. Hmm." He could feel the doctor's fingertips pushing up his eyelids, and although he knew his eyes were fully extended he still could not see.

"Is it . . . is it bad, Doc?" he asked hoarsely.

"You tell me."

He shrugged. "I can't see anything. Haven't seen nothing for two days."

"What've you been drinking?"

"Nothing, not today."

"Well, it's my guess that drinking wood alcohol caused your blindness," the doctor said dryly. "I'd call it whiskey poisoning; I've seen it before."

"We figured that's what it was, Doc," Leo agreed.

"Damn varmints that sell bad whiskey like that need to be shot!" the doctor growled.

"Or worse," the Kid said grimly.

"We'll bandage your eyes. You stay in a darkened room for a few weeks, and if you're ever going to see, we'll know by that time. But you must keep them bandaged or you could spoil your chances for ever seeing again."

Bobby drew a deep breath. "What's my chances, Doc?"

He wasn't sure if he wanted to know the answer. If only he could see the doctor's face, but that was stupid. If he could see the man's face, he wouldn't be asking the question. Blindness seemed to be dulling his wits. He braced himself for the doctor's reply.

"Oh, I'd say fifty-fifty. But if you don't keep them bandaged and stay out of the light for a while, then your chances are none at all."

The doctor wrapped his eyes with some cotton cloth. "Now you keep these on."

"Oh, he will," Leo promised. "Won't you, Ki—Bobby?"

"Sure." He rose and turned toward the sound of Leo's voice. "Pay him, Leo, and we'll go."

"You two just passing through?" the doctor asked quietly.

"Yeah," Leo answered. "Why are you asking?"

"Oh, I was thinking. There's a widow woman who takes in boarders. She's got a little place east of here. She'll put up your horses and take you in. Won't cost you much. Er, Leo, is it? You keep Bobby there for a week."

"That's an idea, Leo," the Kid said considering the notion. At least he had a fifty-fifty chance if he followed the doctor's advice. It was a lot better than no chance at all. And the sooner he regained his eyesight, the sooner he could track down those poison peddlers and square up with them.

"Find out where this woman lives," he ordered.

"Her name's Mrs. Parker," the doctor informed them. "You go east for two miles. She's got a small spread sitting by itself. Can't miss it."

Later, when they arrived at Mrs. Parker's place, the Kid decided that he liked the sound of her voice. The cost was reasonable. For their meals, horse pasture, and bed it was a dollar a day. Her house smelled of fresh bread. The rocker that Leo placed him in felt secure beneath him. He and Leo had decided to use aliases, so they were known to Mrs. Parker as Bobby Jones and Leon Smith. Not very original, but she didn't question them. Her name was Beth.

They settled in quickly. Leo was free to scout around and find out all he could about the Arnold's Store incident. While Leo did that, the Kid, with his eyes bandaged, sat in the rocker and contemplated his entire life.

The rocking chair reminded him of the stage guard

job he had taken with Halbert Coach lines. They both had the same kind of swaying motion. After Peter Townsend's death, he had hired on as a shotgun guard. Made the run from Pueblo, Colorado, to Morton's Station in New Mexico and back. There the line split; one went west to Santa Fe, the other toward the east.

There was nothing on the stage worth robbing. But there were always drifters who from time to time would hold it up for the mail and strongboxes, just in case they held a few dollars.

The stage schedule called for him and the driver, Buck, to make two runs down to Morton's and back, then they had two days off. His serious impotency problems with women began while he was in Pueblo. That was before he met Maria.

In the Largo Bar on his day off, bored to pieces, he sipped on a foamy beer and watched a skirt swisher who was working hard to find herself a customer. The afternoon business was slow, so she crossed the room and sat at his table uninvited.

"What's your story, mister?" she asked in a bored tone.

"Story?" In disbelief, he blinked at her words in his alcohol-induced stupor.

"Come on, you guys all got a story. This is free," she said cynically. "Some guys would rather tell me their life stories than go to bed."

"What kind of story?" he asked curiously.

She shrugged her bare shoulders, then pulled up her low-cut dress with both hands so her thin bare legs were partially uncovered. "Oh, I don't know. Like the guy who killed his wife, I guess. It was back East somewhere, so he said. He really felt bad about it, but said she nagged him all the time. He told me that one day he got tired of it and tied her up in a chair, then stuffed her mouth full of stockings. Then he asked her if she would still nag him, and she nodded her head yes. So he left her like that and went to the saloon for a few beers. When he came back home, she was dead. Blue as a goose, he said. It's crazy to hear all these different kinds of stories."

He looked across the table at her. Hell, he had one to beat that and spoke flatly. "The first man that I killed had beat up my mother."

"What?"

"He did," he confirmed. "It was in Ohio. He was some fancy dresser, and for no reason that I could see he just started beating on her with his cane."

"Ah, that's sad. Did you love your mother?"

Bobby shrugged. "I ain't sure, but I sure hated him. So I went and got one of his own dueling pistols, loaded it and shot him in the back of the head."

"Did he die?"

"Sure he died."

The woman was silent for a moment, then rose and smiled down at him. "Well, you want to come back to my room now?"

He was doubtful. She wasn't that good-looking. Besides, he felt too drunk to be aroused. Finally he rose and followed her wordlessly to her room. It turned out to be a gut-wrenching mistake for him. The whole thing was over before it started, leaving him angry and confused at his failure.

After that episode, his attempts to make love all failed. Because, drunk or sober, no matter how hard he tried it wouldn't get stiff.

It was after one of those distressing events that the stage was held up by two men. The robbers rode out of a dry wash firing their pistols. It surprised him and the driver, Buck Calley. Calley drew up the teams.

"Hands up or you're dead!" the robbers shouted.

"Listen to them, Bobby. All we've got is mail," Buck warned and raised his hands high in the air to caution him from trying something against the robbers.

Bobby threw down his shotgun and climbed down from the seat box. It was humiliating to have to obey the two worthless outlaws. The passengers disembarked, their faces white with fear.

"We want all your valuables," one robber growled. Bobby listened and knew he would never forget that gravelly voice. He fumed silently as the two men took gold watches, wallets, and anything else that looked valuable. He stood there helplessly, gritting his teeth as the robbers pushed the passengers around.

"Guard," the second robber addressed him. "You got anything?" He shook his head. He took note of the man's Colt pistol, observing that it had no front sight. And he noticed the man's eyes were a brilliant blue.

"Should I kill them?" the blue-eyed man asked his friend.

"No, stupid!"

Blue-Eyes chuckled in the Kid's face. His words had caused the passengers to cower together. Bobby decided the man was crazy, and was just looking for an excuse to shoot someone.

"Get up there, driver, and go like hell," the gruff-voiced man commanded. "You look back and I'll shoot your head off. Now everybody load up!"

Buck climbed up and took his place. Seething with rage, the Kid followed him and glanced down to make sure all the passengers were on board. He nodded to Buck, after he made a careful note of the robbers' horses.

At Morton's relay station, the Kid begged the agent for a saddle horse.

"What are you going to do against them two?" the short balding man asked.

"Never mind, I'll get them."

"Oh, I don't know, Kid. I ain't got anyone to go back with you."

He shook his head. He didn't need any help. "I'll get them by myself."

The man scratched his shiny head. "Yeah, I reckon Mr. Halbert would pay a lot of money if you got them dead or alive."

"Loan me a horse," the Kid demanded, filled with impatience to be riding after the two.

"Aw, all right. Take mine, but you only got three days," the agent warned.

"Fair enough." He took a double-barreled twelve-gauge and rode back to the holdup site. There, he found his own pistol where the robbers had tossed it, thinking it was broken.

Through the next day he followed their trail until he reached an isolated building that served as a store. He dismounted at the corral, taking note of the robbers' familiar marked horses in the pen.

He cautiously entered the small building.

"What do you need, mister?" the storekeeper asked.

The Kid glanced around, quickly noting that he and the proprietor were alone. "Two men. One's blue-eyed, the other's got a gravelly voice."

"They ain't here."

Filled with rage, he shoved his pistol in the man's face.

"You're lying and fixing to die." He watched the man's resolve melt and his eyes widen.

"They're in the back room playing with a squaw who works for me."

"You let out a yelp and I'll kill you like I aim to do to them, savvy?"

"Sure. I won't make a sound. I promise." The man's face looked pale as a bed sheet.

"This ain't no idle threat. I'm the Coyote Kid."

"Holy cow! No, mister, I won't." He made a whistling sound through his lips and ducked down.

The Kid reached over the counter and found a sawed-off shotgun. He drew it out and holstered his .38. With a click of the breech, he noted both chambers were loaded. Holding it in both hands, he moved to the curtained door in the back of the store.

He heard the familiar gruff voice in the room ask, "Who rode up?"

"How should I know?" the other robber said testily.

"Well, damnit, go see!"

"Aw hell, you get all the pleasure and I've got to do all the work," the blue-eyed man complained. When he turned toward the door, he screamed. The Kid stood facing him, the shotgun in his hands. Both barrels took the blue-eyed man full blast and threw him backward on a pile of supplies. The Kid dropped the shotgun and quickly drew his own weapon.

The gruff-voiced man rose from a cot while the buck-naked squaw whispered something about escaping and dove behind a pile of crates.

"I give up," the man said flatly. His arms were up in the air, and he stood up naked. "Don't shoot." There was no fear, nor repentance, in his voice. Nothing but disgust at being caught. The .38 barked and the lead bullet took out the outlaw's right eye and smashed through his brain. He fell backward on the cot. Both robbers were dead.

The Kid loaded all the loot he could find putting it in a sack he found on the floor. Then he rode back to the relay station. He had been gone only two days, and Mr. Halbert rewarded him with two hundred dollars.

But his impotency problem with women grew worse. He began to drink more whiskey and less beer. Faintly, he recalled being drunk and sitting on a bed with some doxy. He placed his pistol barrel against her face.

"Tell them that the Coyote Kid is a good lover." She drew back in fear and tried to escape the muzzle of his .38.

"Don't move," he slurred.

"I—I'm not," she stammered.

" 'Cause if you do—"

"What? Oh God, what?"

"If you tell them that I didn't pleasure you, I'll put this little barrel in your nose and blow your brains out."

"Yes. Yes, please put the gun away," she begged.

"All right, but you stay here and keep guard while I sleep. Stay right here in this bed with me."

"Oh, I will, Kid," she promised. "I will."

The whiskey didn't solve his problem. Threatening whores didn't help him, either. He didn't recover his manhood until he met Maria. And Maria had left him for God. After she ran away, he drowned his misery with more whiskey, because he knew it was useless to try another woman.

Now, without his sight, he was alone in his rocker. Clack, clack, the runners crunched on the floor. He rocked in his dark world, waiting for Leo to return. His hearing grew keener with his blindness. He recognized Leo's familiar footfalls when he entered the room.

"Kid—I mean Bobby, Mrs. Parker's gone to milk the cow. I found out a few things." Leo must have hunkered down in front of him. "That little boy died. Word is they don't know for sure if it was us."

The Kid gritted his teeth and clenched his fingers around the rocker arms. "Leo, you listen to me. Stay sober and be ready to leave at any time. Don't leave me unless you don't have any other choice. When these weeks of being bandaged is over, if I'm still blind, then . . . then, Leo, I want you to shoot me."

"Aw, Kid. You're talking crazy. I can't do that," Leo whined.

The Kid lunged out and caught Leo's arm. He held it tightly until Leo at last promised to do his bidding.

"Leo, look at it this way." The Kid tried to inject a little humor into the situation. "It's like a horse with a broken leg. You got to do things you don't like sometimes, savvy?"

"Yeah. Shh, Kid, here comes Mrs. Parker."

"You just remember what I said."

"I will, Kid."

Bobby could hear Leo's boots clumping out the door. He continued his slow rocking until he heard the woman's soft soles cross the room. He looked up as he felt her presence in front of him.

"Mr. Jones, could Mr. Smith fix some of the fences tomorrow?"

"Sure. And call me Bobby."

"Very well. I'll ask him at supper, if you don't mind. Are you—are you in much pain, Bobby?"

"No, ma'am."

"Would you like some company?"

"Yes, I would. Company would be nice. It's lonely in this night I live in."

"Tomorrow, I'll spend more time with you," she promised. After a little while he sensed that she was rising to leave. "Tomorrow I'll sit with you longer," she said, repeating her earlier promise. It made him feel good. He tried to see her in his world without light, but couldn't. Nor could his imagination conjure up a picture to go with her soothing voice.

The next morning, before Leo left to fix the fence for her, he stopped to ask the Kid if he wanted anything.

"I'll be okay, Leo. You stay gone for a while; I want time to get to know this woman. No," he interrupted Leo as he started to speak, "don't tell me if she's ugly or not. It doesn't matter."

Leo whispered in concern. "What if you can't—"

"I'll tell her that it's due to my blindness."

"But for God's sake, whatever you do," Leo said hesitantly, "don't get angry with her."

"I'm only foolish like that when I'm drunk."

"Yes. Here, let me help you to your rocker."

"No." The Kid shrugged off his hand. "I want to walk to it by myself." He felt his way with his hands, then sighed in satisfaction when he lowered himself onto the seat. "See, Leo. I did it by myself."

Leo laughed softly as he left the room. The front door closed with a thud behind him.

"Bobby," Mrs. Parker cautioned from the kitchen, "you be careful. You don't need to fall and injure yourself. Are you hungry?"

"No, ma'am."

"Oh, you men are always hungry, even when you're sick," she retorted lightly, coming into the room. He could smell the food she set before him. Maybe he was hungry after all now that he thought about it.

"Need some help to eat it?"

"No."

"Those biscuits are buttered, but watch out, they are still hot."

He promised he would. Saliva rushed into his mouth at the prospect. Her thoughtfulness made his day a little brighter.

Later she came, took the empty tray, and sat near him in a chair. He tried to detect what she smelled like, but the house was full of rich food smells.

"What are you doing?" he asked curiously.

"Shelling dried beans."

"A blind man can do that."

"Yes, he can." She placed a large pan in his lap. He felt for her hands, grasping them gently between his own. They were long and slender. She did not pull away as he ran his thumbs over the backs of them.

"May I touch your face?" he asked. "I can't see you, of course, but I hear your gentle voice and I wonder what you look like."

"Wait. I'll put the pan out of the way." He heard her move, her dress rustling. He frowned in confusion.

"I'm on my knees, don't worry."

He nodded and she took his hands and pressed them to her cheeks. Slowly his fingertips traveled over her face and her nose. She had thin, delicate skin. His fingers sought her ears beneath the silky softness of her hair. Then he explored her eyes and soft, sweeping lashes.

"Bobby, you know that I'm ugly."

The Kid shook his head. "No, you're wrong—a blind man knows."

"I'd like to sell you a horse," she said with a soft laugh. His hands touched her neck, and he detected a pulse at the base. It beat like a hummingbird's wing.

"What happened to your husband?" he asked.

"He was sick and just died." Her voice suddenly became a little breathless, as though she were excited.

The Kid moved his hands to her shoulders. He felt the soft material of her dress. Then as if on cue, they both rose. No words were necessary. The magnetism between them was mutual.

She led him to the bedroom and undressed him with a gentleness he knew would sweep him away. What was meant to be happened, naturally, and he had no problems. In the darkness of his world, he felt the power of his life return. Again he scented womanhood and curled his lip to let it rush in. Once again he was the master of his own body. She was the vessel and their world was distant from the earth's dust.

He knew that in the evening, Leo would see the success on his face. Later he bathed, put on a fresh shirt, then made his own way to the rocking chair. The bandages were still over his eyes when Leo came in.

"Bobby, you sure look nice."

"Thanks, Leo. You sleep alone in the extra room tonight."

"Yeah, I kinda figured that. Oh—" he spoke to Mrs. Parker—"ma'am, I fixed that fence."

"Did you hear him, Bobby?" she asked, sounding thrilled because it was repaired.

"Yes. He's a good man, Beth. I only ride with good men."

So the Kid began sleeping with Beth. The following week when she had gone to milk the cow, Leo rushed in.

"Kid! Kid!" he shouted, breathing heavily. "They brung in those bootleggers that sold us the poison whiskey. A lawman and a woman had them in irons. They just now rode in; I saw them myself. It was them."

"What?" he asked. He gripped the rocker until his

knuckles popped. Then he tore the bandages from his eyes. The light penetrating his eyeballs burned. He squinted in horror and grabbed for Leo.

"My God. I can see! I can see you, Leo. I mean it." He pounded Leo on the back as tears of relief streamed down his face. "It's a miracle. Oh, Maria, it's a sweet miracle."

"Damn!" Leo chuckled and patted his back. He turned when Beth entered the room. "Look, he can see." Leo's voice trembled and he shook with excitement.

The Kid was shaking, too. He looked at the woman who had given him back his manhood. No, she was not ugly. He stood grinning widely as she put down her milk pail then rushed into his arms.

"This is the best day in my whole life," Leo gasped.

The Kid looked at his friend in rueful amusement. He knew what Leo meant. He had been reprieved from having to shoot the Coyote Kid like he was a lame horse.

Beth held out the bandages. "Let's put these back on, Bobby. I'm sure it will be better if they have a little more time to heal. Remember what the doctor said."

The Kid submitted. He was satisfied that he would not be blinded for life. And now for first time he had seen her. She was not beautiful, but she was nice-looking. When he held her again, he would remember what she looked like. He was so full of gratitude that he forgot about the news that Leo had brought.

CHAPTER 12

John Wesley was relieved to see the sign indicating the sheriff's office. Long before then, he had grown weary of the three criminals. They were a surly crew, and it had been a strain to keep them in line around Mrs. Arnold.

"Well, what have we here?" a tall, lean man wearing a badge asked.

"Whiskey dealers," John said as he dismounted. He noted the quick frown the lawman cast at Mrs. Arnold. "Do you know Mrs. Arnold, Sheriff?"

"She looks familiar." The sheriff turned and bent his frown on John. "Who are you?"

"John Wesley Michaels, an officer of the court."

"Federal?"

"No, sir. Territorial court. I have three John Doe warrants and evidence for you."

"Territorial law?" The man's words echoed with suspicion. John hesitated to show the man his badge. The major had warned him that local law enforcers did not take kindly to anyone infringing on their jurisdiction.

"I believe we work on the same side of the law?" John challenged the man.

The sheriff studied him for a moment, then seemed to reach a decision. "Sure we do. I'm Sheriff Rogers, and I'm glad to see someone run those three down. You did Apache County a real service. I've been trying to get the goods on Gar there for years." He motioned to the prisoners. "Get on inside the jail," he ordered.

John nodded to Dolly where she sat on horseback, then he followed the sheriff inside the jail. In the office, he handed Rogers the three warrants and the bottles of whiskey.

"These are my deputies, Neal and Teddy." The sheriff indicated the two young men in the room. "We'll get your handcuffs off the prisoners, and you can come back tomorrow and fill out the arrest papers on them. I'm sure you're tired."

John dismissed the man's concern and remained silent as the two deputies eagerly used his key to unlock the handcuffs. Then they shoved the whiskey peddlers down the hall to the cell.

"They'll still be here when the judge comes," the sheriff assured him.

"Fine. One more thing, Sheriff." John had started for the door, but he stopped and turned back. "Do you know the Coyote Kid?"

"No, I'm afraid I wouldn't know him on sight. He's the one who allegedly shot Mrs. Arnold's boy, right?"

"Not allegedly, Sheriff. A couple of weeks ago he and his partner were headed south and bought whiskey from those peddlers." John watched the sheriff's face intently. There was something suspect about the sheriff's quick change from anger to cooperation. Sheriff Rogers was, no doubt, a fair-wind man, and right now he had shrewdly guessed that the wind was blowing John Wesley's way.

"No, he hasn't been here, or I'm sure I would have heard about it. Now, Mr. Michaels, if you don't mind I have an important appointment to keep. You will be back in the morning, won't you?"

John Wesley knew he was being dismissed, but as it suited his own purposes at the moment, he let it pass. Nodding to the sheriff, he picked up his handcuffs from the desk, then walked quickly out of the office.

"Well, did he take them?" Dolly asked skeptically when he reached her side.

He raised a brow in surprise at her irritated tone. "Of course." He put the manacles back in his saddlebag, shaking his head in wonder at the way the woman's mood fluctuated.

"Well, I was beginning to wonder if—" She broke off abruptly as the sheriff came sauntering out on the porch.

"Afternoon, ma'am," he said with a hint of amused laughter in his voice. He nodded at John Wesley. "You folks have a good night."

John slapped down the flap of the saddlebag, his teeth clamped in a tight line. He looked over the horse and glared at the sheriff's back as he strode down the boardwalk. There had been such a wealth of insinuation in the sheriff's parting words that John had to fight hard not to scramble up on the porch and knock the man's teeth loose. He hoped Mrs. Arnold had not noticed Roger's meaningful look. He turned to her, keeping his anger well hidden. "Do you want to sleep in a hotel?"

"No, they cost money. We crossed a small stream earlier that would make a good campsite." Her voice was grim, her eyebrows furrowed.

"Why are you angry?" he asked under his breath.

She still glared when she turned to look at him. "That stupid man acted as though you had a disease. You're both lawmen; so why did he act like he didn't want to take your prisoners?" She continued without giving him a chance to reply. "I hate that kind of a man. You're the one who captured those outlaws. He should have been grateful, but he acted as though you were the criminal."

He sighed as he mounted Jacob. She was right, of course, but he wasn't greatly concerned about the lawman's manner toward him. He was more relieved that Mrs. Arnold had not noticed the lawman's knowing grin.

"It doesn't matter, Mrs. Arnold. Let's move on." He also noticed the shocked stares the two of them drew from some of the town women as they rode up the street. Oblivious to their looks, Mrs. Arnold still acted upset on his behalf. The major warned him local sheriffs were liable to resent any intrusion in their business. Turning over the whiskey makers had been a good example. He planned to write a complete report to the major and do the paperwork for the prisoners at the jail in the morning. He also wanted an opportunity to do some checking around town to see if anyone had seen anything of the Coyote Kid.

At the small stream, Dolly was undecided just where to stop, and didn't feel like asking the silent man riding behind her. Irritated by her own indecision, she jutted out her chin and set the mare westward on a cowpath that paralleled the stream. She led Thomas behind her. He had become a docile, well-trained beast of burden ready to go wherever she led him.

"Is this a good place?" she asked defensively as she turned in the saddle to look at John. The water looked deep enough in the small clear stream, and would be perfect for her own intentions. Every bone and muscle in her body cried for release. The odious smell of horse and perspiration saturated her pores. Several times on the trip, she had considered changing into a dress, but she had not wanted to cause more ribald comments from the whiskey peddlers than they had come up with on their own. At the moment, she rebelled at the idea of changing when her skin felt so gritty.

"This is fine. I'll put up the horses this time," he said, gathering the reins in his hand.

"I want my bedroll." She busied herself undoing the leather ties.

He frowned in puzzlement; it was still an hour until dark. "Your bedroll?"

"Yes. After I build a fire I intend to take a bath and I'll need something to wrap around me." She stared at his face defiantly. Perhaps he was shocked at her words, but it should come as no news to him that women, as well as men, took baths.

"Why do you need a fire?" he asked in genuine curiosity.

She closed her eyes and summoned up patience. He certainly did not know very much about women. Although she admitted grudgingly that he did not seem shocked by the idea of her bathing. "I will want to sit by the fire to get warm after I've bathed. And I may even wash my hair. If you want to change, I'll wash your clothes, as well."

"Mine?"

"Well," she retorted dryly, "I don't intend to wash you."

He grunted as his face heated beneath the layer of dust. "I was not suggesting anything of the kind, Mrs. Arnold."

"My name is Dolly. We've been riding together for five days. Call me Dolly!"

"Is that your real name?" He took a good look at her. Somehow the name Dolly did not seem to suit her.

"My real name? No, but I don't use my Christian name."

"Which is?" he persisted in a calm voice.

A smile lifted her chapped lips. "It's Zinnia, like the flower." She frowned in mock fierceness. "But if you ever call me that, I'll shoot you."

"Zinnia?" he echoed in wonder.

"Don't you dare laugh!"

He drew in his cheeks to keep from laughing at her glaring eyes. Hastily he looked away and changed the subject. "Mrs. Arnold, I'll change my clothes, but I can wash them myself."

"And will you bathe?"

"I suppose." The idea was not unappealing, but the lack of privacy bothered him more.

"There are plenty of places to take one." She pointed toward the stream. "That is my bathtub. When I'm finished, you can use it."

"Mrs. Arnold, I'm quite certain I can find my own bathing spot." He closed his eyes; for sheer tenacity this woman took the prize.

After supper, she bathed in the clear water. It was dark, but she didn't mind the enveloping twilight. The soap from her saddlebags and the soft water of the stream eased away the dirt and aches on her skin. All the chafed and sore spots were soothed by the cool water. Running her hands over her body, she discovered strong muscles had already begun to replace the soft ones. Being a housewife was a lot different from riding astride a horse.

She dried herself briskly, causing her skin to tingle. Then she wrapped the blanket around her and tiptoed over the coarse ground to the fire. When she had warmed away the goose bumps, she quickly donned a dress. Then, gathering up her dirty clothes, she went back to the stream.

"All right if I wash my clothes here, too?" Michaels asked quietly as he squatted beside her.

"Yes." She watched warily as he plunged his clothes into the water.

"Don't worry, Mrs. Arnold. This is not a new chore to me," he said with a note of humor.

She shrugged and continued rubbing the dirt from her jeans. "John Wesley," she asked thoughtfully, "where will we go next?"

"South. Fort Apache. Maybe the Kid headed in that direction. We can only follow our noses until we find a solid clue of some kind. You know there are people who might hide him?"

"Hide him?"

"Yes. It might be difficult for you to understand. But the Kid is some sort of a paid vigilante. He works for ranchers and shoots rustlers and thieves. Actually, as far as we know, he rarely shoots innocent people. Except your son," he finished quietly.

Her hands tightened in the wet folds of her clothes. She wasn't ready to talk about Josh. "But he shot Manuel for no apparent reason. Why?"

"I don't know. I've heard stories that when he's drunk, he indiscriminately shoots Mexicans and screams, 'You bloody vaqueros, you killed him.'"

"But what does that mean?"

He wrung out his clothes then doused them in the water again as he related to her what he knew of the Kid. "The Coyote Kid is real, but he's a legend, too."

She waited for him to continue, but there was only the sound of the water squashing in and out of his clothes.

"Here, give me the clothes. You tell me about the Coyote Kid and I'll wash them."

He nodded in agreement, sat back on his heels and looked up at the rising moon. "The Kid once worked for a rancher in New Mexico. This man never wore a gun. Seems a Texan along with his Mexican cowboys drove a big herd north to graze this rancher's range. The rancher met them unarmed and was shot down. They missed the Kid somehow and rumors have it that later he killed all of them. He scattered their cattle, and when he attacked the vaqueros he howled like a coyote."

"What did he do next?"

"Oh, I've heard several different stories. Some say he continued to shoot rustlers and stage robbers for a price. Ironically, the only time he was in jail was under a murder charge later dismissed as self-defense. Word is he was framed over an honest gunfight. They say that when he was let out of jail, he had a gun in his boot. Obviously supplied by someone on the outside."

"You make him sound like a hero," she said, seeming put out at the notion.

"I consider him a killer. But I'm afraid the Kid is a part of the disease called 'vigilante violence' that grips the West. When the law fails, then people write their own rules. And they hire men like the Kid. So many ranchers and even politicians owe him favors. Do you see what we're up against?"

"What does all this mean?"

"I just wanted you to know he has several friends who may hide and help him." He paused, ran his front teeth over his lower lip and stared at a bright star. How many of these people would aid the Kid, he had no idea. Then he continued. "Tomorrow we ride back to Snowflake and fill out an arrest report. I'll write the major and then we'll ride south. We'll find the Kid."

She digested the news slowly as she carried the wet clothes to some willow branches. "Sometimes I wonder if we will catch him," she said tiredly.

He blinked, taken aback by her words. It was the first time he had heard her sound despondent. "Do you want to go back?" he asked quietly.

She ground her teeth in irritation. "There you go, Mr. Michaels," she said, regretting her momentary lapse into feminine weakness. "No, I do not want to go back. I won't go back, not until . . . not until we've arrested the Kid." She felt tired and depressed and angered by his attitude. After all they had been through, he still did not take her seriously. He was ready to send her back without so much as a thank-you.

Glaring at his shadowed face in the starlight, she swept up her blanket and stalked back to the fire. Tomorrow, she vowed, she would poison him. Even the thought of snakes lurking around the camp did not dissolve her anger at the hardheaded marshal. Adjusting the blanket over her shoulders, she wrapped it tightly around her. The star-sprayed sky held her gaze, while she wondered what to do next. It was a long time before she finally lay down in her bedroll and sleep claimed her.

The following morning she boiled some mush and sprinkled brown sugar on it. They ate the meager breakfast in silence. As they sipped their second cup of coffee he finally spoke. "Tell me something."

"What's that?" she asked guardedly.

"Tell me how I'm supposed to write to the major concerning your presence. He's never going to believe that a woman helped one of his marshals round up a gang of whiskey peddlers, or that she rides with that marshal as a sort of assistant." He looked at her as if thoroughly amused by his dilemma.

She wrinkled her nose at his unfamiliar smile.

"Well," she began, " 'Mrs. Arnold' sounds like someone old enough to be your mother or grandma. Just write in such a way that he doesn't learn the truth from that snippy sheriff. You don't have to tell your major everything. Besides, if you refer to me as the motherly Mrs. Arnold, it wouldn't be a lie, would it?"

He sat in silence for a moment, pondering the matter. Somehow he must handle it. Then he prepared to ask her something that had nothing to do with the subject at hand, a serious matter that kept bobbing into his thoughts. Maybe her womanly intuition would answer the question for both of them.

"Why don't you trust Sheriff Rogers?"

She shrugged and gestured helplessly with her hand. "I just don't trust him."

It was strange that her words so bluntly echoed his exact thoughts about Rogers. John rose and threw the remains of his coffee on the dry ground.

"Well, would you like to wait here for me today? If I don't learn anything in Snowflake about the Kid, we'll head south and look for him. In the meantime, you could rest up for the long ride ahead."

The idea of spending a leisurely half-day out of the saddle certainly held appeal. Slowly she nodded, then looked up at him with genuine concern. "John, please be careful in town. That Sheriff Rogers is an odd turned man; he worries me."

He opened his mouth to agree, then clamped it tight. He was not going to give her another reason to get angry on his behalf and he did not want her worrying. He strode off to his horse, contemplating meeting Rogers again.

Actually, the man was about what he had expected. He was a politician and businessman with a thousand square miles in Apache County to control, and only a handful of young deputies to back him up. No doubt he passed out deputy badges in the towns across the county to his political cronies. Some town councils made their own selection for municipal law, but most appointments were made by the sheriff.

It was still early in the morning when John reached Snowflake. He dismounted in front of the office-jail and hitched Jacob to the rack, noting the young deputy who came through the open doorway.

"Howdy, Mr. Michaels."

John made a quick survey of the empty street. "Good morning. Is Sheriff Rogers around this morning?"

The deputy answered with a laughing shake of his head. "Sheriff doesn't get up this early. My name's Neal Tobin. Oh, don't worry, Mr. Michaels, those whiskey peddlers are still here." He stepped aside for John to enter the office.

"I sure hope so. Those three are tough outlaws," John said. The fact had not escaped his attention that those whiskey peddlers were the calculating type of ruthless outlaws that were ruining the West. They reminded him of diamondback rattlers, dangerous within striking distance. Even the youngest of the gang was a threat. All he lacked was experience to be equal to the leader, Gar.

"They're in the cell back there, if you want to check, mister."

John declined the offer. "I don't need to see them, but I do need to fill out the arrest report so the circuit judge will have all the details when he gets here."

"We've got pen and ink and some paper here in the desk," Neal said helpfully. He searched for the supplies and put them out for John. "Anything else you need, just ask."

"Neal, you ever heard of the Coyote Kid?"

"Well sure, Mr. Michaels. Who ain't heard of him? He's the one who shot that little Arnold boy."

John sat down behind the desk, then raised his head and smiled at the young deputy. "You can call me John. Now listen, Neal, I want to ask your opinion." He had carefully chosen his words so as to get the deputy's complete cooperation and attention. "Do you think the Kid's come through Snowflake?"

Neal looked down at his dusty boot toes and shifted uncomfortably. "If I said no, I might be lying, 'cause to tell you the truth, Mr. Michaels—er, John—I don't really know what he looks like. I'm sorry."

"Thanks." John had his answer. He dipped the pen in the inkwell and began the painstaking task of writing an arrest report. "Don't worry about it, Neal. Just keep your ears open, and if you hear anything about the Kid let me know." He didn't doubt this young deputy was honest, but he worried about what little chance he would stand against the Coyote Kid.

"You need any more light?"

"No, Neal, the light's fine. I detest paperwork. I'll be a while so you might as well get on with whatever you were doing."

"Thanks. I'll go over to Claire's and get some breakfast, if you don't mind watching the jail while I'm gone. Can I bring you back something?"

"No, thanks, I've eaten."

After Neal left, John continued with his carefully worded testimony. He wrote:

Your Honor:

The three men that I arrested—Gar Doe, John Doe, and the younger one who has refused to give me his first name—were in possession of a large store of untaxed whiskey at a cabin two days' ride north of Snowflake. They did fire upon my person and that of a person assisting me. Although the arrested men intended to kill us, I and my assistant were unharmed. I destroyed the store of whiskey with the exception of two bottles preserved as evidence for the court. If I am not available at the time of the trial, please accept this letter as my sworn testimony.

> Your servant,
> John Wesley Michaels
> Arizona Territorial Marshal Commission

John laid down the pen and blew on the ink to dry it. Then he searched for another piece of stationery to write to the major. After locating a clean sheet, he picked up the pen and wrote:

Dear Major,

I spoke to the parents of the youth who was murdered. I arrested three whiskey peddlers and destroyed a large stock of whiskey. The criminals are in the Apache County Jail awaiting trial. The Kid's trail is dim but I will follow whatever leads that I have. Mrs. Arnold is accompanying me.

John stopped writing and reread the letter. He felt concerned about mentioning Mrs. Arnold's presence, but decided in the end that he had said enough. He signed his name, folded the letter and pushed it in an envelope, then sealed it with some wax from a candle. Carefully he wrote the major's name and address on the outside.

His task complete, John began tidying up the sheriff's desk, and his gaze fell on an opened letter that was addressed to the sheriff. He quickly glanced around, then reassured that Neal was not returning, he drew the envelope toward him and removed the letter. Purposefully he read the contents.

To: Sheriff Rogers of Apache County
There are numerous reports circulating in the Capitol here in Prescott concerning Governor Sterling's secret police force. I know how serious this matter is to our rightfully elected law enforcement officers such as yourself. Please keep me informed of any news or information on this executive move to usurp the territorial legislature and elected law enforcement officers.

Sandford Tucker
Legislative Clerk

John pushed the letter back inside the envelope. The major would need to know about this new development. Sounds of approaching leather soles caused John to hurriedly place the letter on the desk and turn with a bland face.

"Did you find everything you needed, John?" Neal asked.

John nodded then stood. "My letter to the circuit judge is here." He indicated where it lay on the paper-strewn desktop. "Tell Sheriff Rogers that I was sorry I missed him but I must get on the trail of the Kid."

"Oh, I will, sir. The sheriff is a very busy man," he said hastily as if in apology.

"Yes, I'm sure he is." It was difficult to keep the dryness out of his voice. Then looking at the young man's earnest face, he recalled his concern for Neal's safety and cautioned him. "Neal, watch those three men in there. They'd stop at nothing to escape."

"Oh yes, sir. I'll watch them." Neal glanced at the door as a woman suddenly appeared, bearing a tray of food. "Oh, come this way, Claire." She seemed a pleasant woman, but her face was scarred with pockmarks.

"Claire, this is John Wesley Michaels." Neal made the introductions. "He is an officer of the court. He brought in those three back there."

"Nice to meet you, ma'am," John said. "If you'll excuse me, I'll be going."

"Ride careful, John," Neal said. "And good luck in capturing the Coyote Kid."

John smiled and lifted his fingers to his hat in farewell. He pulled the wide brim of the hat over his forehead and left the jail. The post office was directly across the dirt-packed street and he headed for the open door. The clerk inside appeared very efficient, but looked at the address on John's letter with critical eyes.

"It'll take a few days to get to Prescott."

"That's fine." John studied the man's thin face for a moment, then decided it was an honest one. "Say, do you have a general delivery letter for Bobby Budd?"

"No, why?"

"I'm a lawman, and I'm looking for this Bobby Budd." There was only a slim chance that the Kid might have received a letter here, but as he had told Dolly, he could not afford to leave any stone unturned.

"If one comes by, I'll be sure and let you know, Mr.—"

"John Wesley Michaels. I'll check back with you," he assured the man.

Next he went to the store beside the post office. A congenial woman waited on him and assured him that a few Indians and freighters were all the strangers that she had seen lately. He took his purchases of beans, bacon, and hard candy with him in a cotton sack when he left.

Outside on the boardwalk again, he glanced quickly at the saloon. It had not yet opened for the day. John hung the sack of provisions on his saddle then mounted and rode leisurely back to the campsite by the stream.

"Any news?" Dolly asked when he was near enough to hear her. She was sitting on her bedroll. He immediately noticed that her hair was brushed into a shiny wave of chestnut silk, and the dress she wore looked very fresh and feminine. Obviously, the morning's layover had been good for her. For the first time, she appeared rested.

At the sight of him, her heart lifted in relief. "Well, did you learn anything?" she repeated with a frown.

"No. No sign of the Kid. The deputy on duty admitted that he wouldn't recognize him if he saw him. But I didn't learn anything else either in Snowflake."

"Where do we go next?" She took the sack from his outstretched hand.

He uncinched his saddle. "According to the map that the major gave me there is a place or two south of here. We can start checking them tomorrow."

"Tomorrow? What's the matter with today?"

He frowned in annoyance at her nagging persistence. "Mrs. Arnold, if the man is in the territory, he's not racing away. Please allow me to know my own business."

"How do you know he's not hurrying out of the territory?" she asked, feeling slightly taken aback by his fatherly words.

"Trust me."

"Trust you?" she repeated like a small explosion. "You sit on your rump all day and I'm suppose—"

"Yes?" he asked in a dangerously quiet tone.

"I . . . I . . . do you accept apologies, John Wesley?" she asked, suddenly subdued.

"It's not necessary. Did you renail the loose shoe on the packhorse?" he asked abruptly.

She blinked her eyes, trying to follow his quicksilver mind. Trust him to remember that Thomas's shoe had made a ringing noise on the road to Snowflake. Wordlessly she shook her head.

From the pannier, he removed a small hammer and a few nails. She followed him over to the packhorse. He caught the hobbled horse, tied a lead rope on his halter and hitched him to a small pine. She stood back, arms folded. When he squatted down to remove the hobbles, she came closer.

"About that apology. I really am sorry. By the way, what did you tell your employ . . . er . . . the major about me?"

John stood up and put the buckskin's hind foot on his knee. He removed the nails from his mouth so he could answer her. "I simply wrote that Mrs. Arnold is accompanying me."

"Oh well, that's all right, then. It sounds just like what I said, your grandmother or someone equally staid."

"No, you are not—" John stopped abruptly and tried again. "Now, what I mean to say is that you are not old." Then he busied himself shoeing, deciding there was no good way to verbally escape the matter.

"So there was no Coyote Kid in Snowflake?" she asked in disappointment, ignoring his comment on her age.

He set the horse's hoof down. "I did see a letter to the

sheriff from a legislative clerk in Prescott. It warned the sheriff that a secret police force might take over his job. That might explain the sheriff's attitude."

"Secret?"

"Yes, the governor's secret force."

"Oh!" Her eyes widened in understanding. "That means you!"

"Yes, Mrs. Arnold." He smiled at her in genuine amusement. "I'll have to write the major about the matter, though. Would you hand me a few more nails? They're in my saddlebags."

"Yes, John Wesley Michaels," she said sharply.

He frowned after her, watching her stalk over to his saddle. What had he done now?

She muttered under her breath as she searched in the saddlebags for the nails. That stiff-necked man was never going to unbend long enough to call her Dolly. Mrs. Arnold! The very idea of his stubborn ways made her fume. She'd show him. She needed some way to take the wind out of John Wesley's sails.

CHAPTER 13

The Kid was jubilant over regaining his sight. It was as if he had been reborn and had his whole life to relive. The light that crept in from the edges of his bandages continued to build his confidence.

Satisfied that Beth was out milking the cow, he began to question Leo. "Is that lawman and the woman still around?"

"He was in town this morning. It seems strange for a woman to be traveling with him."

The Kid was pondering the situation when he realized that Leo had grown unusually silent. "What's wrong, Leo?"

"Nothing."

"Bullshit! Something's wrong, I can tell."

"Well, Kid," Leo finally said, sounding reluctant. "The woman with that lawman is the Arnold boy's mother."

"I see." The Kid fidgeted restlessly in the rocker. "And you're sure that ain't Ben Arnold who's with her?"

"No, the word's out that this guy with her is a special

agent. Arnold was the one with the rifle who came out of the store. No, it ain't him."

Special agent? He'd never heard of one of them in Arizona before. Must be a Pinkerton man or a U.S. Marshal. No matter, he and Leo really needed to ride now. If his sight continued to improve as swiftly as it had been, they could slip across into Mexico and be beyond the grasp of the law until things settled down. Right now he desperately needed a drink. It had been several days since he had had any whiskey, which brought back the irritating thought of those whiskey peddlers. He was not sure he would get a chance to settle with them while they were in jail.

"At sunup, we're riding south," he abruptly informed Leo.

"Where to?"

The Kid grunted impatiently. "Just south, damnit! I may be blind, but I can still decide what we do."

"Sure, Kid," Leo quickly agreed. "She's coming back."

The Kid heard her enter the room. He wasn't eager to leave Beth, but he knew there were always more females to be found. He thought about the Arnold woman who was accompanying the lawman. The whole idea of her and this so-called agent made him uncomfortable, and for some inexplicable reason the notion ate at him.

At dawn he and Leo struck out for the south. Their horses were well rested and frisky. The pair covered several miles before midday. The Kid frequently lifted his blindfold to peek at the bright world of rolling grass and pines.

"How far are we going?" Leo asked.

"Oh, a good ways yet. We need some whiskey. Wonder how far it is to the next town?"

"Beth said there was a little community called Poker Town," Leo said. "Maybe we can get us some there."

"Sure." The Kid peered again from beneath his bandages.

By late afternoon they rode into Poker Town, an assortment of rough lumber and log buildings. Leo guided the horses to the front of a low-eaved log saloon. "We going in?"

"Why not? Nobody knows us." The Kid began to untie his blindfold, then squinted against the harsh sunlight.

"You sure you should do that, Bobby?"

He frowned at Leo. "Yeah. I got to start sometime. Come on, let's go in the saloon."

Once they were inside the sour-smelling interior, the shadowy light made Bobby's eyes water, but he was thoroughly grateful that he could see. He sauntered to the bar and smiled at the grim-faced, bearded bartender. "A bottle of good whiskey for me and my friend."

Although Bobby's vision was not completely clear, he could still detect the tough, ice-cold glare of the bartender.

"Good whiskey's five dollars a bottle. You can use tin cups for free, but glasses cost fifty cents, so if you break them I can buy some more."

"We'll try one shot in a glass and see how good it is," the Kid said, enjoying the eye-to-eye contact with the man.

"It's good."

"I'll be the judge," the Kid said. He lifted the glass containing a finger of the liquor. It was good whiskey.

He nodded his approval and slapped the money down. The man was still as antagonistic as before, but he drew out the second glass from beneath the bar. Then he picked up the money. The Kid expected him to sink his teeth into the coin, but to his surprise the man merely dropped the money in a metal box behind the bar. Shrugging, he took the bottle and both glasses and moved to the corner table where Leo was already seated.

He and Leo drank easily at first. The whiskey on their empty stomachs mellowed their mood. "It sure feels good to be on the move again," Leo said, smiling. "I get kinda itchy anymore if we stay in one place too long."

The Kid nodded more in understanding than agreement. "Yeah, I know how you feel. But I could have stayed back there with Beth a lot longer. What was her place like? I didn't get to see the layout."

Leo shrugged. "Hell, it was just a two-bit outfit. Had a stream and some pine trees and a barn. I don't know; it was just a regular place."

The Kid raised his glass to eye level. "Leo, if there was a way to change my face so nobody knew who I was, I'd go back there and stay for a long time."

"You mean forever, Kid?" Leo whispered in shock. He set his glass down.

"What's so bad about that?"

"Nothing, nothing," Leo said quickly. "Hell, I was just bored. You know there's women like her all over, Kid?"

"Maybe. But hell, Leo, I really could have stayed and grown to like it."

Leo poured himself another glass of whiskey. "Me, I'm glad we got the hell out of there. Now, where's this rancher's place? You know, the one who wants us to do a job for him?"

"Oh yeah, I almost forget about him. Guess he's east of here. We'll go look him up."

"Say, this is good whiskey," Leo commented after taking a long swallow.

"Real good. We'll buy us a stock of it." The Kid was pleased with his steadily improving eyesight. Things were getting back to normal, and in a moment of honesty, he silently admitted that he was anxious to be working again. Tomorrow, they'd go look up Cyrus Edgar. He doubted Cy had solved his problem. Men in his line of work weren't that plentiful.

That night he and Leo slept in an old barn filled with the pungent odor of horse manure and urine. Not even the strong fumes of the whiskey completely obliterated those powerful smells.

At first light, the pair rode east. Edgar's place turned out to be a smattering of log corrals, haystacks, and a low-sided set of buildings. A dog barked a welcome. A grim-mouthed woman in her fifties came out on the porch.

"Is Cy Edgar here?" the Kid shouted.

"Not now. He'll be back directly. But he don't need any hired hands," the pinched-mouth woman said.

"Thank you, ma'am," the Kid said with an amused smile. The woman's hard eyes indicated her disapproval of their obvious inebriated state. Hell, her opinion didn't bother him. She might look down her beaky nose at them, but she wasn't the one that was going to pay them. The Kid deliberately reined his horse around and tipped the bottle to his lips. He motioned to Leo and they began riding away from the house. When they were a hundred feet up, he reined up Buster.

"This is far enough to wait for him."

When Cy arrived a few hours later, the two of them were sitting cross-legged on the ground, empty whiskey bottles scattered about them. Both men rose to greet their potential employer.

"Cy Edgar?" The Kid squinted up at the man, who was on horseback. He was a tall lean man with a frown beneath his beaver hat.

"Yes?"

"I'm the Coyote Kid. You got a problem?"

"I sure do." The man smiled broadly and dismounted. "I've got a real problem. Are you who you say you are?"

The Kid laughed. "That's me. Oh, you have to excuse our appearance. Me and Leo have been celebrating. See, I had a real problem with my eyes, but now I can see pretty good again."

Obviously, the man had no idea what he was talking about, but he did not press the issue. "Come on with me while I put the horse up. No one will hear us down at the corral."

Almost an hour later the Kid and Leo set out to end the man's problems. Cy Edgar told them several head were missing, but he was unable to capture the rustlers. He added sourly that even if he caught the people red-handed, it was doubtful he could get them tried and con-victed.

The rancher sounded certain who the rustlers were. He named a half-breed, Jacko; the other was the breed's brother-in-law Nat Milner. A squaw rode with them, too. Edgar wanted them stopped. He paid the Kid two hundred and fifty dollars in advance with a promise of a hundred more upon completion of the deal. As much as the Kid's conscience urged him to go on to Mexico, he kept think-ing how they needed Edgar's money to stay south of the border.

"Kid, you sure you're seeing good enough for this job?" Leo asked worriedly as they rode east.

"Don't worry about me. We'll get these rustlers and then be in Mexico in two or three days."

Leo shook his head. "It ain't like you to just ride over and do a job without some planning first. What if they're a tough bunch?"

"Ah, Leo, take a drink and quit your whining. I can see good enough to do the job." More confidence returned. With each passing hour, he felt more like his old self. Al-though his vision had not been completely restored, he felt certain that he would be able to see the scum and get rid of them.

The rustlers' place was in a canyon on the side of a pine-covered mountain. Leo led the way up the trail and stopped abruptly at the sound of barking dogs.

"Yeah, I heard them, too, Leo. Just keep moving."

A squaw looked up from a washtub at their approach. She was a full-blood Indian with long black braids hanging down her back. From behind her, a copper-faced buck stepped out of the small house with a rifle in his hands. Following him came a hatless, shorter white man.

"Howdy," the Kid greeted them with a warm smile. "We're lost. How far is it to Poker Town?"

The white man smiled back. "Boy, you're lost. This road ends here unless you're a billy goat." He indicated the sheer bluffs behind the house.

"See, Leo, I told you we took the wrong fork," the Kid said over his shoulder, and turned back to the man with a shrug as if in apology. "Say, do you drink whiskey?"

"Sure."

"This here's Leo. I'm Bobby." The Kid made the introduction casually as he dismounted. A quick glance around showed him that the woman had continued her scrubbing and the Indian buck was standing in a relaxed pose. He drew a bottle out of his saddlebags.

"Well, howdy. Nat Milner's the name. This is Jacko. Come on inside." Milner invited them in with a gesture of his arm. "We'll drink some of that whiskey."

The Kid's gaze was drawn to the Indian girl. In her late teens, he guessed. The turn of her hips and shape of her breasts under the buckskin dress aroused him. So the others didn't suspect his designs on her, he clapped Leo on the shoulder. "Found us some drinking buddies."

Leo agreed with a nod.

Inside the small homestead, they took seats around a rough homemade table. The Indian and Milner drank cautiously at first, but the alcohol soon melted their wariness.

"Where you guys going?" Milner asked.

"Poker Town."

"Aw hell, there ain't nothing there worth seeing," Milner said, dismissing the idea contemptuously. As the girl entered the room he bellowed at her. "Silver Belle, fix us some food." The girl nodded, but she ignored the bottles of whiskey on the table.

"You hungry, Bobby?" Milner asked.

"Sure, but not for beans. You got any venison?"

"Ha! Venison!" Jacko's crack of laughter was unsteady. Milner's sharp look of disapproval silenced the Indian.

"No venison, huh?" the Kid lamented.

"We got real meat," Milner said guardedly.

The Kid splashed more whiskey in the mens' cups, noting that Leo seemed very tense and quiet. Leo tossed down the glass of whiskey and frowned at the Kid. Bobby ignored him.

"Does your woman want a drink?" the Kid asked generously.

"Silver Belle, want some whiskey?" Milner asked her.

She shook her head, scowling in disapproval.

The Kid grinned at her. For a damn Indian, she was a real looker. In fact, her beauty improved with each swallow of whiskey. He made up his mind that later he would possess her.

After a couple hours of drinking, the notion to have the woman became a growing obsession with him. He had two more bottles in his saddlebags. Eventually he got around to asking the men about the beef—Edgar's beef.

"You got many cattle?" The Kid slurred the question.

"Oh. We got a few." Milner shrugged. "It's tough to get started. Big guys like Edgar don't like us small ranchers."

"Yeah, big ranchers get pushy," the Kid agreed, thinking silently to himself, especially with the rustling kind.

The meat in the stew that the woman served was not venison. The Kid knew beef when he tasted it.

"What do you guys do?" Milner asked, looking from Leo to Bobby.

"Oh, we hire on sometimes. Actually, we've been looking for a ranch of our own. You wouldn't sell this one, would you?"

Milner did not answer right away. The Kid interpreted his hesitation as indecision. Finally Milner said with what seemed like forced reluctance, "No, guess not."

"It's a rough way to start, Milner, with no money and all," the Kid said sympathetically.

"That's right," Milner slurred. "Why hell, I ain't seen any money in six months. Ranchers won't hire us on even for roundups."

"Oh well," the Kid said, "you got a good-looking woman. Look at me; all I got is ugly old Leo."

"Yeah, what 'bout me?" Leo joked. "All I've got is you." The men guffawed loudly, banging the table with their fists.

The girl hurriedly came to the table and began stacking the dishes as if she feared for their safety. Milner caught her by the waist, the action nearly unseating him. She stood in a resigned pose, but seemed to shrink away from the newcomers as though afraid she would contract some disease.

"She's a good-looking woman, ain't she?" Milner boasted proudly.

The Kid nodded. At the moment he would pay a twenty-dollar gold piece to lay her. Leo obviously knew what was going on in his mind, because after giving him an uneasy look, he jerked up his glass, spilling the contents.

The Kid raised his brows and grinned at Leo. Then he turned his attention back to her. She twisted away from Milner and moved toward the dry sink, her hands filled with dirty dishes. The Kid knew she would not loosen up, not unless Milner could get her to drink.

Jacko rose clumsily to his feet. His foolish actions betrayed his purpose. He obviously needed to relieve himself of a bladder full of whiskey. The Kid noted that he did not wear a gun. His only weapon was a knife in a sheath on his belt. Milner had a Colt in his holster. But Bobby doubted that he was very proficient with it.

The afternoon crawled by, slipping into evening. There was only one full bottle left on the table. Jacko hummed some tune off-key. Milner's attention span was almost nil. Leo was becoming restless.

The Kid looked at them through a whiskey haze. "Hey, Milner." He had to hit the man on his forearm to get his attention.

"Hmm? What's that?"

"Do you eat that big rancher's beef?" the Kid asked.

"Hell yes, all the time." Milner waved his arms around. "He's got plenty . . . ain't gonna miss a few head."

"Yeah, reckon so," the Kid agreed as he rose. "I need some air." He looked around the room. The woman was already outside. Bobby nodded at Leo, indicating that he should stay with the two men.

Outside in the starlit yard, Bobby tried to steady his wobbly legs. He checked his saddlebags, searching for his last bottle of whiskey. It was gone. He frowned, trying to remember. Yes, he knew there had been one more bottle in there. Where the hell was it?

He looked around in the dim light, but could see no one. Then he heard her voice.

"You were looking for this?" she asked from beside the corral, holding up the last bottle.

Bobby could see by the glint of light on the glass that she had his whiskey. "Yes," he said, laughing as he swayed toward her, "but I want both of you." Briefly he wondered if he had frightened her off by saying the words out loud. The idea sobered him somewhat. He glanced toward the house then shrugged. Leo could handle the two drunken rustlers. He had other plans.

The woman backed away as he drew nearer. But he saw the flash of her white teeth as she smiled broadly. "Who are you, mister?" she asked, holding out a hand as if to keep him at bay.

"Bobby Joe," he said as he stepped forward.

"No, no. You are not Bobby Joe. I am not stupid. You're a trader, huh? You give them whiskey so you can steal something?"

"Yeah, but I want you!"

"No, you think of me when you are full of whiskey."

"No," he protested, "I thought of you when I first rode in here."

She lowered her outstretched arm. "Did you give him some money?"

"Who?"

"My man."

The Kid shook his head in slight confusion. "You mean for you?"

"It already cost you plenty whiskey," she said mockingly. Then with slow deliberation she raised the bottle and took a long swallow. The Kid waited silently, controlling his basic urge to rush her. She wagged a finger at him to stay back. "Not yet, Bobby Joe. Silver Belle needs more whiskey. I see you look at me, then you get my man drunk. You're a big trader?"

"No," the Kid said softly as he closed the gap between them. He stumbled over a pole, then righted himself with a vivid curse.

"Wait, Bobby Joe. I take one more drink." She raised the bottle again.

While her head was tilted back to drink, Bobby stepped to her and took the opportunity to raise her skirts, then he drew her against him.

"Wait," she protested. "Put the whiskey down first so it not spill."

Confident that she was ready for him, Bobby shrugged and placed the whiskey against a corral post. Then he went willingly into her outstretched arms.

At sunup, the Kid awoke in shivering stiffness. He was lying on the cold ground, wearing only a shirt. His bare legs were dirt smudged; pine needles clung to his skin. The squaw was sprawled beside him on her side, her skirts bunched around her waist. Her shapely copper legs were dirt-caked and coated with pine needles. He grinned and closed his eyes in satisfaction.

Vaguely he recalled the previous night. A smile lifted his mouth as he remembered the pleasure he had derived from her. Sighing aloud, he rose and began to dress. He shook his dusty wadded-up pants then hurriedly pulled them on. Buckling on his holster, he looked at her but she still slept. With care, he spun the cylinders and checked the .38's loads.

A grim line edged his mouth as he walked purposefully toward the house. Inside loud snores filled the room. The Indian was asleep at the table. Leo on a bed to the right. Milner lay on a cot in the far corner, his face turned to the wall.

The Kid took a deep breath and pointed the gun at the Indian's head. The blast was deafening. The buck fell off the chair and slumped onto the floor.

"What!" Milner shouted as he jerked up in the bed.

His eyes were focused on the barrel of the Kid's smoking gun.

"Milner, you rustlers never learn," he said softly.

"Rustlers!" Milner shouted.

The .38's hammer fell on a dud cartridge. Milner reacted instinctively, grabbing his own revolver from his holster overhead. The Kid backed toward Leo, facing the menacing barrel of Milner's sidearm.

"Shoot him, Leo!" the Kid shouted. He knew he was between Milner and Leo's gun. Milner's shot missed the Kid, whose second shot hit Milner high in the shoulder. The Kid tried to see through the thick cloud of gunsmoke. His sore eyes watered and his vision blurred.

Leo screamed in pain. The Kid jerked around, shocked at the sound. Leo was hit. Milner was making noises like a crazed animal. He lunged at him, clawing at his face.

In the chaos, the Kid raised his pistol and forced it into the rustler's midsection. The .38 exploded this time. Milner drew back and grabbed for his side. The Kid's next bullet punctured the center of Milner's chest. His hands flew to the new wound, then he coughed and fell over some chairs onto his back.

Bobby stepped over him and rushed to Leo's side. Blood poured out between Leo's fingers as he tried to stem the flow. Seated on the edge of the bed, he stared up at the Kid and spoke in a hoarse whisper. "I'm a goner, Kid. You tell them señoritas that I love them when you get to Mexico." He collapsed back on the bed. Leo was dying.

"Leo, Leo, I'll get a doctor." The Kid was trembling.

"No use, Bobby."

"How in God's earth did you get shot?" the Kid growled as he clenched his fists in frustration.

Leo smiled tiredly. "It wasn't your fault. Go on. Kid, you better clear out."

"I'm staying. I aim to bury you."

Leo shook his head weakly and choked on his own blood. "No. You better go on. That marshal . . . he's coming."

The woman's screams forced him to look toward the door. The noises coming from her throat were an Indian death chant. She looked wide-eyed beyond the Kid and renewed her screaming.

When he looked back around, Leo was dead.

He rushed past the woman. She was not crying, but her pain-filled eyes looked heavenward, as if seeking relief. He hurried outside to escape her curse. Her haunting moans followed him.

His head pounded violently as he mounted Buster. He lashed the horse with the reins, keeping rhythm with the throbbing in his head.

He did not know how long he had been riding before he realized he was lost. Then he turned west and raced the weary animal across the open grassland, until the lathered horse began to stumble with exhaustion. How long would Buster last at this pace? He regretted the fact that he had not fed or watered the beast while he had been at Milner's place.

In a small draw, he let the horse drink and graze while he crouched in a ball. The memory of Leo dying was vividly implanted on his mind. Trembling from head to toe, Bobby drew out his gun. At every little sound he whipped around, searching the landscape for his unseen pursuer. There was no one. He was alone. Leo was gone.

Whiskey would help him, he decided hopefully. He

needed some good, strong whiskey. He recalled the insolent saloonkeeper in Poker Town. The man had good whiskey.

His decision made, Bobby jerked the horse's head up and mounted. The water and short rest had restored some of the horse's energy.

It was still twilight when he dismounted at the log saloon. A few hip-shot horses stood tied at the rail. He noticed a tall buckskin horse under a pack across the street with several more ponies tied over there. Busy place. As he started for the batwing doors, he fell into a deep coughing fit and he used the porch support to hold himself up until the breath-depleting spell passed. Lightheaded and still determined to find enough liquor inside to drown his loss of Leo, he pushed through the double doors.

At the bar, he motioned to the bartender and slapped some money down for a bottle. He was oblivious to everything around him but the brown bottle that the man set before him. His one thought was to drink enough brainnumbing whiskey to forget—

He ripped out the cork, turned his head back, and tilted the bottle to his lips. The fire of the liquor burned as it slid down his throat. At last, he set the bottle down and gasped for breath. Good . . . he had found a sanctuary.

"Bobby Joe Budd?" a quiet voice of authority said from behind him. "I'm arresting you for the murder of Josh Arnold, by the power invested in me by the courts of the Territory of Arizona."

When the Kid turned, the man placed the muzzle of his Colt in Bobby's stomach and deftly removed the .38.

The Kid sagged wearily. "One more drink and you can kill me or do whatever you want. But I'm having one more drink." One more to forget Leo's dying face.

CHAPTER 14

Dolly glanced out the dry-goods store window. Her eyes widened in surprise as she watched John Wesley follow a thin cowboy inside the saloon across the street. John walked purposefully with a determined gait that she knew well. She swallowed hard as she realized what was happening. The Coyote Kid. That thin hatless man just had to be the one they were seeking.

The dress fabric that she held bunched in her hand slipped from her grasp as her mouth tightened in pain. Jerking her head up, she strode quickly through the store. Outside on the boardwalk, she drew her gun and quickened her pace toward the saloon. The memory of her son's lifeless face urged her onward, oblivious of the stares she was generating. A vein throbbed in her temple as she raised the gun and cocked it.

Her shoulder brushed the batwing doors aside as she entered the saloon. A red-hot need for vengeance was kindled in her mind. She raised the pistol and took aim at the man leaning against the bar next to John Wesley.

The first shot from her pistol crashed into the bottles

behind the bar. Everyone in the room shouted and ducked for cover. Everyone but John Wesley.

"Mrs. Arnold!" he shouted. "You can't shoot him; he's my prisoner!" He walked toward her, blocking her view of the cowering, handcuffed Kid at the bar.

Dolly stared at him with burning hatred in her heart. "Get out of my way! I'm going to kill him!" She tried to move sideways to get a clear view of the Kid. The pistol was clutched tightly in both of her hands. "Get out of my way, John Wesley Michaels. I want that son of a bitch dead. I don't want to hurt you, but he is going to pay for killing Josh."

John Wesley moved swiftly and wrenched the gun from her grasp before she could protest. "No. Let the law handle it now. Do you hear me?"

All the fight went out of her. Her face crumpled like a child's and she leaned against him. "I saw him come in. I was in the store, and I knew you were going to get him. Oh John, he has to pay." Tears spilled down her wind-burned cheeks as she looked up at him imploringly.

John stifled a grunt of frustration. He jammed her pistol in his waistband and held her by the shoulders. "It's over, we have him now. Get a hold of yourself."

She raised her head and looked over his shoulder. Her eyes widened in disbelief. The bartender held a shotgun, but John noted with relief that it was aimed at the Kid.

"Dolly," he said softly, the name slipping out in a moment of compassion. "It's really over now."

She stared at him, numbed with shock. "Yes. Yes, you're right. I . . . I won't try anything. I promise." The last words came out in a whisper of defeat.

John fought the anger inside him. He was angry with himself, with the Kid, and even with her. He released her shoulders and said coldly, "I'll meet you outside. We're taking him back to Snowflake tonight."

"All right, John," she said wearily and turned to leave.

He noted her slumping shoulders as she walked outside. Then he strode to the bar and tore the bottle of whiskey out of the Kid's hands. In a gesture of frustrated rage, he smashed the bottle against the bar railing, sending a shower of liquor and glass over him and the prisoner. His cold glare bored into the Kid. "I don't want any tricks out of you."

"Well, well," the bartender drawled, "so he's the Coyote Kid, huh?"

John nodded curtly. "Do I owe you anything for damages?"

"Nah. This ought to be good for business. What's your name?"

Unable to see any way out of it, John answered, "John Wesley Michaels." He jerked the Kid around by his elbow and pushed him toward the door.

"Hey!" the saloonkeeper shouted, "Are you a U.S. Marshal?"

"No, just an *officer* of the court."

"Oh. And the lady with the gun is your missus?"

"No," John growled, "her name is Mrs. Arnold." He hoped that the man would make the connection without additional explanation.

"I see. That's the reason she wanted him dead—" The man stopped abruptly, obviously having heard about the Arnold boy being shot. "Well, thanks, mister. Arresting the Coyote Kid in here will sure be good for my business."

John cringed. His contempt for liquor and what it did to a man made him angry, but it disturbed him more to think that what he did would support such a vice. He guided the Kid out to the boardwalk, moving past the crowd of dismayed onlookers on the porch.

"Hey, lawman. Is that woman out here in the crowd?" the Kid asked in a gruff voice.

"Don't worry about it. I've got her gun in my belt." His tone was sharp, not inviting any more comments.

"You might not worry about it, but the woman's out for my blood."

Despite his irritation at her foolhardy actions, John was relieved to see Dolly beyond the crowd, sitting on her gray, the packhorse in tow. "Which one is your horse?" he asked his prisoner.

"That one." The Kid pointed to an exhausted-looking animal tied to the hitch rail. "He's about gone."

John could see that. He shoved the prisoner toward the spent animal. His lips tightened as he walked toward the beast. He stripped the saddle off and unbridled the horse.

"What the hell are you doing?"

"Do you want the saddle?" John asked flatly.

"Of course."

"Then pick it up, 'cause this horse is about to die. And I'm not letting it fall down here in the street." He lightly slapped the horse's rump, then watched it amble down the street in the growing darkness.

In dismay, the Kid looked at his freed horse then at John Wesley. "Well, the hell with it!" He threw the saddle down in disgust.

"Suit yourself." John shrugged as he noted the action. He removed Jacob's bridle and fashioned a halter from his lariat for him.

"Get aboard," he told the Kid.

Unsure what to expect next, Dolly watched the two. Once the Kid was in the saddle, John came over to her.

She looked down at him in puzzlement. "Surely you're not going to walk?"

"No, I'm not. If I may, I'm going to ride with you."

"Oh, oh certainly." She looked hard at the Kid and scowled. "You ought to put a noose around his neck and drag him back."

John handed her the lead to his horse and hung his bridle on her saddle horn. Then he stepped into the stirrup and swung up behind her.

Feeling his solid form against her back, Dolly automatically stiffened. "Are you ready?" She tried to ignore the curious and knowing stares of the many people milling about in the street.

"Hey, you boys get a good look!" the Kid shouted. His manacled hands held on to the saddle horn as he boasted. "You're looking at the Coyote Kid. You'll see him again."

Her hands tightened on the reins and leads as she listened to the braggart. With deliberation she dug her heels into her horse's side. Her intentional jump-start nearly unseated the prisoner. He jerked in the saddle, but held fast.

The Kid smiled sardonically in her direction. "Come on, boys, they're selling tickets to my hanging." The crowd laughed at his careless attitude. John grimaced with disgust at the circus atmosphere. He was forced to reach past her in an almost intimate way in order to stay seated behind her.

"I'm not poison, John Wesley. You can hold on to me." When he resisted, she shrugged. "Then fall off, see if I give a damn, you stubborn devil."

He was already regretting his decision to ride double with the sharp-tongued woman. Behind them the Kid was singing off-key. The smell of liquor still clung to John's clothes from the smashed liquor bottle. But the most disturbing thing of all was riding behind a woman on the gray with its swinging gait. It was next to impossible to hold on without bumping her. His legs rubbed hers because he could not keep back or hold them straight down and maintain his balance at the same time. It was going to be a long night. The fact that he had been celibate for too long only increased his discomfort.

Glancing at the darkening twilight sky, John tried to detach himself from his surroundings. He wondered about the whereabouts of the Kid's partner. Had they parted company or was he waiting somewhere in the distance for a chance to ambush them? He twisted in the saddle but saw nothing threatening as they left the village.

What about Dolly? Her part was over; surely she would see that and return to Arnold. A nagging doubt irritated him. He wasn't entirely confident that she would agree to that solution, but he would meet that problem when it arose. Hopefully things would work out. His present assignment was nearing completion. Bobby Joe Budd could await trial in the Apache County jail. Dolly Arnold was free to return home, and he would be alone at last. He looked forward to a less fettered state.

She kept the horse at a steady pace. John's silence behind her didn't surprise her. But her conscience plagued her with guilt because of her earlier impulsive actions. She regretted taking a shot at the Kid. Not because she had missed him, but because of the reproach of the silent man behind her on the mare. Perhaps he was right; the law could handle Bobby Budd. It was probably better that way. Besides, she sighed wearily, what had her actions accomplished? Well, she conceded, John Wesley had called her Dolly for the first and probably the last time. But she admitted that he had lapsed only because he momentarily lost his composure.

"How did you know it was him—back there?" she finally asked. "I mean, he's thinner than I recall."

"Plain luck. I was walking by when he had that coughing fit on the porch, and drew my attention. I looked over at him and noticed that guardless .38. He was the right height and his clothes were sure a mess. Figured it was him."

She nodded to indicate that she had heard him and felt him shift around some more. A faint smile lifted her lips. She found this law business an exciting occupation. It was a lot more interesting than cooking, washing, and being a housewife. An idea took root in her mind. Perhaps when John rode out on a new case, she could help him. Of course, persuading him that he needed her would be a little difficult, but she was fairly confident that she just might manage to do that.

The Kid sang in a slurred voice. Feeling warmed by the whiskey that he had consumed earlier and yet confused about how to handle his arrest, he took refuge in song. He had gotten out of worse deals before. Something would work out. If only Leo was with him, but poor Leo was dead. His *compadre* was gone. The Kid shook his head to keep from remembering. He looked ahead at the two people riding double. Just who in the hell did that Mrs. Arnold think she was? Her taking a shot at him like she had back there. His whiskey-laden brain refused to make a connection between her hatred and the cause for it. She was simply a good-looking woman. But it had sure been a blessing that she was such a poor shot. Hell, maybe it simply wasn't his time yet to join Leo.

"Oh, cows move along. We got miles to go," he sang aloud.

The twilight soon turned to darkness and stars lit the way. They would never make Snowflake before midnight,

John decided. He pushed himself back on the saddle for the umpteenth time. A faint scent tickled his nostrils. She emitted a slight smell of perfume. He made a dogged attempt to wipe the smell from his senses. More and more he regretted his foolish idea to ride double with the woman.

"John, when will they have a trial?"

"Soon, I hope."

She made a face at his unhelpful answer. But it was typical of him, she knew. He never gave away his emotions or thoughts.

"We may need to rest the horses," he said, as he noted while checking on his prisoner that the moon had begun to rise.

"All right," she agreed tiredly. "When would you like to stop?"

John shrugged, immediately regretting the action since it caused more body contact with Dolly. "Oh, anytime. Would you like to stop now?"

"That would be fine." She wondered why they were still talking like polite strangers, but she was too weary to work out the reasoning. With a deep sigh, she reined up the gray mare and waited while John dismounted. He did not offer to help her down; for once she would have welcomed his strong helping hands. But she recalled she had told him long ago that she was perfectly capable of dismounting alone. Her eyelids closed for a restive second over her weary pupils as he took both lead ropes. Feeling irritated with him for some inexplicable reason, she straightened her back and short-loped her mare toward the dark shadowy thicket of junipers.

A few moments later she staggered in relief to be off the horse for a while. More than that, she was longing for a few moments of privacy away from both men. The gentle night breeze cooled her face as she brushed her hair. Standing in the silvery light, she pulled on the tangles, vowing that tomorrow she would find a way to take a bath. It was a luxury that she had taken for granted at Ben's place. Anytime she wished she could draw water and bathe, but out here water was a rationed commodity. A bed would feel heavenly, but she was becoming accustomed to curling up in a warm bedroll on the ground. Besides, she admitted silently, she was so tired it would not matter where she slept.

The lonely sound of a yapping coyote startled her. She suddenly realized how vulnerable she was out in the darkness away from the men without her gun. It was time to ride back to them.

The Kid was seated on the ground, his hands still manacled. He looked up at John Wesley who had his head cocked as if listening for the woman's return. "So your name's John Wesley Michaels, huh? Have we met before?"

"No, we haven't," John said flatly. He searched over the dark landscape for sight of her. What was she doing out there that was taking so long?

The Kid clucked his tongue. "That's a shame. I always figured some famous lawman would arrest me."

"Why? Do you fancy yourself as someone special?"

"No, not me. But I know there are stories about me. A lot of lawmen have rode the wrong way looking for me. Guess I was too smart for them."

John ignored the boasting. "Where's your partner, Leo Jackson, alias Leon Smith?"

The Kid hung his head and closed his eyes in pain. "Now, why did you have to ask about poor Leo?"

John took a deep breath, striving for patience. "It's part of my job. I'll have to go find him."

The Kid shook his head. "You can't."

"What do you mean I can't?" John tried to read the prisoner's face in the moonlight, but he couldn't.

"Ain't no reason to go after Leo. He's dead."

"How?"

"In a shootout this morning."

John tried to gauge his voice, wondering if the Kid was telling the truth.

"Why in the hell do you think I came back by myself for the whiskey?" the Kid challenged, looking up at him with a smile.

John's instincts told him that the Kid was telling the truth. He let the matter drop as his thoughts and concerns returned to Dolly's absence. Where was she? A coyote howled, and at last he heard the sounds of her horse's hooves returning.

Masking his relief, he glared down at the Kid. "You better not try anything. And watch your mouth around the lady."

He took Dolly's pistol out of his belt and turned, waiting for her to rein up beside him.

"Is everything all right?" he asked as she dismounted and stood beside him.

"Fine. I want my pistol back. There's damned coyotes out there."

"Did they frighten you?"

"No." She gave him an indignant look. "They just sounded eerie. I hate those yapping critters." She peered beyond him, trying to see the Kid's face in the firelight.

John bit back a word of caution as he handed her the revolver. "Here."

"Thanks." She braced herself, expecting a long lecture on her shooting exploits. When he said nothing, she felt let down. Maybe she had grown to enjoy their bickering. But John never did what she expected him to.

"His partner Leo is dead," he informed her. "Or so he says."

"Do you believe him?"

John frowned. "Maybe, but we'll keep an eye out anyway. As for him"—he jerked a thumb over his shoulder at the Kid—"I want him in the Apache County jail."

"Do you think we'll reach Snowflake by morning?"

"Yes. If you're ready to go now, I'll get him mounted. Oh, and Mrs. Arnold, I'm sorry about the inconvenience of having to ride double."

So he was back to "Mrs. Arnold." She sighed in exasperation, but her sense of humor came to her rescue. He was obviously still worried about having to ride behind her. His dismay was almost comical. "Well, John Wesley," she said pointedly, "it's not as if we were rubbing bellies, is it?"

"Pardon?"

"Oh, never mind. Go load that singing idiot." She remounted the mare, wondering why she could not build up a fierce hatred for the Kid. Somehow he seemed a different man from the one who had shot her son. It was difficult to reconcile this drunken, thin man with the reckless killer of her child. Her brow furrowed as she tried to understand her own reactions toward their prisoner.

John returned, leading Jacob. The Kid was sitting resignedly on the horse's back. John stepped toward the gray. "You ready, Mrs. Arnold?"

She nodded, bracing herself for the extra weight on the mare. She closed her eyes when John swung aboard in the same restrained manner that he had assumed before. "Don't fall off," she said to taunt him.

When the horses moved at a fast trot, the Kid slowly began to sober up. He decided it would be wiser not to sing the bawdy songs that came to mind. Mrs. Arnold seemed like two different people. Her words were those of an experienced woman, yet she was strangely reserved like a lady. It was an odd mixture. As for the lawman, he surmised Michaels would be a difficult man to trick. He also knew that Michaels would shoot him if he found it necessary. That was a sobering fact. He had no intentions of trying to escape from John Wesley Michaels. The time for attempting an escape would come after he was no longer in the lawman's custody. With that thought came the memory of the silver pistol that was lowered into his cell on the rope. He would need one of those for sure this time.

Snowflake came alive when John and Dolly led the Coyote Kid down the street. Word must have been telegraphed ahead of their arrival, because onlookers, big and small, crowded the boardwalk watching in the first light of dawn as they moved up the main street toward the jail.

Neal stood in front of the sheriff's office, a Winchester repeater in the crook of his arm. He greeted them with a polite nod. "How do, Mrs. Arnold, John."

John Wesley slid off the horse and helped the prisoner down. He noted how Dolly pointedly looked away from the Kid. Wordlessly, he marched the prisoner inside the jail.

Stiff and sore, Dolly dismounted to seek some relief from her tight muscles. Standing beside the gray, she watched Neal, who was searching the crowd as if expecting trouble. Then he turned and hurriedly followed John inside the jail. At the sound of an approaching wagon, she turned. A soft snort of displeasure escaped her throat as she noted the new arrival. Sheriff Rogers, she observed with cynicism, had arrived just in time to bask in the glory of having the notorious Coyote Kid in his jail.

A cold chill swept over her as she stood in the early morning sun holding the reins to the horses. It was strange to feel so numb. Her son's killer was in jail, but the fact did not fill her with half the satisfaction that she expected. And it was oddly discomfiting that she had no hate or thirst for revenge left in her heart. She seemed to be observing herself with an odd detachment. She saw a tired, disheveled woman smelling of horse and sweat. A chill ran through her shoulders and she shivered as she waited for John Wesley Michaels to come out of the Apache County jail. The feeling of detachment passed. She closed her eyes, wondering why she was so depressed at the thought of her future and what it held for her.

CHAPTER 15

The deputy called Neal gave the Kid a shove toward the doorway. When he entered the cell block, Bobby instantly recognized the burly whiskey peddler behind the bars. The other two lined up to watch him were also members of the gang. How damn convenient for him, he mused. The rotgut makers were right there.

"Ha! So they got you, too, Kid?" Gar sneered. "That damn preacher-lawman and woman ran down the great Coyote Kid. Sounds like a joke, huh, Kid?" Gar taunted. His loud laughter grated on Kid's nerves, but he smiled back at the big man. It was the kind of warm smile that hid all the hate and anger raging inside him. He had not forgotten the poison they had sold him. Still, he continued to grin as if this whole episode, his arrest and seeing them again, amused him.

"Is the room service here any good?" he asked Neal.

"Sure." The deputy grinned. "Just ask them birds." He jerked his head toward the peddlers.

"Yeah, nice fellows." In a lower tone the Kid added,

"Just don't drink their damned old whiskey. It could kill ya."

Neal nodded and unlocked the empty cell. "Now, don't try nothing, Kid. We ain't fools here. We heard about your tricks in New Mexico, and there ain't nobody going to sneak you a gun in this jail."

The Kid grinned at the deputy as he entered the eight-by-six cubicle that he considered would be his home for a while. But he didn't believe for one moment that sometime there wouldn't be an opportunity for gaining his freedom. They wouldn't think about his escaping twenty-four hours a day like he would. That would make the difference. He needed one little slipup—all jailers made them—and it would be up to him to use it to his advantage.

Down the hall, inside the sheriff's office, John Wesley filled out the report for the judge. He ignored Sheriff Rogers's pacing, but listened resignedly to the man's sharp questions.

"Just who in the hell are you, John Wesley Michaels?" Rogers demanded. "And why is Mrs. Arnold outside on my street?"

"Because she—" John broke off and frowned at the sheriff. For a long moment he considered telling the man that she was none of his business, then a better answer came to him. "I suggest you go out there and ask her yourself."

"I will. I'll do just that," Rogers declared, although he made no move. He peered with evident suspicion at John's face. "Are you part of this damned secret force of the governor's?"

"Hardly secret!" John scowled. "And I certainly don't want your job, Sheriff Roger."

"My job?"

"Sure, you're the man who captured the Coyote Kid." John stood up. "Just sign your name to this arrest report. I'm sure there will be a lot of reporters here in a few days to interview you. I can see the headlines now: 'Sheriff Rogers Brings in the Coyote Kid.'"

"What kind of trick is this?"

"No trick." John shook his head wearily. "We have one goal, you and I. To get all the Coyote Kids, whiskey peddlers, and crooks into jail. It doesn't matter who gets credit for doing it. I'm not here to take over your job. And I don't want to talk to any reporters."

"I suppose that Yankee son of a bitch of a governor hired you and sent you here."

John sighed inwardly, growing heartily sick of the man. "I'm leaving now."

Rogers nodded uncertainly, but John could see that the sheriff was still suspicious. There was nothing more to say. It was depressing to bring in a killer like the Coyote Kid, and be met by a supposed comrade in arms who was as distrustful as Sheriff Rogers. It was degrading, as well, and at that moment John Wesley was fed up with the whole system. Dolly was right about him. Sheriff Rogers was indeed a strange man. Ignoring Rogers's searching look, John stalked outside. He scanned the crowd until he spotted Dolly.

When he reached her side, she asked flatly, "Is he all locked up?"

"Yes."

"Good, let's ride."

He nodded, but wondered if she was as satisfied as she sounded with her son's killer being locked up. A bigger question irritated him. Why was he so grateful that she was still out here waiting for him, instead of riding off on her way back to the store?

After a week in jail, the Kid felt totally defeated. The cause for his dejection were the leg irons that the sheriff had ordered put on him. Rogers had told him, "Kid, this ain't no New Mexico joke. We're going to make damn sure that you don't get a gun or any chance to escape."

Each time Bobby took a walk around the small cubicle he was forced to carry the heavy chains that bound his feet. Every trip to the outhouse behind the jail was a grim reminder that he could not run away while he was so encumbered.

It galled him because the whiskey gang laughed at his predicament when he paraded by them lugging his chains.

"Hey, Kid," Gar shouted, "they really got you this time. All chained up like a damn old dog."

Their constant harassment was a dull knife stuck in his side. He promised himself some form of vengeance for every one of their digs at him.

The only bright spot regarding his captivity was the fact that he knew the woman who delivered their food. The first time she brought the prisoners their meals, he recognized Claire. She barely glanced at him, but he knew she remembered him. For one fleeting moment their eyes met, then she hurriedly looked away.

"Don't get too friendly with the guy in the next cell," Gar had warned her. "That's the Coyote Kid; he's a killer."

"Go to hell," the Kid had shouted at him, scooting his feet and holding up the chains so he wouldn't trip. That was the first time he had seen Claire. He had to find some way to talk to her. Maybe she could get him a gun. It had been years since he had pleasured himself with her. Hell, he had staked her with money long ago, enabling her and her man to get away from the desert. She certainly should remember that good deed. Best he could recall, she even enjoyed him. Now all he needed was the opportunity to speak to her in private.

To while away the time, the Kid played checkers with Neal. The table was set up outside the cell. The deputy was a good enough player, yet a lot of the time the Kid let him win, hoping Neal would lower his guard sometime. At least he was capable of silencing Gar's loud mouth. For that alone, the Kid was grateful to the young man. Obviously, there had been some kind of altercation between Neal and Gar before he got there.

"Gar!" Neal would say. "Get over there on your bunk and shut your mouth!" Oddly enough, that was all it took for the burly man to retreat in silence.

Each day, morning, noon, and night, Neal individually marched the prisoners to the outhouse behind the jail. His sawed-off shotgun discouraged any escape attempts. It was while the Kid was seated over the outhouse's rough-cut opening that he spied the obvious place to stash a pistol. The ledge above the door would provide the perfect hiding spot. The idea rejuvenated him. Now he simply had to get word to someone. Claire? he wondered. But how? At the moment he did not know, but it was enough that he had a half-formed plan. Somehow he would get someone to hide a pistol in the outhouse.

Days dragged by like weeks. A reporter from Santa Fe came to interview him. Neal handcuffed Bobby to a chair and allowed the reporter to question him. Delbert Rawlings was a four-eyed little man, timid as a rabbit. He scrawled the Kid's answers on a sheaf of papers.

"Did you kill the outlaw Jim Nance?" Rawlings asked.

"Nah." He shook his head. "Apaches must have killed him. I heard he was scalped; that ain't my style."

Rawlings swallowed so hard that the Kid could see his Adam's apple bob up and down.

"Sure, everyone has their own way of handling things like that, and that ain't my way." The Kid spoke offhandedly as he studied the rack of Winchester repeaters hanging on the wall.

"How many men have you killed?"

"Well, how many do they say I've killed?" the Kid asked in amusement.

Rawlings gazed at him intently before answering. "Oh, a dozen or more."

Pained, the Kid frowned. "Must be more than that," he said in disappointment. "Hell, I've been doing this work for years."

"You have?"

The Kid felt weary of this wimpy reporter, but he was grateful for the opportunity to study the outer office. "Sure. Haven't you heard of me in Santa Fe?"

"Yes, but how do I know what's true and what's legend!"

He lifted his left hand, his eyes glittering in rage. But the chair held him and the handcuffs restrained him. He dropped the chains from his clenched fist. The sound startled Rawlings and he bolted upright.

"They say you shot two stage robbers in Colorado?"

The Kid shook his head in disgust. "They say. Who the hell are 'they'?"

"Mr. Budd, I'm merely using the term 'they' as you would a word to represent all the legends about your life."

"Legends? Legends are fairy tales, ain't they?"

Rawlings nodded. "Sure they are. That's one of the

reasons that I'm here. I would like to separate fact from fiction."

"You came from Santa Fe, huh?" he asked thoughtfully, rapidly forming a plan in his mind. "Hey, if I wrote a letter to a sister there at the convent—" The Kid stopped and glanced around to make sure no one could overhear his question. "Could you deliver it?"

"Oh, sure."

"I mean a secret letter. I want to be sure this sister is the only one who reads it."

Rawlings smiled and pushed his glasses back up on his nose. "Certainly."

"I tell you what, Rawlings, I'll make a deal with you. You'll hear all about the Coyote Kid so you can have your story, if you promise to deliver this letter for me without reading it."

"To your sister?"

"No! To a sister. She's a nun in a church, goddamnit!"

Rawlings's mouth formed an O and he blinked several times. "Oh yes, I see now. We have a deal, Mr. Budd."

He tried to read the newspaperman's face, wondering how trustworthy he really was. It was a risk, but he decided he would have to take a chance on the reporter. He knew that if he wrote a letter to Maria and tried to send it the regular way, Sheriff Rogers would read it. But Rawlings seemed the type of man to respect privacy—for a price. If he told the reporter enough so that he sounded like a big hero, the newspapers would buy the story and pay Rawlings well.

Bobby knew the newspapers back East ate up stories like his. The more improbable the lies, the more willing they were to believe them. He recalled a story about a gunman in the Silver City jail who told a reporter that he had shot lots of famous people. The story made headlines, even though one of the men he had supposedly shot was a lawman who was not even dead. Yes, he decided, Rawlings would agree to his deal. He would mail a secret letter to Maria. She would bring him a gun just like the last time he had been in jail. Maria knew how important his work was.

So he began his story for an enthralled Rawlings. "I was born in Missouri. I ain't too sure, but I believe my mother was a stage actress. It was while she was touring with those actors that she had me."

"And your father?" Rawlings questioned, as he scribbled furiously.

He glanced around as if to be certain no one would hear his revelation, then lowered his voice to a confidential whisper. "Well, President Hayes was in St. Louis about nine months before I was born. It was the same time my mother was there on an acting tour. Of course, he wasn't president then. He fell in love with my mother. Oh, it was sad. He was a Republican Yankee and, of course, she couldn't marry him, her being a Southerner and all. My poor mother went to her grave clutching a picture of President Hayes."

With a concerned frown, Rawlings glanced up from his scribbling and studied him. The Kid quickly continued before he could pick holes in his story. "That's fact, Mr. Rawlings. 'Course, you can't print that. I wouldn't want to embarrass the president, but I'm telling you confidentially, it's the gospel. Maybe you could just say that my father was a politician who could not marry my mother because of his family."

"But that makes you a—"

"A bastard," the Kid inserted grimly. "It's better to say that than to smear a good man's name. Right?"

Rawlings nodded without looking up from his writing.

The Kid was pleased with the beginning of his life.

He began to look forward to the time he spent telling Rawlings tall tales. He grinned at the thought of the papers carrying edition after edition of tales about the Coyote Kid episodes.

That evening back in his cell, he was surprised to see Beth Parker in the jail although he made no sign that he knew who she was. She brought him clean clothes, calling it an act of mercy.

"These belonged to my late husband," she explained to Neal. "Since Mr. Budd seems to have no one to take care of him, I shall suffer my Christian duty and tomorrow take his clothes to wash them."

Neal carefully inspected the clean clothing for a concealed weapon. "Ma'am, you certainly do good work for the Lord."

"Yes, ma'am, you sure do," the Kid agreed. "I'll pay you from the money that the deputy is holding for me until my release."

"Yeah, Kid, I'll pay her for you," Neal agreed.

"That would be good of you. And ma'am, thank you for your kindness."

She nodded without expression and quickly hurried away.

With the fresh shirt and pants in his hand, the Kid shuffled back to his bunk. He was glad Neal had searched the clean clothes because he would never think of searching the dirty ones for a message. He would consider that he had done his duty by inspecting the incoming ones. All the Kid had to do now was to write a message to Beth as he had written one to Maria. And somehow he would also find a chance to ask the pock-faced Claire for the same help. One of the three women would surely get him a gun. Things were working out to his satisfaction.

His spirits were revived. He stretched out on his back and stared at the ceiling, a smile on his lips.

"Hey, Kid!" Gar yelled, disturbing his tranquillity. "You're going to be famous before they hang you, ain't you?"

"Sure, Gar, sure I am."

There were times, the Kid knew, if there had not been a vacant cell between them, he would have strangled Gar with his bare hands. But there would always be time for that later. First, he needed a gun. He had three chances of getting one. Two days earlier he had thought things were hopeless. Now he was confident they would work out. Killing Gar could wait for a while. He would get a chance to do that, too.

The early morning light slanted in the upstairs window at the Harrington House. Seated on the edge of the bed, Ella Devereaux cringed in pain as Doc Simmons probed her side.

"Hurt bad?" he asked.

"Yes," she managed. "I can't even raise my arm."

"You've broken some ribs," he said sternly. "That Waddle do this to you?"

"Doc, it has to be a secret. I don't know what to do. But he's moved in and taken over my business."

Acting uncomfortable, Simmons looked around the room, then he nodded, satisfied that they were alone. He pulled up a chair and sat on the edge of it, close to her. He produced a snow-white handkerchief and began to polish his glasses. For a moment, he appeared to be in deep concentration about the matter of her problem.

"Have you spoken to the sheriff about him?"

"No, I don't need a scandal over it, either. Besides, who would they believe in court, him or me?" She raised her brows, then shook her head to dismiss such a foolish notion. "Whores and madams are fair game, you know."

"Well, I'd goddamn sure stop him if he was doing that to me. You have plenty of friends. Get them to help oust him."

"Waddle is a tough man. He won't go easy."

Doc glanced over at her, then strapped on his glasses. "I'll think on a way—"

"I don't want you hurt, Doc. You've been so nice to my girls and me. No need to involve you in my problems. I'll think of a way." She really meant what she told the man. There had to be a way to get rid of Waddle.

"Wear a corset. That will help until it heals." Doc still acted put out when he stood up. "I'll check around. Might be a way to get rid of him without a scandal." He ran his palm over his white mustache and mouth. "There's a way. Until then, you stop aggravating him."

"That's not easy, either."

"Try hard. We'll find a way," he said, sounding upbeat, and grabbed his satchel. "Painkiller will let you sleep. You have that?"

"Yes," she said and with a sharp ache rose to better hear the noise in the hall. She opened the door and blinked in disbelief.

Two burly men had labored up the stairs and were coming down the hall with a large trunk. She frowned at them.

"What's this?" she asked.

"Mr. Waddle paid us to deliver it right to his room. It's his," the first man said. "That black gal said his room was up here."

"Down at the end of the hall. Put it in there," she said with a wave. Her anger grew with each second at the thought of his taking over her apartment and shunting her off to one of the bedrooms.

"See you." Doc waved his hat at her and went off down the hallway.

Something came to her as she forced a smile and acknowledged his departure. What was so damn precious in that trunk? Maybe she should investigate. First, she needed a lookout, so Waddle wouldn't discover her trying to open it.

Not Sassy, the black girl might give it away if pressured. Strawberry, the redhead, would do. She'd keep her mouth shut. Besides, the girl had some finishing-school education. She'd made herself a bad choice of men and climbed over the fence one night to abscond with a gambler who had the same qualities as Waddle.

Ella hurried down the hallway after the two men left. She stuck her head in the girl's room. Strawberry sat before the mirror brushing her hair and jerked around to look at her mildly.

"I need your help," Ella hissed.

"Sure, what are we doing?"

Ella held two fingers to her mouth to silence the girl and slipped inside the doorway with a twinge of pain shooting from her sore ribs.

"I've taken my last beating," she said with her back to the door.

"Good, I wondered when you'd wise up," Strawberry said, then she set the brush down, rose, and tied the belt of her dressing gown. Glancing down to check her appearance, she looked up and nodded her head that she was ready.

"They just brought his trunk upstairs," Ella said. "I want to open it and see if I can find anything inside it to incriminate him." She drew a shuddering breath up her nose. "I want rid of him."

"I knew he got on you hard." Strawberry grimaced in disapproval.

"No reason for me to take that. Will you be a lookout while I try to unlock it?" She shrugged, discovering that hurt, too.

"Sure, where is he now?" the girl asked.

"Down on Whiskey Row." She had to force down her rage, knowing he was blowing more of her money at the gambling tables. "Come on."

Ella searched up and down the hallway. Then they hurried to the room.

The smell of stale cigar smoke struck her nose when she opened the door. Her precious apartment had taken on the smells of an old saloon. The musk of a man's sweat permeated the room's closed interior.

"Can I open a window?" Strawberry asked, wrinkling her nose at the offensive odors.

"Yes, that one." Ella indicated the side window. "If he comes we can close it. Whew, it smells bad in here. No one's emptied the pot, either." She knelt before the camel back steamer.

"You have a key to the lock?" Strawberry asked, taking a place behind the lace curtain for a view of the courthouse and street. From there Ella knew the girl could see Waddle approaching the house from Whiskey Row.

"I have several to try," she said. Her knees gave her discomfort as she tried each key on her ring, one by one. But she had no success. Discouraged, she at last dropped back on her heels.

"It's no use. If we break in, he'll know who did it."

"Maybe I can open it. One time I watched that sorry Earl open some trunks by picking the locks with a wire."

"Good girl, but do we need to get a wire?"

"I could find one downstairs and be right back."

"Not a word to any of them—" Ella frowned at her.

"Hey, I can keep a secret."

"I know. That's why I chose you."

Strawberry swished out of the room and was gone. Ella pushed herself up and took the post at the window. She didn't expect him that early, but one never knew. It would be just like him to lose a lot, then come back and demand more money from her. She clenched her jaw muscles tight enough to make them hurt, and shook her head in disgust. He had to be stopped.

The redhead came swiftly through the door holding a short piece of wire. Grinning with a determined look at Ella, she dropped down before the trunk and began probing the lock. Ella turned back to observe the street below. She closed her eyes. There had to be a God up there who heard her, and she prayed for her deliverance from Waddle's tyranny.

"I've got it!" Strawberry exclaimed and the audible click made Ella's heart jump inside her sore chest. She quickly checked the street and rushed over.

"Oh, my God!" Strawberry said and drew back.

Ella could hardly believe her eyes at the sight. The chest bulged with pads of money. Hundreds, maybe millions of dollars. So why was he using up hers?

She picked up a bundle of twenties and began to fan them. The crisp new feel of them thrilled her. There was an unbelievable fortune in this trunk. It all made no sense.

Strawberry brushed the edges of a bundle on her freckled cheek. The bills fanned out as she grinned in shocked disbelief. Excitement danced in her green eyes as she waved the money.

"Wait," Ella said, and tore the band off the packet in her hand. She blinked at the top bill, sliding it up so she could compare the serial number with the one on the second bill. "Jesus, oh, Jessica, it's the same. They're all counterfeit!"

"What?" The girl leaned over to look at the proof in Ella's hands. "They look so damn real; they can't be."

"They are," Ella said in numb shock. "They damn sure are."

CHAPTER 16

Five days later John received a letter from Major Bowen. He read it to Dolly as she cooked their dinner at the campsite outside of Snowflake.

Dear John,

The capture of Bobby Joe Budd is commendable. I understand that Sheriff Rogers has taken precautions to make sure he remains in jail, but the Kid is cunning. The men who have hired him in the past may attempt a jail break if they fear he will inform on them. The governor and I agree that you should stay in the area to be on hand to thwart any attempt to free him.

Judge Elbern Monroe, who is presently handling cases in Tucson, should be able to hold court in Snowflake in a few weeks. He is a very tough judge, and the one we would like to see take charge of this case. John, try and be as inconspicuous as possible. I appreciate your letter regarding the legislative clerk Tucker. Governor Sterling sends his thanks, as well.

I feel certain that by now you will have delivered Mrs. Arnold safely back home to her husband. Thank you for a job well done.

Sincerely,
Major Bowen

"Delivered me home?" Dolly echoed the words with a laugh. Squatting beside the fire, she busied herself stirring a pot of beans. "Well, John Wesley, he must not have believed that I sounded like a grandma."

"No." He sighed and paced in front of the fire. Deep in his own thoughts, he folded the major's letter and placed it in his shirt pocket.

"Well, it's not as if we were living in sin, is it?"

"Mrs. Arnold, that is beside the point. You are an attractive woman, and . . ."

"Well . . ." She raised her brows in surprise that he had noticed. "I figured that in your book, John, I was as ugly to you as one of those whiskey peddlers."

He spun on his heel and stalked away, not trusting himself to speak.

She watched him disappear in the night and turned back to her cooking. For the moment, she found only a small satisfaction in penetrating his tough hide. His most recent attempts to ship her back home had irritated her the most. He had begun the day they put the Kid in jail. Bone-tired, they had stumbled back from Snowflake to their present campsite.

"Mrs. Arnold," he had started in a weary tone, "the murderer is now in custody. You can return home; your part is done. I'll arrange for you to have an escort or a wagon for the journey."

She never bothered to answer him; instead she had untied her bedroll, and unsaddled her horse. Then she'd ignored him by lying down on her bedroll with her back turned toward him. Curled up in a tight ball, weary and upset, she closed her eyes. Why, she wondered, was staying with John becoming such an obsession? If she went home, she mused sadly, she would be haunted by memories of Josh. She needed a new life. And despite John's persistence in calling her "Mrs. Arnold," he was still just a man. Somehow she would have to convince him of that fact.

Now they were back to their bickering again. She rose from her cooking resolved to get her emotions under control and to restore some tranquillity in their camp. "John Wesley," she shouted, "come and eat. There's no sense in letting the food go to ruin just because you're angry."

He soon strode back to the camp, his face blank. "I wasn't aware that I was angry. Something smells good." He ignored her skeptical look and took the plate of beans and corn bread that she held out to him.

"Mrs. Arnold," he said hesitantly, "perhaps you might be of assistance to me for a while longer."

She hid her surprise and delight. "Oh?" she asked quietly. Avoiding his keen gaze, she filled her plate.

"It might be dangerous. The thing is, we need to be aware of every visitor the Kid has. If anyone tries to get a message to him, we have to be prepared. Some visits might seem trivial, but we have to be ready for anything. The more we know about his visitors, the better off we are."

"So I am of some value?"

He nodded. She could be very valuable. She had a sharp mind along with her sharp tongue, he acknowledged wryly. Since Major Bowen had hinted at some kind of conspiracy to break the Kid out, it would be to their benefit if they could find out who saw the Kid in jail and find out something about them. Dolly might be able to question the townspeople. Besides, the two of them could cover more range than one lawman.

"First thing to do is to talk to the woman at the cafe. The one who takes the prisoners their food," he said between bites. He cocked his head. "This is good."

She shrugged. "Same as yesterday's menu, but I'm glad you like it," she added. "What exactly do we need to know?"

He left his spoon on his plate and gestured with his hand. "Someone may have already gotten to the woman who sends over the food for the prisoners since she's in a position to see him every day."

"And they may have bought her off, or gotten her co-operation somehow?"

"That's a possibility." He looked at her in admiration for her quick thinking. "The major's concerned that there might be a move to get the Kid out of jail. We need to be very careful. You may be right about this woman being bought off." He took a long swallow of coffee, then continued. "Oh, by the way, there's a reporter from Santa Fe in town getting the Kid's life story. His name is Rawlings. Try and avoid him; he asks too many questions."

She rose and refilled his plate then sat cross-legged beside him, careful not to actually touch him. "I'll figure out a way to find out if this woman at the cafe knows anything. Is there another way to find out if anyone's planning to spring him?"

"Word gets around if you listen in the right places. I'll trust my judgment and perhaps find a greedy informer."

She sighed. "I suppose I'll have to put on a dress to go into town."

"It might be a good idea. You'll be less conspicuous. We have to be careful not to tip our hand at this game."

She was silent for a moment as she gathered her wits, then she spoke quietly. "John, do you really understand why I haven't gone back to the store?"

"Yes. But I do think you should consider another arrangement."

"Another arrangement?" she asked, genuinely puzzled.

"Yes. You should stay in town alone. It would be more proper."

She was torn between laughter and exasperation. "Don't worry about my reputation, John Wesley. You are a perfect gentleman, but I am not a fancy lady from a house in town, I'm from a house all right, but not the right kind."

John put down his plate, regretting his suggestion. "You don't have to tell me anything."

No, she guessed shrewdly, he wouldn't want to know about her past. "It seems strange, doesn't it? Most women want a house, a stove, and a roof over their heads. But I'm content to cook on a campfire and ride a horse."

He gave no answer. He feared that she expected a commitment from him. The notion made him feel trapped. She was a good cook, and good with the horses, but he wasn't ready to take on a partner of any kind. He spoke gruffly. "It's no place for a—"

"A woman, you were going to say!"

"Exactly. Besides, the major is not going to put up with one of his marshals traipsing around with a woman."

"I'll talk to him."

"Oh, no you won't!"

"All right, then." She knew she was beaten for the moment. "But until you've finished your job with the Coyote Kid, I'll ride with you and assist you."

He knew nothing he could say would persuade her otherwise. "Maybe."

She pushed the beans around on her plate. Her appetite had disappeared during their tense conversation. She studied his rigid profile, wondering about him. "John," she said softly, "may I ask you one personal question?" When he nodded, she continued. "Have you ever been married?"

"No."

"I'm not going to ask you why," she stated, feeling snubbed.

He turned toward her, frowning. Then after putting up a shield against her pity, he spoke quietly. "I considered marrying a woman in Colorado, where I came from. But the salary I made at the time wasn't adequate. She found a better provider and married him."

"Oh, I'm sorry."

John shrugged. "It was probably for the best."

Dolly could feel his withdrawal and regretted her question. She rose and spoke briskly. "It's pretty dark already. I'll do the dishes in the morning, just leave them." Anxious to escape from the tense situation building between them, she hurried toward her bedroll. Tomorrow she had something meaningful to do, something other than herding the horses. Taking care of their stock had kept her occupied the last few days, but the thought of actually doing law work, almost like being a detective, was exciting. Besides, it would be nice to go into town as a woman.

Under the starlight, he washed the dishes in the stream, grateful for something to do. He did not want to dwell on their conversation. He deliberately detached his mind from the woman and thought about his job. In the morning, he planned a wide swing around the area on horseback.

Perhaps he would discover if the major's worries had any foundation.

She awoke before dawn and slipped away to the stream, leaving him asleep in his bedroll across the camp. The cold water splashed on her skin awoke her quickly, then with chattering teeth, she hurriedly dried with a flour sack and dressed. With her wet hair bound in the sack towel she hurried back to camp in the chilly air.

He was already up and moving about when she stoked the fire to life. The radiant heat warmed her as she made coffee and put on a pan of Dutch-oven biscuits. While they baked, she brushed her hair dry. She noted he was busy hobbling the horses, avoiding her as usual. Every time they spoke intimately or personally, he acted as if he regretted it afterward and ignored her.

John walked slowly back toward the fire. He noticed her clean hair and slightly wrinkled dress; it was obvious that she had bathed earlier. He squatted down on his boot heels beside the fire and studied the orange flames licking up from the logs.

"I'm going to ride east of town today. I've never been in that area." He picked up a fresh biscuit she offered on a long fork, speared from the Dutch oven. With a warm grin of gratitude, he juggled it between his hands before biting into it.

"Hmm. These are good."

She nodded to acknowledge his words. "See if you can find some butter from a farmer. They usually sell their surplus." She laced her town shoes, knowing they were probably going to make her feet sore, but cowboy boots were hardly suitable to wear with a dress.

"Yes, butter would taste good on these." He looked up

at her, his mouth full of hot biscuit. After he chewed and swallowed it, he asked, "Are you riding a horse into town?"

"No, it's early yet, so I'll walk. Besides," she added with a smile, "I'm a woman today, not a horse herder."

His lips tightened. Was she making a dig at him? She certainly was a woman today. He frowned, wondering if he were making a mistake sending her on a mission that might prove dangerous. What if something happened? He shook his head at his thoughts as he absently took another biscuit from the pan. The heat of it seared his fingers and he dropped the bread into his lap with a soft oath.

"Did I hear you say 'damn'?" Dolly blinked in astonishment.

John raised his gaze and squinted at her golden sunlit silhouette. "You be careful out there."

"I will. And John, don't burn yourself on the rest of those biscuits."

There was a spring in her step when she left him. The cool morning air brushed her cheeks as she trudged to town. She felt conspicuous in a dress, and the shoes were already pinching her feet.

When she neared the small frame houses scattered at the edge of the settlement, she slowed her pace. She passed the swaying shingle of the doctor's whitewashed house, then went around the weed-choked pens that served as a gathering place for cattle buyers at roundup time. At the cafe, she mounted the steps and stood on the boardwalk. A quick glance at the jail and saloon assured her that no one was stirring. For a fleeting moment, her vision clouded as she thought of the Coyote Kid sitting in that cell. Then she shook her head to dismiss the notion and tried to see inside the cafe. The sun glinting on the window prevented her from seeing the interior.

A woman, bearing a tray of food, came through the front door.

She noted the woman with interest. About thirty years old with brown hair, but her face was scarred with pock marks.

"I'll be right back, ma'am," she addressed Dolly. "If you like you can go inside and wait. I'm sorry, I doubt that my new Indian helper can wait on you, but I will be back in a few minutes."

Dolly smiled. "Thank you, I'll wait inside." She watched the woman cross the street with the food. There was only enough food on the tray for one person. No doubt the tray was for a guard rather than the jail prisoners.

A bell tinkled as Dolly entered the cafe. An attractive Indian woman, who stood at the stove, turned and smiled blandly. Then she returned to her cooking. Dolly looked around at the empty tables, before selecting one in the middle of the room. She watched the Indian woman, who seemed to be very intent on her cooking. A good-looking girl, perhaps still in her teens; her braids hung in shiny black ropes down her slender back. Her beauty would appeal even to a white man; it seemed odd to her that this girl was working for a woman.

The cafe owner returned. She smiled at Dolly and offered her a cup of coffee as she put up the empty tray.

"Yes, please." Dolly suddenly felt uncomfortable. It had been so long since she'd had a conversation with another woman, she had forgotten how to act. She wrung her hands in her lap, wondering if she should put them on the table or hold them primly.

The woman returned, carrying two steaming cups of aromatic coffee. "Here you are. Gosh, you must be new in town. I've met most of the women."

"Yes. My name is Mrs. Dolly Arnold."

"And I'm Claire Fenton. I own this place. I lost my husband, Chester, a year ago. We had a farm, but we sold it to buy this place. Do you need something with your coffee?"

"No, thanks. I guess you're pretty busy with having to feed the prisoners?"

"I am, but I have a few minutes today to visit, before the crowd rushes in here for breakfast. I hired that Indian girl yesterday. Her name is Silver Belle. Isn't that a pretty name? She's frying the prisoners' mush right now, so that helps a lot."

Dolly agreed.

CHAPTER 17

"Now I know where I've seen you before," Claire said with a look of recognition on her pocked face. "You rode in with that man who arrested the Coyote Kid."

Dolly considered the coffee cup on the table before her. She saw see no reason to deny it. She nodded quickly. "Yes."

She felt the woman's eyes studying her intently. "Are you working for the law, too?"

How should she answer her? Dolly blinked in confusion. "You, I mean, the man that I rode in with . . . He's not Mr. Arnold. It . . . it's very complicated."

The woman's slow nod only added to her frustration. Looking Claire in the eye, she finally confided, "John Wesley Michaels, the man I rode in with, is an officer of the territorial courts. I'm his cook."

"Oh, you cook for him?"

"Yes," she said with some relief. "I also herd and hold horses," she added with a wry smile.

"I see. He isn't your husband—" Claire broke off, her face flushed with obvious embarrassment. "Oh, I'm sorry. I remember now. The Kid shot your little boy, didn't he?"

Dolly nodded and tried to keep her gaze on the coffee cup. Sharing her loss with another woman made it more real, and caused tears to well up in her eyes. Until this moment, she had put her grief in a deep hole in her heart, protecting it and hiding it from the world, but nothing could contain it. She fought hard, but quickly the sorrow surfaced.

"It was such a terrible thing," Claire said softly. "I knew the Kid before he became a killer."

"Oh?" Dolly struggled to regain her composure so she could do the job that John had sent her to do. This woman had known the Kid before—how well?

"Yes. He worked for a rancher then. Chester and I stopped on a big ranch where the Kid worked. He was some sort of a guard against folks homesteading the ranch land." Claire looked away, a faint smile on her face as if the memory pleased her. "We were almost out of supplies and money when the Kid first showed up. Of course, he was Bobby Budd back then. Bobby told me that his job was to move people off the land. He gave us some money, so . . . well, we could go on," Claire said haltingly. "But that was before he went on to this shooting business."

"Yes." Dolly nodded. "I'm sure that he wouldn't be that nice now."

Claire looked toward the front window, a dreamy smile on her face. "But he was nice . . . then."

It did not take someone with a great imagination to know that there was more to the story than Claire was telling her. Dolly sipped her coffee, then spoke quietly. "Did he recognize you?"

"No." She avoided looking at Dolly as she spoke. "I've

taken trays of food over there, but he doesn't give any sign that he knows me."

"I suppose he's been on the run a long time."

"Yes." Claire shook her head sadly. "I would never have thought that he would turn out this way."

Filled with suspicion, Dolly vowed to keep a close watch on the woman. There were too many gaping holes in Claire's story, and it did not require a shrewd mind to guess at the lapses.

"I . . . I'm sorry, Mrs. Arnold, but I have to take those prisoners their meal now."

"Dolly," she corrected her with a friendly smile. "Let me pay you for the coffee."

Claire shook her head as she rose from the table. "No, Dolly. It's my treat. You know, that newspaperman would really like to talk to you about how you helped capture the Coyote Kid."

Dolly was shocked by the idea. "Oh no, Claire. I—I couldn't talk to a . . . a man about the matter. I'm sure you understand."

"Of course. I have to hurry. I hope you'll come again."

"Yes, thank you." Dolly looked toward the kitchen area. "That Indian girl is very attractive."

"Yes, she seems to have no family," Claire confided. "She hired on for very little pay. Well, Dolly, goodbye for now." Claire moved gracefully away from the table to the kitchen.

Dolly rose, her curiosity piqued. As she stood and smoothed her dress, she once again took a moment to study the Indian. Had she ever seen her at Ben's store? Many Indians came by and traded there, but she couldn't recall ever seeing her before.

Shrugging inwardly, Dolly walked toward the door and went outside in the sunlight.

At the dry-goods store, she selected some baking soda. She really didn't need it, but it gave her an excuse to be in the establishment, where she could watch the street. The merchant allowed her to browse unaided through some bolts of material.

She took up a position near the window so she could observe the jail as she fingered the various dress material. She noted Deputy Neal leaving the jail a few moments after the sheriff arrived. Down by the saloon, a swamper came outside and leaned sleepily on a broom. He was a grizzled-bearded old man. Dolly recognized the type. They usually worked for free lunches and a few drinks, then slept in the storeroom of the saloon.

Having grown weary of spying, since she had learned nothing that would help John, she moved to the counter and paid for her baking soda.

"Didn't find a piece of fabric to suit you?" the store-keeper asked politely.

"No, not today, but I'll be back again."

"Fine, come look all you want. You new here?"

"Yes." She smiled and quickly hurried outside to escape further questioning. Already she grew tired of wearing a dress and the shoes she had stuffed her feet into pinched her toes. But since she could not sit on the bench outside the store and whittle like some old man, she supposed she had better head back toward the campsite. It seemed to her that being a woman was inconvenient at times.

Walking carefully past the houses at the edge of town, she sighed in relief on reaching a grassy slope. Seating herself on the ground, she removed her shoes and wiggled her freed toes in relief. Then, barefoot, she walked back to camp.

She was glad when she caught sight of their campsite.

Her gray mare and Thomas were grazing across the small stream. There were no signs of John or Jacob.

Dolly quickly located her jeans and shirt in the pannier then moved to her willow-walled dressing room. A few minutes later, feeling more comfortable, she busied herself with the campfire. The gun on her hip was a reassuring companion.

Perhaps, she mused, she should start some kind of meal. He would be home sometime. Home? It was sure something that she could think of a shady grove of young ponderosas as home. Laughing softly at her thoughts, she began to put together a meal.

When John Wesley had left that morning he had taken the road east. The way consisted of two narrow dry ruts that wound through the small checkerboard farms fronting the wagon-track scars. In the cool of the morning, John studied the farmsteads and the lay of the land.

He noticed a woman hanging out some laundry. Remembering Dolly's request, he reined the gelding up the path to the house and removed his hat.

"Good morning, ma'am."

She turned and squinted at him in the sun. "Oh, good morning. May I help you?"

"The name's John Wesley Michaels, ma'am. I noticed your brindle cow and wondered if you had any butter to sell?"

She nodded. "I'll have some later," she said as she hung a man's shirt on the rope line. "I still have to churn it. Will you be passing this way again later?"

"Yes. Is your husband around?"

"No." She hung out a soggy pair of jeans. "I'm a widow, Mr. Michaels."

"Oh, sorry. I was judging by the washing."

The woman looked at the laundry, then at John Wesley, her eyes suddenly alert. "Th . . . they belong to that prisoner Bobby Budd. He needed someone to do his washing. I have taken the task upon myself."

"I see, Mrs. . . . ?"

"Beth Parker."

"My pleasure, Mrs. Parker. I'll stop by later for that butter."

"It'll be ready."

He speculated about the woman as he rode away. She seemed pleasant enough, but she had acted odd about the Kid's laundry. Almost defensive, he decided. He wasn't sure if she had assumed the role of a martyr or if she actually knew the Kid. It was something to keep in mind.

He rode past the farms and onto the rangeland. The high country, studded by an occasional stand of pines, rolled away.

Later, he topped a ridge. The mountain air was clear, except for a few clouds that resembled ripened cotton bolls. In the road ahead, he spotted a disabled wagon. Three men labored with one of the wagon wheels. Perhaps they would have some information that he could use.

John short-loped his horse down the grassy incline. As he neared the wagon, he could see that a large load of fresh-cut boards were stacked on the rig. John reined up beside them and greeted the men.

"Good afternoon. You fellows having trouble?" The pungent odor of resin from the lumber assaulted his nostrils.

The eldest man looked up. "If it isn't one thing, it's two more. Me and the boys were counting on us having a payday today. We got this lumber sold in Snowflake, but we'll be two days getting the wagon fixed."

"You must have a sawmill," John said conversationally.

"Sure do. You need some lumber cut, mister?"

"No, not today."

"The name's Jeremiah Tombs. This here," he said, indicating the two younger men, "is Ned and Radford, my sons."

"How do." John dismounted and extended his hand. "My name's John Wesley."

The men all shook his hand, then the father spoke. "What manner of business are you in, John Wesley?"

"I work for the courts."

"Hmm," Tombs commented, "I thought you was some kind of preacher; you could pass for one."

"No," John said with a laugh. "I'm not a preacher, but I could use your help. Have you seen anything of a bunch of cowhands or ranchers riding this way?"

"No, why?"

"To be frank with you, Mr. Tombs, I'm concerned that some of the Coyote Kid's friends may be planning to break him out of jail."

Tombs nodded. "Well, the boys and me ain't seen or heard nothing like that. I was in Poker Town a couple days ago. Never heard a word down there, except that the Kid was captured in that bar. Oh, they're saying that he shot two men south of there."

John frowned at the new information. "Who were they?"

"A squaw man by the name of Nat Milner and his half-breed brother-in-law. And the fellow who rode with the Kid got it too. Leo somebody. They brung their bodies down to Poker Town."

John frowned in thought. So, the Kid had been telling the truth about his partner. "Did Sheriff Rogers go down there and investigate the shootings?"

Tombs laughed as if John had made a joke. "No way.

He has a rancher down there who wears a badge. And another who's the magistrate. They held court in the saloon, if you want to call it that. Said it was obviously a case of self-defense."

John's teeth clamped down hard at the information. "Who were these ranchers that posed as the law?"

"One was Cy Edgar. He's a kind of law around Poker Town. He's got a crony by the name of Tom Howard who has a magistrate's license."

John knew how that system worked. Those kind of men were the result of the lack of law that ranged the West. Their existence was one of the reasons the governor had appointed a secret security force. The thought caused him to recall the letter he had found in Sheriff Rogers's office. Major Bowen had explained how sheriffs passed favors out to their political supporters in the form of badges and magistrate licenses. Any big backer could become a lawman if he knew the right people. It was a tyrannical system that had little to do with real justice.

John pulled his grim thoughts back to the present. He watched the two strapping Tombs boys unhitch the team.

"Mr. Tombs, I would appreciate it if you hear anything to send me word. Will you?"

"I sure will, John Wesley. You're the one who brought in the Kid, ain't you?"

He nodded. "But that's not the important thing. What is important is the fact that he's in jail, and I want him to stay there to stand trial."

"By Gawd, John Wesley, you're as modest as a preacher. Me and the boys surely will keep our eyes peeled."

"I'm camped north of Snowflake on the first stream to the west."

"I'll send word if'n we hear anything. Good luck to you, sir."

He thanked the man and mounted Jacob. As he passed the front of the wagon, he said goodbye to the sons. The lumbermen would be his allies. Before this matter with the Kid was over, he knew he would need all the friends he could find. There was a chance that some of the Kid's rancher buddies would band together to get him out of jail.

Riding along back to Snowflake, John tried to piece together every possible means of a jailbreak. Nothing shaped in his weary mind. All his ideas led to blind canyons with sheer walls.

When he rode up the lane to her place, he absently noted that Mrs. Parker had taken all her clothes off the line. He dismounted and tied the gelding to the fence. When he heard the door opening, he turned.

"I have the butter here in a jar for you, Mr. Michaels." She moved out on the porch as she spoke. "You do have a place to keep it cool?"

"I'm sure my, er . . . the woman does," he stammered in confusion, instantly regretting his slip.

"Tell your missus that I would like to meet her. You folks must be new around here."

He nodded helplessly. The woman had trapped him. He paid her for the butter and hurried back to his horse.

When he reached town, he immediately noticed that a crowd had gathered on the porch of the jail. He rode up to the saloon porch trying to see and stopped short.

"What's happened?" he demanded of the gray-whiskered swamper.

"The prisoners have been poisoned. Two of 'em are dead, and the other two are sick as horses." The old man interrupted his speech to spew a brown stream of tobacco from his wrinkled mouth. "It's like the colic. Yes, sir. Two died and them others are sicker than a dog."

John fought down a fiery rage inside him and asked, "Who died?"

He dismounted, his hand still holding the jar of butter. Hitching the horse with one hand, he looked at the man impatiently.

"That Kid and the big one, Gar, are bad off. But hell, I reckon they're too damned mean to kill."

Turning sharply on his heel, John strode toward the jail. He forced his way through the crowd on the porch and stopped in front of Neal, who was cradling a Winchester.

"Oh, come in, Mr. Michael."

"Thanks, Neal. Is Sheriff Rogers here?"

"Yeah, him and the doc both." He stood aside for John to enter the jail.

Inside, John noted how haggard Rogers looked. Another man, who was holding a coffee cup, turned toward him.

"Doc, this is John Wesley Michaels. He's the one who brought the prisoners in." The sheriff looked warily at John. "They've been poisoned. In my own damned jail. And I ain't sure how in the hell it happened," he admitted in a defeated tone.

"Doctor, is the Kid dead yet?" John asked curtly.

The doctor swallowed his coffee and shook his head. "He'll probably survive. Him and the big whiskey peddler weren't as bad off as the others were. Maybe they didn't get as much poison, or maybe their systems are stronger. The others only lasted a few hours. It was some kind of fast-acting poison."

"Well, just what kind of poison was it?"

The doctor sighed. "That's the problem. We don't know, but we think it was some Indian stuff."

"Indian?"

"Yeah," the sheriff said. "Some squaw went to work for Claire yesterday at the cafe. Claire provides the meals for the prisoners."

John nodded as he recalled the conversation with the lumberman about the shooting of the squaw man and Indian in Poker Town. "Was this woman living with a white man and a half-breed over south of Poker Town?"

The sheriff nodded with obvious reluctance. "Some squaw man and a half-breed."

"And," John said, glaring at Rogers. "You knew those men were killed by the Kid?"

"I heard something like that," Sheriff Rogers said evasively.

John fought the anger growing inside his chest. He was not letting this lawman get off that lightly. "Sheriff Rogers, three men were shot, not two days' ride from here. Your specially appointed deputy up there held an inquest in a saloon, and the whole episode was swept under the rug. You knew about that, didn't you?"

"What in the hell are you getting at?" Rogers's face reddened in outrage.

"Just that I'm holding you responsible for the death of those prisoners. You and your so-called law are accountable."

"It was a mistake! They made an error in judgment. Hell, Michaels, it's a wonder that Neal wasn't killed, too. How in hell was I supposed to know about the squaw?"

John sighed, never bothered to answer Rogers, and turned toward the doctor. "The Kid going to be well enough to stand trial?"

"It's too soon to tell, but I expect he'll recover." The

doctor looked at John and rubbed his jaw thoughtfully. "You know, it's a funny thing. Over three weeks ago this Kid and another man came to my place. He was blinded by some bad whiskey he'd been drinking. That blindness seems to have completely healed." Under John's steely gaze, he hastily added, " 'Course, I didn't know at the time it was the Coyote Kid."

After removing his hat, John ran his fingers through his hair. "The Coyote Kid poisoned by an Indian," he said in disgust. Was she hired to poison him to keep him from talking or had it merely been an act of revenge? They might never know.

"Well," Rogers commented sullenly, "the whole world'll know about it in a day or two. That newspaperman, Rawlings, is already writing a story about it."

Feeling frustrated by the careless law system, John glanced at the jail cells and then at the sheriff. "Sheriff, I'll be back. You better double the guard here."

"What the hell for?" Rogers demanded belligerently.

"The Kid has a lot more enemies than just one Indian squaw."

Rogers agreed glumly. "I suppose you're right. I'll be goddamn glad when this whole thing is over."

John Wesley never replied as he stalked past Neal. He ignored all the questions that the crowd shouted at him. Rogers was the politician, let him answer their questions.

Mounted on his horse, John noticed that he had been carrying the jar of butter all this time. He almost laughed at the absurdity. As he took one last look at Sheriff Rogers, the man was making placating gestures with his hands as he tried to silence the crowd.

As the horse picked his way up the path to the camp, John heard the other horses nickering at their approach.

Dolly waved and came to meet him. "Well, John Wesley, you've returned," she said as she took the reins.

He nodded and waited until he dismounted and faced her to say, "They poisoned the prisoners today."

"Who did?"

"An Indian woman."

She was shocked. "Not the same Indian woman who was at the cafe?"

"I guess." He frowned at her in puzzlement. "Did you see her?"

She nodded. "Claire, who owns the cafe, said this Indian girl just showed up, was looking for work and willing to do it very cheap. Did they arrest her?"

"Not yet. They can barely mount a two-man guard at the jail."

"Will we . . . will you go after her?"

"I really can't afford to leave here in case the ranchers try something. Although I haven't seen anything of them, they could still be on their way here."

"I can't believe that girl poisoned the Kid."

"Well, he's not dead yet, him and Gar. But the other two didn't last very long. The doctor thinks the Kid will probably recover."

She looked at him with a frown, uncertain whether she was glad the Kid hadn't died so that he could stand trial, or if she would have preferred him to suffer in agony by slow poisoning. Too, she could not believe the Indian woman she had seen earlier was a murderess. But she had had no way of knowing what was in the squaw's mind. Despite telling herself that, Dolly somehow felt that she had let John down. She shook her head, trying to rid herself of the guilt.

"I have some food ready," she said in a subdued voice. "Oh, I see that you got some butter."

"Oh, yeah." He gave her the jar, relieved to have it off his hands. Noting her unusually depressed expression, he felt a flicker of compassion. Most women did not affect him one way or another. But she was a different matter. If nothing else, he felt that they had almost become friends. At least they shared respect for each other. Being friends with a woman was a totally new concept for him, but he was surprised to admit he was not averse to the feeling. She was the first woman he had ever really trusted—what she said he believed. He closed his eyes; some things were just too complicated, like their relationship.

The Kid felt too groggy to even raise his head off the iron bed. His mind wallowed in a deep fog and his guts felt on fire. Curled up in a ball on the bunk, he considered his depleted condition and how it had all happened. He could hardly believe that the Indian bitch had poisoned him. That damn Silver Bell had drank his whiskey and laid him. She belonged to those two rustlers that killed poor Leo. God, he missed Leo. If only Leo was alive, he wouldn't be rotting away in this stinking cell.

A violent eruption began inside his stomach, causing him to rise weakly to vomit. He was denied even that small comfort. Nothing was forced from his stomach. Nothing but the powerful depleting action that gagged him. A putrid stench rose in his nostrils and he lay back exhausted by his efforts.

Two of the whiskey peddlers had died, their bodies hauled away like yesterday's chamber pots. Gar was reduced to a growling, twitching mound on his bunk in the next cell. It was a shame, he lamented, that the son of a bitch wasn't killed, but he was a hard case. And now that Gar had been moved to the adjoining cell, he was too weak to reach through the bars and choke him to death. He surmised that he and Gar had not taken in as much poison as either of the other two. Who knew why they had been spared?

His plan to escape was still intact. The letter to Maria asked for her help. He had borrowed paper from that reporter and now his note to Beth was hidden in the pockets of the dirty pants that would be sent to her for washing. Soon he would slip a note to Claire with the same request for help as the other two. Surely, she hadn't been in on the plot to poison him. He did not think she would do that, not when he had helped her long ago.

Now, he needed sleep and plenty of it. If he didn't strangle on his own gagging, he would make it another day. God, he could sure use some good strong whiskey to soothe his sore throat. The poisoning episode seemed as though it had taken place days ago, not merely earlier that day. And that stupid Deputy Neal had wondered if it had been part of an escape attempt. The Kid smiled to himself. Actually, Neal wasn't too far off, the Kid admitted. If he hadn't been so damned sick, he just might have taken a chance to make a break for it in the confusion. That damn copper-hided bitch needed to be taught a lesson. Oh well, tomorrow he would feel better. Maybe he'd get some kind of sign from one of the women he had written to for help. He just had to get through this night without dying.

At the Harrington House in Prescott, Ella Devereaux laid her plans well. Waddle won several pots while gambling that evening and he came back to Harrington house, roaring drunk, well after midnight. She had waited up for him.

"There you are—" he slurred, and swung his arms

around loosely. "Had us a real streak of good luck tonight, darling. I got money in all my pockets." He grinned foolishly and she stepped in close for fear that he would fall down.

"My girl—" he mumbled and hung on to her. Supporting his weight hurt her injured ribs, but she wanted him upstairs in his bed, not retching in her fine parlor.

"I'm coming, missy," Strawberry said, raising her skirt in her hands and charging down the stairs.

"Yeah, I like redheads." He smiled and dropped his head as if he had passed out, hanging between the two women.

"How did he ever get home?" Strawberry hissed.

Ella shook her head. This was the drunkest he had been since he came to Prescott. The two started up the stairs supporting him between them.

"You know I won lots tonight," he confided to Strawberry, while they strained to haul him up to the second floor.

"That's nice." She looked at the ceiling for help.

"Both of you getting in bed with me?" He giggled, then snorted through his nose.

"Sure," Ella said, "if you're man enough."

"I damn—sure—am."

"You sure are," Strawberry said to soothe him.

At last they reached the head of the stairs and both girls were breathing heavily. One of the other girls peeked out of her door, but Ella's disapproving shake of the head made her slam it shut.

Minutes later they dumped him on the bed. He groaned and passed out.

"Get his clothes off quick," Ella said. "I want him to think he had a party up here."

"Sure," Strawberry said, tugging on his coat sleeve.

Together they stripped it off him. Then, while Ella planted some of the counterfeit bills in the large roll she took from his coat pocket, Strawberry took off his shoes and more bills floated out of them.

"I'll put a few in there, too," Ella said, bending over to pick them off the floor. Though it hurt when she leaned over to reach for the scattered money, she felt so confident her plan would work, the adrenaline numbed her.

Soon they had him undressed. Buck naked, he lay sprawled on top of the bed, his arms spread out. The trace of black hair that grew down the middle of his chest and stomach outlined his stark white skin. He was so vulnerable, so defenseless, she wanted to smash him with a chair, stab him a thousand times, even shoot him with her .22, again and again. She drew a deep breath up her nose. How had she ever loved him?

Oh, for the innocence of youth.

"What else do we need to do?" Strawberry asked, breaking into her thoughts.

"Nothing my dear, nothing. He'll do it all by himself tomorrow."

"Wouldn't you like to be here when it happens?"

"Yes, but I'll hear the story over and over again in my parlor."

"You think it will work?"

Tired of looking at his pot-bellied anatomy, Ella motioned her toward the door, and blew out the lamp. "Yes, it has to."

CHAPTER 18

"If that Indian girl isn't a ghost, I don't know what she is. We haven't spoken to one person who has seen her," Dolly said with a scowl of disapproval as they rode toward camp. All their searching of the countryside surrounding Snowflake had produced nothing.

"No, she's not a ghost, just elusive," John commented. "The major once told me that an Apache could hide from an army and even escape from them though completely surrounded."

"Hmm. Well, we can't surround her, 'cause we can't even find her," she grumbled.

He looked over at her, mildly amused. "You must be telling me you're tired." He bit back the comment that she looked weary, as well.

"No, I'm not tired," she said defensively. She scowled at him from beneath the brim of her hat. No doubt he was planning to ditch her again. All he needed was one little excuse, and he was back on his soapbox. "I'll still be in this saddle until you're ready to call it quits."

"Mrs. Arnold—"

"Mrs. Arnold!" she mimicked him acidly. "I'm damn tired of 'Mrs. Arnold.' You called me by my given name once and it didn't kill you!"

"Yes, ma'am," he said quietly, startled by her sudden outburst.

"No, John Wesley, you are not getting off that easy. The name is Dolly. Say it, Dol-ly!"

"Dolly," he mumbled. His eyes stared ahead as he rode. The name did not fit her, but he admitted silently that he had been thinking of her as "Dolly" for some time now.

"Oh, forget it," she retorted angrily. "You aren't interested. And I damn sure would have a hard time putting up with you." She put her heels to the gray and raced ahead.

He exhaled hard and shook his head. For a long moment, he tried to retrace the conversation, wondering what had set off her fiery temper. He honestly did not know what he had done wrong. She was one of the few people that he felt comfortable with, but if he told her that, she might take it the wrong way. Besides, he thought, frowning, he wasn't sure he would know how to phrase the words so they sounded respectful.

By the fourth day after the poisoning incident, the Kid felt back to normal. He was once again playing checkers with Neal through the bars of the cell.

"They ain't caught that murdering Injun yet, have they?" he asked the deputy.

"No. But that lawman, Michaels, and Mrs. Arnold have been scouring the country for her with no luck."

The Kid moved a checker, his mind not on the game. "Where did that Mrs. Arnold come from originally?"

Neal shrugged as he jumped two of the Kid's pieces.

"Some say she just showed up at Arnold's Store a few years ago. I heard that she was a saloon girl before, but I reckon folks are just guessing about that part."

"She ain't bad-looking," the Kid said. Neal had him in a bad position on the board. Almost as sorry as his position in jail. Beth Parker had probably found his note by now. Claire had taken hers without a sideways glance and pushed it inside her dress. And that wimpy Rawlings reported that he had mailed his letter to Maria.

Neal smiled at the Kid's careless move. "Yeah, she's a good-looking woman. Your mind ain't on the game, Kid. Must be on Mrs. Arnold." Neal swept the board clear of Bobby's checkers with his next move.

"Yeah," the Kid said, "let's quit for a while. Besides, I need to go out back." He cast a glance over at Gar. The whiskey peddler was asleep. It was a period of time that the Kid savored because he was spared hearing the man's grumbling.

Neal pulled the keg back that held the checkerboard. He shouted at the new guard, "Check the street, Whipple. The Kid's coming out."

Every trip to the privy was now a suspenseful journey for him. The smelly, fly-buzzing frame outhouse was the key to his freedom. When someone delivered that gun in the slot above the door, the Coyote Kid would be able to escape. He would be rid of those damn leg irons that made him shuffle. He would ride to the country of the señoritas.

Rattling his chains, he scooted along in the gap between the saloon and jail to the unpainted privy. Behind him, armed with a shotgun, Neal marched with a glint in his eye.

Despite their friendly games, he knew that Neal would shoot him if he had to. It was his job.

He opened the outhouse door, trying to control his thundering heart. He pulled the door shut, then reached over the ledge above the door. His fingertips touched something familiar, the cool metal of a pistol. A shout of triumphant laughter nearly escaped him.

In a swift movement he checked the gun, relieved to see it was loaded. Then he raised his pant leg and shoved the pistol inside his boot. It was a small revolver, but just right for his needs. He did not have time to gloat over his success. He must make plans.

He unbuckled his belt and dropped his pants. No longer would he be a condemned dog on a chain. At last, he had the means of deliverance. Seated on the raw boards, he planned his escape while a hoard of flies buzzed in the breathless interior. The old Coyote Kid would soon be on the prowl again, howling his lonesome song and riding for Old Mexico like a prairie fire. He just had to decide when to make his move. There would be a right time to make a break for it, but he must plan every step very carefully.

Wearily they dismounted and unsaddled their horses at the end of another uneventful day. Dolly's bones ached while she stripped out the latigos. She glanced over at John. His endurance amazed her. When he set out to do something, he certainly stuck to it.

"We keep coming up with nothing," she complained. A quick inspection of the camp told her that the carefully banked fire was out. "Maybe, we're looking in the wrong places."

"Where else would you look?" he asked, then added, "Oh, your fire seems to be out."

"My fire? Well, it's your damn fire, too. I'm going to go take a bath in the stream. You can build it or eat raw food." She grabbed a flour-sack towel and stormed off.

She felt gritty, and the smell of horse in her nose was so strong that it burned her nostrils. Maybe a bath would soothe her flaring temper. Everything irritated her. She needed to escape from John, as well, maybe even from her own thoughts.

Concerned about her obvious distress, he dared not follow her. He busied himself turning the horses loose to graze, knowing that they were so weary they would not leave the area. That chore completed, he decided to rebuild her fire while she was gone. It might help her get back to normal. She had been edgy for two days and he suspected he knew the reason. In a short while, the "Kid business" would be over. They would have to return to a normal life—go their own separate ways.

Hunkered down on his boot heels, he soon had tinder burning in the firepit. The flames licked at the small pile of needles and twigs. The time they'd spent together tracking down the Kid had consumed both of them like a raging fire. He nodded his head as he considered the matter of what was wrong with her. She didn't want that fire to die.

The Kid had considered his options. He tried to conceal his impatience. It was time to get out of the jail. Sheriff Rogers was gone somewhere, and he'd overheard Neal tell Whipple that Marshal Michaels was off again looking for the squaw.

Whipple was a dour-faced man whom the sheriff had hired to help Neal. Some dumb farmer, the Kid figured, would be easy to run over. He planned to coax Neal into a game of checkers, then with the gun, get the keys that the deputy carried, and let himself out of the cell. Then he would release Gar. As much as he disliked him, he knew he might need his assistance to pull off the jailbreak.

At the moment, Neal was gone to take Gar to the out-house.

The Kid quickly pulled up his pants leg. He glanced around to be sure that Whipple was not at the door. Hastily, he double-checked the small-caliber pistol, reassuring himself that it was loaded. He returned it to his boot and dropped his pants leg over it.

The damn leg irons were at the ankles of his boots, but he would soon be free of them. Seated on his bunk, he daydreamed of a blue sky above him and freedom.

Neal returned the grumpy Gar back to his cell. Bobby watched the deputy put up his shotgun.

"You ready to get beat again, Kid?" Neal asked. The deputy smiled as he set up the checkerboard in front of the bars.

"Sure am." The Kid seated himself on the nail keg and scratched his leg. His gaze was on the deputy, who was placing the checkers on the board. A quick glance in that direction assured him that the cell-block door was closed. There was no sign of the other guard.

"Where's Whipple?" he asked casually.

"Oh, he's gone to order something at the store."

The Kid nodded. Then in one lightning sweep, he stuck the pistol in the deputy's face. "Don't try anything, Neal. I ain't wanting to kill you. Just give me the keys, careful like, and don't try nothing."

"Where in the hell—?" The threat of the pistol silenced Neal.

"Shut up. The keys, damnit! Where's the leg iron keys?"

His face white, Neal woodenly handed over the cell keys. "Sheriff Rogers has the ones to the leg irons in his pocket."

"Shit," the Kid swore and rose to insert the key into

the lock. It clicked with a sound that thrilled him. But Neal, who was still seated, made a move. A fatal one for his holstered gun. It pained the Kid to pull the trigger. He hadn't wanted it this way.

The gun barked in the Kid's hand, and Neal pitched over on his back. Outside the cell, the Kid looked at Gar's shocked face.

"Get me out, Kid. I'll help you," the big man begged.

It was good to hear the bastard whine, the Kid noted with satisfaction. The chains restricted his steps as he hurried to the door and unlocked Gar's cell.

Gar held his own leg chain in his hands and looked at Bobby. "What now?"

"Whipple's out of the office. Get Neal's gun. We've got to find a blacksmith," the Kid said as he shuffled down the hall. "There's no keys here for these leg irons."

"Oh, hell," Gar swore in disgust.

No one in the office. "Grab a shotgun," the Kid ordered. "Whipple and the whole damn town will be here after hearing that shot."

"Yeah. Hey, Kid, here comes he now!" Gar shouted. He picked up a shotgun and dragged his chains to the door. There was one blast from the shotgun. The Kid glanced up in time to see Whipple bowing over from the shot and crumpling to the street.

Frantically, the Kid searched through the sheriff's desk, but could not find the keys. "Is there a blacksmith's shop here?" he asked as he loaded a Colt .45 from Rogers's desk. He jammed the revolver in his waistband, and quickly drew down a Winchester rifle from a rack. The chamber was loaded.

"No, I don't think there's a smithy close. Seems he's at the edge of town," Gar said. "Hey, what are you doing?"

"Trying to open the safe," the Kid said, his hand on

the set handle under the combination. "It's got my guns and money. The damned thing's locked."

"Come on, Kid. Let's just get some horses and ride."

"You know what your problem is, Gar?" The Kid ducked down to see out the window and examine the street. No one was in sight. The notion filled him with confidence. A smile formed on his lips. "You're in too much of a hurry. Ain't there a saloon next door?"

"Yeah, but what are you up to now, Kid?" Gar sounded edgy.

"We'll go over there, and get us a drink. I'll sign for the drinks and Sheriff Rogers can pay them back when he returns. It'll be credit."

"You're crazy. I want out of this town now!" Gar shouted in wide-eyed disbelief.

The Kid picked up the leg iron chain in his left hand, and the Winchester in his right one, then he shuffled past Gar. To hell with that grisly lunatic; he was having himself a drink.

Gar tagged along. "This is crazy, Kid."

"Wait, Gar. We need to get these damn chains off. We can't ride a horse like this. There ain't one damn horse out there in the street to ride anyway. And if you call me crazy one more time," the Kid threatened, "I'll blow your brains out."

Gar shook his head. "I want to get the hell out of here."

"We will, we will. Just stay calm," the Kid assured him as they entered the saloon.

"Hey!" he shouted at the bartender. "Get those hands on the bar. And you!" The Kid turned toward a swamper. "Old man, go get us an axe and find us two saddled horses. Wait a minute." He turned back to the shaking barkeeper. "Pour him a drink first. He needs it."

"And drink it fast," Gar said sourly. He had positioned himself by the door so that he could watch the street.

"Bring an axe first, before you get those horses," the Kid ordered the swamper, who was spilling whiskey as he lifted the glass with his trembling hands. "And tell them at the livery that no one will get hurt. We've got money in the sheriff's safe to pay them. We ain't crooks."

"Bullshit!" Gar swore. "You just hurry, old man, or I'll blast your ass off."

"Gar!" the Kid shouted. "We ain't killing innocent people. Give him time to go get it. He's working for me."

Gar swore under his breath. "Bartender, bring me a bottle of whiskey."

The Kid nodded assent, and the saloonkeeper hurried to comply. Casually, the Kid lifted the bottle that remained on the counter. He drank his first draught, then sighed in satisfaction. It was good whiskey. Real good.

"The swamper's coming back with the axe," Gar said.

"Good. He can chop off these chains, and we'll worry about getting the cuffs off our legs later."

It required several whacks by the nervous man to separate the chains. Gar was growling impatiently, but soon his leg irons were separated.

The Kid stood nearby, the bottle of whiskey in his hand "Now, Gar, you cut mine." He turned toward the swamper. "Now go get us two good horses and saddles, old man. Tell the livery man we've got the money to pay for them."

"Holy shit, Kid. Just tell him to go get some damn horses. We're wasting time. Besides, it's clouding up like it's going to rain."

The Kid shrugged. "A little rain ain't going to hurt." He laughed aloud. The rain would aid them in their escape by erasing their tracks. The Kid stood with his feet wide apart so that Gar could chop his leg iron chain in two. The third whack brought a rattle of separated chains—it was sweet music. Soon he would be free. There would be plenty of time to shoot Gar later. For the moment he still needed him.

"What do you figure, Kid?" Haggard-looking, Gar tossed the axe aside. "There ain't no one in the street. Where's that old man?"

The Kid shook his free legs. The chains on the cuff rattled, but he was free at last. "He'll be back, if you didn't scare him out of his wits."

"I see him. He's coming with our horses."

"Gar, get all the bartender's money, but count it out. We ain't common thieves. Let me know how much there is so I can give him an IOU against my money in the sheriff's safe."

Gar frowned in disgust. "The hell with you and your goddamn ideas." He stood by, watching impatiently as the bartender counted out the money.

The Kid scowled at Gar's barely restrained impatience. He was not Leo, although he was as good at worrying as Leo.

"S-seventy bucks," the bartender stuttered.

"I'll make a chit on paper."

"Yes, sir."

"Are you coming?" Gar asked, as he stuffed some of the money in his pocket.

"Sure, Gar." The Kid signed the paper that the bartender laid on the bar. "You collect your money from Sheriff Rogers, savvy?"

"Yes, sir, Mister Kid."

"Put another bottle of whiskey on my bill. You want one, Gar?"

"Hell, no. I can drink later. Let's go."

"Oh yes," the Kid said as an afterthought. "Give the old man a bottle on me."

Outside in the sunshine between the clouds, they mounted the horses. When he reined his around, he noted how Whipple lay on his back in the street. Dead. The shotgun blast had made a great black-red hole in his chest. Frantically, Gar rushed off lashing his poor horse in a frenzy and the Kid booted his horse after him A final look around, and he tipped his hat, smiling. Goodbye, Snowflake.

It had begun to rain. A grumble of thunder complained, giant clouds boiled in the sky. Dolly had covered the pack supplies and pulled on an oil slicker over her own clothing in preparation for the storm.

John had built the fire up to burn through the approaching summer shower. "It's going to be really raining in a bit," he prophesied.

"Yes, I can smell it already." Dolly smiled, welcoming the rain.

He sat down on a log in his slicker. "Wish I had a tent for you."

"That would have been nice. I might even have let you sit in it." She poured coffee in an enamel cup and handed it to him. "I would have called it Dolly's Tent, and you would have had to call it that or sit out in the rain."

"Yes, ma'am."

She drew a deep breath and poured herself a cup of coffee. He called her "ma'am" just to aggravate her. Who did he think he was?

As the rain began to increase, a man on horseback rode up the creek toward their camp.

"It's Doc," John said. "Something must be wrong in Snowflake."

"What could be wrong now?" she asked.

He shook his head, then rose and moved forward to greet the man. "Hello, Doc. Get down and have a cup of coffee."

The doctor waved the offer away. "Kid's broken out of jail. He killed Neal and Whipple, the new deputy. Him and Gar hightailed it out of here a while ago. I sent word with a boy to notify Sheriff Rogers. Then I rode up here myself to get you."

News of the escape and the dead lawmen was a slap in the face for John. Raindrops drilled the rubber-coated slicker and blurred his vision.

"I'll be ready to go in a few minutes," he said. "Doc, I'm sure sorry about all this. Did they have outside help?"

The physician wearily shook his dripping hat. "Danged if I know."

"Good enough," he said and grabbed up his saddle.

"I'm going with you," Dolly said and raced off to capture their horses. Raindrops ran down her face as she hurried down the grassy slope. The Kid was loose and had killed some more innocent people. Would he ever be stopped?

She returned with the animals. He saddled hers without an argument.

"I'll cinch it," she said, "saddle yours."

"Fine. Get some jerky; we may be gone a while."

She nodded in response to his request. Her wet fingers fumbled as she threaded the latigo through the rings. That deputy Neal was the best one of the bunch; his death caused a pain in her heart.

"I was afraid of something like this," he said grimly. "I would bet he got help from an outsider."

She looked at the doctor, who had dismounted and

stood huddled in her canvas coat waiting for them. "Did he?"

"I don't know much about it. When I got back from seeing Mrs. Murphy, the bartender came and got me. Said there was nothing I could do for the two dead men, and wondered what they should do with all the officials out of town. We sent the boy to get word to Rogers and I rode up here. Things are a mess."

Lightning blazed across the sky and more thunder boomed over their head. Involuntarily, Dolly ducked, clutching the reins to the startled mare in her fist. A cold chill ran down her spine. A real fear of what lay ahead for them filled her thoughts as she climbed in the saddle to ride to town.

They rode into Snowflake in a light drizzle. A dozen riders wearing slickers sat on horseback in front of the jail. Sheriff Rogers turned his horse and came over to meet with John.

"Did Doc tell you what happened here?"

"Only that the Kid and Gar escaped. How did they do it?"

"I ain't sure. Neal was shot in the cell block. Whipple was gunned down in the street. We can't find out if they had any help." Rogers glanced at Dolly, his eyes narrowing with displeasure. "This posse ain't no place for a woman."

"Dolly's coming along," John stated, his voice brooking no refusal. She felt warmed by the tone and his casual use of her given name. Although she felt clammy cold under her slicker, her goose bumps magically disappeared. John Wesley had actually defended her right to be there.

Ella Devereaux opened the front door and smiled at the man standing in the lamplight. "Major Bowen, so nice of you to drop by." She stepped back to admit the straight-backed man in the brown business suit. He removed his hat and came inside.

The piano music and voices from the parlor drifted into the entry hall. She graciously pointed to the adjoining room where they could talk in private. He nodded and took her bidding.

"Have a seat. Will you have something to drink?" she asked, going to the decanters on the buffet.

"Whiskey's fine." He set his hat aside and took a seat on a stuffed chair with rosewood arms.

"You want your whiskey straight?" She held up the fine crystal tumbler.

"That would be okay, Mrs. Devereaux."

"Ella, call me Ella," she said, her back to him as she fixed the drink.

"Yes, Ella. Regarding this Ash Waddle?"

"You did find the counterfeit money on him and arrest him?" Her heart stopped. She turned with his drink in her hand.

"U.S. Deputy Marshal Burke did and has him in custody."

"Good," she said, looking up toward the ceiling squares in gratitude. At last, Ash Waddle was out of her life. She handed Bowen the glass. He was nice-looking, handsome for a man past fifty. But shorter than she had imagined him when she had watched him from her apartment window trek up and down the hill.

"I also discovered there is a murder warrant for his arrest back East as you suggested. So I doubt you will see him again. Why did you contact me and not Sheriff Strope?"

She swept her dress under her and took a chair opposite him. "Major, we—you and I have been at odds in the past. But the word is out about your marshals—that they get the job done."

"Thanks," he said, uncomfortable at her praise. "Yes, but counterfeiting is a federal offense and the U.S. Marshal's office handles such cases."

"Major, my daddy always said 'Don't get a boy when you need a man.' I have a trunk upstairs full of those bills that is Waddle's property."

"I'll tell Burke and he'll come relieve you of it." He sat back in the chair as if finally appraising the room. "You said we had been at odds?"

"Yes. Quite frankly, I spied on you."

"I like frankness, Ella. From now on, let's be more frank with each other. I have an agency to run, you have a business that no doubt depends on the trade of many important men. There should be some middle ground we can attain here."

"There will be," she promised, meeting his cold gaze.

"Excellent." He rose to his feet and handed her the empty glass.

"Want another?"

"No, but it was damn good whiskey." A sly smile creased his thin lips.

They both laughed and she showed him out. For a long moment she considered the man. The major and his marshals would be a force in the territory's future. She had done the right thing by joining forces with him. When at last she closed the door after him, she wanted to shout. With a tug to pull up her dress front, she charged into the parlor and shouted, "Break out the free champagne. Drinks are on me!"

Ella could see the luster in Strawberry's green eyes. The "we did it" look on her face told all. Ella threw back her head and gave a yell: "Wahoo!"

CHAPTER 19

The shower soon passed overhead and the thunder rumbled like some distant dragon as they left town. John Wesley and Dolly rode side by side at the rear of the posse. Two horse tracks, half melted by the rain, led them southward. Sheriff Rogers rode at the head of his assembled army.

This was not John's idea of how to capture an escaped prisoner. These men from town and farm were poor substitutes for experienced lawmen. Politically elected sheriffs drew great support from such moves, and they all used the system. John mused on what Rogers might say in the future. Probably something like, "Remember when you and I rode together after the Coyote Kid? I need your support again." It was an old political trick that worked all too often for reelection. The criminals knew they were being pursued by a trigger-happy bunch. John felt there was one small consolation in this case—at least the posse members weren't drunk.

He knew how these kinds of posses worked. In a few hours the excitement of the chase would wear off.

"Where do you think the Kid is headed?" Dolly asked quietly.

"No telling. He's no fool. He'll be hard to capture, if he gets ahead of us a good distance. I suspect that his drinking problem, which enabled us to catch him last time, stemmed from the loss of his partner. He won't repeat that mistake."

She sighed and opened her slicker. The rain had stopped again. "You don't like posses, do you, John?"

"No, but perhaps if this posse gives up, then you and I can catch the Kid."

Flattered by his inclusion of her in his plans, she watched Rogers rein his horse out and ride back toward them. Something about the man still grated on her.

Sheriff Rogers nodded curtly at her, then spoke to John. "We can get some food at the Bar L, which is just a little ways up ahead. Then we can push on until dark."

"Good idea," John agreed. He wondered how far ahead those two were at the moment. Instinct told him something wasn't quite right. He had missed something or forgotten to take something into consideration, although he didn't know what it could be. After Rogers rode back to the front of the posse, Dolly glanced at John's frowning profile.

"What's wrong?" she asked softly.

"I have a feeling that maybe we're riding in the wrong direction, despite the tracks."

He shook his head as if deeply concerned about the matter. She did not question him further. Since Sheriff Rogers had now given the order to lope, she and John pushed their horses and fell in with the others.

At the ranch, several dogs heralded their arrival. Everyone on the place turned out to greet them. A woman with some small children, a few ranch hands, and a man who was obviously the owner stood in the yard. John pushed closer to hear the sheriff's conversation with the rancher.

"You seen two riders?"

"I seen one west of here. He was a big, bearded guy leading an empty saddled horse. He was headed toward Cannon Creek in a big hurry.

Rogers turned to John. "That sounds like Gar. You reckon he's shot the Kid?"

"No," John said grimly. "But I think we've been following one man and two horses. You all go after Gar. I'll swing back and see if I can locate the Kid's trail."

"You want some of the posse to go along with you?"

John shook his head. "We'll try it alone."

Rogers looked back at Dolly doubtfully, then shrugged. "Well, good luck. Wonder what the Kid has in mind?"

"With him it's hard to guess. He's probably headed for Mexico, "John said evasively.

"You two be careful," Rogers said, sounding concerned.

"We will." John turned his horse, nodded to the other men, and rode back so that he could speak privately to her.

She saw deep concern on his face. "I heard him," she said at his questioning look. "What now?"

"I think I know where the Kid's hiding."

"Where?" She glanced around to make sure no one was close enough to hear her words.

"A widow's place near town. Come on, let's push on. It'll be dark soon."

"Let's ride then; my mare can take it."

"Yes," John said. "We'd better ride." It was long shot

the Kid would be at the widow's farm, but the best one
he knew about.

A dog barked. In the distance, a bull bellowed. Afoot,
they had left their horses in the dark timber and stood at
the corrals behind the shed of a barn. There was a yellow light in the Parker house.

"The woman's home anyway," she whispered, trying
to make things out in the silver moonlight.

"Good thing she doesn't have any dogs," he commented softly. "We'll slip through the barn then stay low
along the fence. We need to separate her from the Kid."

"Why?" she said as they cautiously entered the barn
and traveled the dark cavernous length of it.

"In a minute," he hissed.

Metal clanged beneath his foot. He put out an arm to
halt her. Then bending low, he picked up a broken leg-
iron cuff. Even in the dim light, he could identify the object. "He's here. Be careful."

"Yes," Dolly agreed. Her mouth was dry, and several
questions flashed through her mind. This was no time to
voice them. She felt for the butt of her .32.

They ducked low and moved along close to the fence.
The back door of the house opened. They froze. A figure
outlined by the light from inside, obviously a woman,
stepped out. They watched for a moment. She was headed
for the privy. Perfect, he decided. The ideal opportunity
to separate the woman from the outlaw. It was a dangerous situation, and for a fleeting second he regretted
having Dolly with him, but the feeling passed. He would
have to use her to hold the woman captive. If Mrs. Parker
shouted, it would sure give the Kid enough warning.

Dolly turned to John and pulled on the kerchief around

his neck. John nodded and quietly untied it. He was slightly reassured by the glint of gunmetal in her hand. Gesturing her toward the outhouse, he moved carefully toward the door.

When he swung the door open, John quickly clamped the kerchief on the shocked Beth Parker's mouth. Dolly shoved her pistol into the woman's midsection.

"Shut up, lady," she ordered. "And get back inside."

He not so gently pushed the widow onto the rough seat. Dolly pointed her gun at the woman's face. Even in the dimness, he could see that Mrs. Parker's eyes were open in fright as he gagged her with the kerchief.

"Where's the Kid?" Dolly hissed.

He released the gag long enough for her to gasp out, "Asleep in the front bedroom." That was all the information that he needed. He quickly trussed the kerchief around her mouth. "Don't let her try anything," he warned Dolly.

"I won't. You be careful, John Wesley."

"I will. If he's asleep, maybe I can take him alive."

"Yes," Dolly agreed, her attention on the prisoner. "Don't even think about moving a muscle," she said to her.

John crossed the yard and silently climbed the steps. The door creaked lightly when he pushed it open with the Colt in his right hand. There was a lamp on in the living room. He closed the door gently so that a night breeze would not alert the Kid. Gun ready, John crept across the living room with careful steps. He stopped at the edge of an open door.

He could make out a figure on the bed. Stepping inside the room, he aimed his pistol at the sleeping outlaw.

"Kid, wake up!"

He knew immediately that the Kid would try for the .45 on the nightstand. The .45 in John's hand belched an orange flame. The explosion was deafening and rocked the outlaw back on the bed. Acrid black powder smoke billowed up John's nose. Death's hold twisted the Coyote Kid.

"Damnit, Kid," he swore as he looked down at the lifeless body of Bobby Budd. "Why did it have to be me, Kid? A hundred men could have shot you."

"John?" Dolly called from the back door. Her heart was hammering in her chest. Was he all right?

He ran a hand over his face and sighed deeply. "Yes, I'm all right." Slowly he backed out of the room and turned to face her and the ashen-faced Mrs. Parker.

"He's dead. It's over," he managed to say.

He holstered his revolver and shifted his gaze away from the accusing look in Mrs. Parker's eyes. A man was dead. In many ways, the Kid was not unlike himself. This was not the time to judge him. His ways were all wrong, but he too rid the West of the criminals. It was over. The Coyote Kid was gone.

"John?" Dolly asked quietly, placing her hand on his forearm. "Are you sure you're all right?"

"Yes. Let's go find the doc. He seems to serve as the undertaker around here."

"What about her?" She indicated the unmoving woman sitting stone-faced on a kitchen chair.

"She's suffered enough. I'm sure he held her hostage."

"But she—" John's fingers on her lips silenced her protest. He shook his head and frowned.

"Do you want to go with me, Dolly?" he asked quietly as he looked directly into her eyes.

"Oh yes, John Wesley. Should I get the horses?" she asked eagerly.

"No. Let's walk. We'll get the horses later. Right now I want to walk and think."

"Do we need anything?" she asked in a softer tone.

"No." He opened the door, then followed her outside.

Dolly smiled at him. She tentatively reached out and lightly clasped his hand. When he did not resist but closed his hand on hers, she felt a renewed hope. It was a small thing, yet the easy connection that joined them seemed a major victory.

"There will be newspaper reporters and photographers here soon," he began. "They'll take pictures of the Kid propped up with a gun in his arms as if he were alive."

Dolly spoke softly as they walked in the starlight. "And you disapprove of all that?"

"The man is dead. It's over. I can't see any good served by that kind of a circus."

She nodded, then closed her eyes. Her son's killer was dead. Josh's death had been avenged. Yet she could not derive any satisfaction from the knowledge. She would think about it later, she promised herself. "John?"

"Let's just forget about it for a while, Dolly. It's been a strange sort of job since it started."

She squeezed his hand. "I guess my presence hasn't helped any."

"No, that's not true," he said, as if surprised. "Quite frankly, I'm not sure I could have managed without your help."

She did not allow her happiness to show. "What's next?" she asked quietly.

"You can return to Ben," he began, but immediately added, "Of course, you don't want to do that."

He was silent as they walked, their linked hands the only communication between them.

"Dolly," he said hesitantly. "Let's get this matter of the Kid settled and then . . . then we'll just have to wait and see."

"Yes." She knew this was not the time to press him.

She had a major concession literally at her fingertips. For the present, that small connection would have to suffice. But somehow, she vowed, she would win him. She knew him well enough to know that he was strangely hurt by the Coyote Kid's death. And in an odd way she understood the feeling.

His prophecy came true. At the flash of powder, another photograph was made. She stayed on the opposite side of the street in the shadows of the cafe roof. Several newspapermen and photographers were assembled at the jail. The Kid was mounted on a board. Sheriff Rogers strutted like a pigeon in front of his jail. Even Gar was dragged out of the jail and photographed with an empty rifle. The posse had brought him in the previous day.

Dolly watched the activity, yet remained inconspicuous so that the reporter Rawlings would not recognize her and start asking too many questions. John had gone to the post office to mail his report and to get the letter he was expecting from the major.

He returned carrying one in his hand. When he reached her, he spoke flatly. "The major wants me to hurry back to Prescott." He avoided her eyes and looked away toward the road leading out of town.

"What are you going to do next for the major?" she asked as they walked to get the horses that were hitched at a nearby rail.

"He says that killers are operating near the Utah line. They've murdered a Prescott man. He wants me to investigate the case."

"Are you taking the stage to Prescott?" she asked absently.

"Yes."

"I'll bring your horses up there for you."

' "No. The horses are yours. I'm giving you both of them for helping me."

"Thank you." She carefully made her voice sound neutral. She didn't trust herself to look at him as he explained the stage route. How it ran from Fort Apache to Globe to Phoenix and then north to Prescott.

"I'll take you to Fort Apache, and then the horses will be mine?" she questioned him quietly.

"Yes." They undid the reins and started to mount up. When he was in the saddle he looked across at her. "Where will you go?"

"Oh, I have a little money saved," she said brightly, "and with three good horses I can go anywhere."

"Yes." He noticed that a nun was walking away from the jail. He hadn't remembered seeing a Catholic church anywhere. Somehow her appearance there seemed strange in this town, but he shrugged away his concern.

They turned their horses and rode out of Snowflake for their camp. He was not happy with Dolly's answers. She acted too smugly congenial and it niggled him as they rode. It was over, they would soon part. He hated it in many ways, but in truth, he was not responsible for her. There simply was no place for her on this job of his.

She enjoyed the mare's lope, and the wind in her face. Yes, she could go anywhere she liked. But she already knew her destination. She would arrive in Prescott after his stage had had time to get there. She glanced at him and smiled. I'll be at the Capitol, John Wesley, she said silently.

He noted the smirk on her face, then he looked off at the rugged distant peaks. His new job had proved to be quite different from being a town marshal, lots of riding, being in the back country, but he liked those parts of it better than what he had done in the past. Open country, freedom, and lots of clear sky.